DIAL M FOR MURDER

Wolfe picked up his extension, and I put mine back at my ear.

"Nero Wolfe?"

"Yes."

"I've mailed you a letter, but you're responsible for this, so I think you ought to hear it. I hope you'll hear it in your dreams the rest of your life. This is it. Are you listening?"

"Yes, but—"

"Here it goes."

It busted my eardrum, or felt like it. It was a combination of a roar and a smack. By reflex my wrist moved the receiver away, then I moved it back. There was a confused clatter and a sort of thump, then nothing. I told the transmitter, "Hello hello!"

Nothing. I cradled it and turned. Wolfe was sitting with the instrument dangling from his hand, scowling at me.

"Well?" he demanded.

"Well yourself. How do I know? I suppose he shot himself."

MURDER BY THE BOOK

Bantam Books by Rex Stout
Ask your bookseller for the books you have missed

AND BE A VILLAIN
THE BLACK MOUNTAIN
CHAMPAGNE FOR ONE
CURTAINS FOR THREE
DEATH OF A DUDE
DEATH OF A DOXY
THE DOORBELL RANG
A FAMILY AFFAIR
THE FATHER HUNT
FER-DE-LANCE
THE GOLDEN SPIDERS
HOMICIDE TRINITY
IF DEATH EVER SLEPT
IN THE BEST OF FAMILIES
MIGHT AS WELL BE DEAD
THE MOTHER HUNT
MURDER BY THE BOOK
OVER MY DEAD BODY
PLEASE PASS THE GUILT
PRISONER'S BASE
THE RED BOX
A RIGHT TO DIE
THE SECOND CONFESSION
THE SILENT SPEAKER
THREE FOR THE CHAIR
THREE MEN OUT
THREE AT WOLFE'S DOOR
TRIO FOR BLUNT INSTRUMENTS
TRIPLE JEOPARDY
TROUBLE IN TRIPLICATE

Murder
by the Book

by Rex Stout

A Nero Wolfe Mystery

BANTAM BOOKS

TORONTO • NEW YORK • LONDON • SYDNEY • AUCKLAND

MURDER BY THE BOOK
*A Bantam Book / published by arrangement with
The Viking Press, Inc.*

PRINTING HISTORY
*Viking edition published October 1951
Dollar Mystery Guild edition published January 1952*
*Bantam edition / September 1954
13 printings through May 1985*

*Bantam Books are published by Bantam Books, Inc. Its trade-
mark, consisting of the words "Bantam Books" and the por-
trayal of a rooster, is Registered in U.S. Patent and Trademark
Office and in other countries. Marca Registrada. Bantam
Books, Inc., 666 Fifth Avenue, New York, New York 10103.*

1

SOMETHING remarkable happened that cold Tuesday in January. Inspector Cramer, with no appointment, showed up a little before noon at Nero Wolfe's old brownstone on West Thirty-fifth Street and, after I had ushered him into the office and he had exchanged greetings with Wolfe and lowered himself into the red leather chair, he said right out, "I dropped in to ask a little favor."

What was remarkable was his admitting it. From my chair at my desk I made an appropriate noise. He sent me a sharp glance and asked if I had something.

"No, sir," I told him courteously, "I'm right on top. You just jolted that out of me. So many times I've seen you come here for a favor and try to bull it or twist it, it was quite a shock." I waved it away tolerantly. "Skip it."

His face, chronically red, deepened a shade. His broad shoulders stiffened, and the creases spreading from the corners of his gray-blue eyes showed more as the eyelids tightened. Then, deciding I was playing for a blurt, he controlled it. "Do you know," he asked, "whose opinion of you I would like to have? Darwin's. Where were you while evolution was going on?"

"Stop brawling," Wolfe muttered at us from behind his desk. He was testy, not because he would have minded seeing either Cramer or me draw blood, but because he always resented being interrupted in the middle of a London *Times* crossword puzzle. He frowned at Cramer. "What favor, sir?"

"Nothing strenuous." Cramer relaxed. "A little point

about a homicide. A man's body fished out of the East River a week ago yesterday, off Ninetieth Street. He had been—"

"Named Leonard Dykes," Wolfe said brusquely, wanting to make it brief so he could finish the puzzle before lunch. "Confidential clerk in a law office, around forty, had been in the water perhaps two days. Evidence of a severe blow on the head, but had died of drowning. No one charged by last evening. I read all the homicide news."

"I bet you do." That having slipped out by force of habit, Cramer decided it wasn't tactful and smiled it off. He could smile when he wanted to. "Not only is no one charged, we haven't got a smell. We've done everything, you know what we've done, and we're stopped. He lived alone in a room-and-bath walk-up on Sullivan Street. By the time we got there it had been combed—not torn apart, but someone had been through it good. We didn't find anything that's been any help, but we found one thing that might possibly help if we could figure it out."

He got papers from his breast pocket, from them selected an envelope, and from the envelope took a folded sheet of paper. "This was inside a book, a novel. I can give you the name of the book and the numbers of the pages it was found between, but I don't think that has a bearing." He got up to hand the paper to Wolfe. "Take a look at it."

Wolfe ran his eyes over it, and, since I was supposed to be up on everything that went on in that office so as to be eligible for blame if and when required, I arose and extended a hand. He passed it over.

"It's in Dykes's handwriting," Cramer said. "The paper is a sheet from a scratch pad there on a table in his room. There were more pads like it in a drawer of the table."

I was giving it a look. The paper was white, ordinary, six by nine, and at the top was the word "Tentative," underscored, written with pencil in a neat almost perpendicular hand. Below it was a list of names:

Sinclair Meade
Sinclair Sampson
Barry Bowen
David Yerkes
Ernest Vinson
Dorian Vick
Baird Archer
Oscar Shiff
Oscar Cody
Lawrence McCue
Mark McCue
Mark Flick
Mack Flick
Louis Gill
Lewis Gill

I handed it back to Cramer and returned to my chair.

"Well?" Wolfe asked impatiently.

"I was on my way uptown and dropped in to show it to you." Cramer folded the sheet and put it in the envelope. "Not so much to get help, it probably has nothing to do with the homicide, but it's got me irritated and I wondered what you'd say, so I dropped in. A list of fifteen names written by Dykes on a piece of his scratch paper, and not one of them can be found in any phone directory in the metropolitan area! Or anywhere else. We can find no record anywhere of a man with any of those names. None of Dykes's friends or associates ever heard of a man with one of those names, so they say. I mean, taking the first and last names together, as they are on that list. Of course we haven't checked the whole damn country, but Dykes was a born and bred New Yorker, with no particular connections elsewhere that we know of. What the hell kind of a list of names is that?"

Wolfe grunted. "He made them up. He was considering an alias, for himself or someone else."

"We thought of that, naturally. If so, no one ever used it that we can find."

"Keep trying if you think it's worth it."

"Yeah. But we're only human. I just thought I'd show it to a genius and see what happened. With a genius you never know."

Wolfe shrugged. "I'm sorry. Nothing has happened."

"Well, by God, I hope you'll excuse me"—Cramer got up. He was sore, and you couldn't blame him—"for taking up your time and no fee. Don't bother, Goodwin."

He turned and marched out. Wolfe bent over his cross-word puzzle, frowned at it, and picked up his pencil.

2

CRAMER'S crack about no fee had of course been deserved. Wolfe hated to start his brain going on what he called work, and during the years I had been on his payroll the occasions had been rare when anything but a substantial retainer had jarred him into it. But he is not a loafer. He can't be, since his income as a private detective is what keeps that old house going, with the rooms on the roof full of orchid plants, with Theodore Horstmann as tender, and Fritz Brenner serving up the best meals in New York, and me, Archie Goodwin, asking for a raise every time I buy a new suit, and sometimes getting it. It takes a gross of at least ten thousand a month to get by.

That January and the first half of February business was slow, except for the routine jobs, where all Wolfe and I had to do was supervise Saul Panzer and Fred Durkin and Orrie Cather, and for a little mix-up with a gang of fur hijackers during which Fred and I got shot at. Then, nearly six weeks after the day Cramer dropped in to see what would happen if he showed a piece of paper to a genius, and got a brush-off, a man named John R. Wellman phoned on Monday morning for an appointment, and I told him to come at six that afternoon. When he arrived, a few minutes early, I escorted him to the office and sat him in the red leather chair to wait until Wolfe came down from the plant rooms, sliding the little table near his right elbow, for his convenience if he needed to do any writing, for instance in a checkbook. He was a plump short guy, going bald, without much of a nose to hold up his rimless glasses. His plain gray suit and haberdashery didn't indicate opulence, but he had told me on the phone that he was a wholesale grocer from Peoria, Illinois, and there had been time to get a report from the bank. We would take his check if that was on the program.

When Wolfe entered, Wellman stood up to shake hands. Sometimes Wolfe makes an effort to conceal his dislike of shaking hands with strangers, and sometimes he doesn't. This time he did fairly well, then rounded the corner of his desk and got his seventh of a ton deposited in the only chair on earth that really suits him. He rested his forearms on the arms of the chair and leaned back.

"Yes, Mr. Wellman?"

"I want to hire you," Wellman said.

"For what?"

"I want you to find—" He stopped short, and his jaw muscles began to work. He shook his head violently, took off his glasses, dug at his eyes with his fingertips, put the glasses back on, and had trouble getting them adjusted. "I'm not under very good control," he apologized. "I haven't had enough sleep lately and I'm tired. I want you to find the person who killed my daughter."

Wolfe shot a glance at me, and I got my notebook and pen. Wellman, concentrating on Wolfe, wasn't interested in me. Wolfe asked him, "When and where and how did she die?"

"She was run over by a car in Van Cortlandt Park seventeen days ago. Friday evening, February second." Wellman had himself in hand now. "I ought to tell you about her."

"Go ahead."

"My wife and I live in Peoria, Illinois. I've been in business there over twenty years. We had one child, one daughter, Joan. We were very—" He stopped. He sat completely still, not even his eyes moving, for a long moment, and then went on. "We were very proud of her. She graduated from Smith with honors four years ago and took a job in the editorial department of Scholl and Hanna, the book publishers. She did well there—I have been told that by Scholl himself. She was twenty-six last November." He made a little gesture. "Looking at me, you wouldn't think I'd have a beautiful daughter, but she was. Everybody agreed she was beautiful, and she was extremely intelligent."

He got a large envelope from his side pocket. "I might as well give you these now." He left his chair to hand Wolfe the envelope. "A dozen prints of the best likeness we have of her. I got them for the police to use, but they weren't using them, so you can. You can see for yourself."

Wolfe extended a hand with one of the prints, and I arose to take it. Beautiful is a big word, but there's no point in quibbling, and if that was a good likeness Joan Wellman had been a good-looking girl. There was slightly too much chin for my taste, but the forehead and eyes were all any father had a right to expect.

"She was beautiful," Wellman said, and stopped and was still again.

Wolfe couldn't stand to see people overcome. "I suggest," he muttered, "that you avoid words like 'beautiful' and 'proud.' The colder facts will serve. You want to hire me to learn who drove the car that hit her?"

"I'm a damn fool," Wellman stated.

"Then don't hire me."

"I don't mean I'm a damn fool to hire you. I mean I intend to handle this efficiently and I ought to do it." His jaw muscles moved, but not through loss of control. "It's like this. We got a wire two weeks ago Saturday that Joan was dead. We drove to Chicago and took a plane to

New York. We saw her body. The car wheels had run over the middle of her, and there was a big lump on her head over her right ear. I talked to the police and the medical examiner."

Wellman was being efficient now. "I do not believe Joan was walking in that secluded spot in that park, not a main road, on a cold evening in the middle of winter, and neither does my wife. How did she get the lump on her head? The car didn't hit her head. The medical examiner says it's possible she fell on her head, but he's careful how he says it, and I don't believe it. The police claim they're working on it, doing all they can, but I don't believe that either. I think they think it was just a hit-and-run driver, and all they're doing is to try to find the car. I think my daughter was murdered, and I think I know the name of the man that killed her."

"Indeed." Wolfe's brows went up a little. "Have you told them so?"

"I certainly have, and they just nod and say they're working on it. They haven't got anywhere and they're not going to. So I decided to come to you—"

"Have you any evidence?"

"I call it evidence, but I guess they don't." He took an envelope from his breast pocket. "Joan wrote home every week, hardly ever missed." He removed a sheet of paper from the envelope and unfolded it. "This is a copy I had typed, I let the police have the original. It's dated February first, which was a Thursday. I'll read only part of it.

"Oh, I must tell you, I have a new kind of date tomorrow evening. As you know, since Mr. Hanna decided that our rejections of manuscripts must have the personal touch, except when it's just tripe, which I must say most of it is, I return quite a lot of stuff with a typed note with my name signed, and so do the other readers. Well, last fall sometime I did that with the manuscript of a novel by a man named Baird Archer, only I had forgotten all about it, until yesterday there was a phone call for me, at the office, and a man's voice said he was Baird Archer, and did I remember the note I had sent him returning his manuscript, and I said I did. He asked if anyone else had read it, and I said no, and then he propositioned me! He said he would pay me twenty dollars an hour to discuss the novel with him and make suggestions to improve it! How do you like that? Even if it's only five hours, that will be an extra hundred dollars for the exchequer, only it won't stay in the exchequer very long, as you know, my darling and doting parents, if you know me, and you ought to. I'm to meet him tomorrow right after office hours."

Wellman waggled the paper. "Now she wrote that on—"

"May I see it, please?" Wolfe was leaning forward with a gleam in his eye. Apparently something about Joan Wellman's letter home had given him a kick, but when Wellman handed it to him he gave it only a brief glance before passing it to me. I read it clear through with my eyes while my ears recorded their talk for the notebook.

"She wrote that," Wellman said, "on Thursday, February first. Her appointment with that man was the next day, Friday, right after office hours. Early Saturday morning her body was found on that out-of-the-way road in Van Cortlandt Park. What's wrong with thinking that that man killed her?"

Wolfe was leaning back again. "Was there any evidence of assault? Assault as a euphemism for rape?"

"No." Wellman's eyes went shut, and his hands closed into fists. After a moment the eyes opened again. "Nothing like that. No sign at all of that."

"What do the police say?"

"They say they're still trying to find that man Archer and can't. No trace of him. I think—"

"Nonsense. Of course there's a trace. Publishers must keep records. He submitted a manuscript of a novel last fall, and it was returned to him with a note from your daughter. Returned how and where?"

"It was returned by mail to the only address he gave,

General Delivery, Clinton Station. That's on West Tenth Street." Wellman's fists became hands again, and he turned a palm up. "I'm not saying the police have just laid down on the job. Maybe they've even done the best they can, but the fact remains that it's been seventeen days now and they haven't got anywhere, and I don't like the way they talked yesterday and this morning. It looks to me like they don't want it to be an unsolved murder, and they want to call it manslaughter, and that's all it would be if it was a hit-and-run accident. I don't know about these New York police, but you tell me, they might do a thing like that, mightn't they?"

Wolfe grunted. "It is conceivable. And you want me to prove it was murder and find the murderer, with evidence?"

"Yes." Wellman hesitated, opening his mouth and closing it again. He glanced at me and returned to Wolfe. "I tell you, Mr. Wolfe, I am willing to admit that what I am doing is vindictive and wicked. My wife thinks it is, and so does the pastor of my church. I was home one day last week, and they both said so. It is sinful to be vindictive, but here I am, and I'm going through with it. Even if it was just a hit-and-run accident I don't think the police are going to find him, and whatever it was I'm not going back to Peoria and sell groceries until he's found and made to pay for it. I've got a good paying business, and I own some property, and I never figured on dying a pauper, but I will if I have to, to get the murderous criminal that killed my daughter. Maybe I shouldn't say that. I don't know you too well, I only know you by reputation, and maybe you won't want to work for a man who can say an unchristian thing like that, so maybe it's a mistake to say it, but I want to be honest about it."

Wellman took his glasses off and started wiping them with a handkerchief. That showed his better side. He didn't want to embarrass Wolfe by keeping his eyes on him while Wolfe was deciding whether to take on a job for such an implacable bastard as John R. Wellman of Peoria, Illinois.

"I'll be honest too," Wolfe said dryly. "The morality of vengeance is not a factor in my acceptance or refusal of a case. But it was a mistake for you to say it, because I would have asked for a retainer of two thousand dollars and now I'll make it five thousand. Not merely to gouge you, though. Since the police have turned up nothing in seventeen days, it will probably take a lot of work and money. With a few more facts I'll have enough to start on."

"I wanted to be honest about it," Wellman insisted.

When he left, half an hour later, his check was under a paperweight on my desk, along with the copy of Joan Wellman's last letter home, and there was an assortment of facts in my notebook—plenty, as Wolfe had said, for a start. I went to the hall with him and helped him on with his coat. When I opened the door to let him out he wanted to shake hands, and I was glad to oblige.

"You're sure you won't mind," he asked, "if I ring you fairly often? Just to find out if there's anything new? I'll try not to make a nuisance of myself, but I'm like that. I'm persistent."

"Any time," I assured him. "I can always say 'no progress'."

"He *is* good, isn't he? Mr. Wolfe?"

"He's the best." I made it positive.

"Well—I hope—all right." He crossed the sill into an icy wind from the west, and I stood there until he had descended from the stoop to the sidewalk. The shape he was in, he might have tumbled down those seven steps.

Returning down the hall, I paused a moment before entering the office, to sniff. Fritz, as I knew, was doing spareribs with the sauce Wolfe and he had concocted and, though the door to the kitchen was closed, enough came through for my nose, and it approved. In the office, Wolfe was leaning back with his eyes closed. I picked up Wellman's check, gave it an admiring glance, went and put it in the safe, and then crossed to Wolfe's desk for another look at one of the prints of Joan Wellman's likeness. As near as you can tell from a picture, it would have been nice to know her.

I spoke. "If you're working, knock off. Dinner in ten minutes."

Wolfe's eyes opened.

I asked, "Have we got a murder or not?"

"Certainly we have." He was supercilious.

"Oh. Good for us. Because she wouldn't go for a walk in the park in February?"

"No." He humphed. "You should have a better reason."

"Me? Thanks. Me have a reason?"

"Yes, Archie. I have been training you for years to observe. You are slacking. Not long ago Mr. Cramer showed us a list of names on a sheet of paper. The seventh name on that list was Baird Archer. The evening she was killed Miss Wellman had an appointment with a man named Baird Archer. Leonard Dykes who wrote that list of names was murdered. It would be silly not to hypothesize that Miss Wellman was also murdered."

I turned on my heel, took the two paces to my swivel chair, turned it so I would face him, and sat. "Oh, that," I said carelessly. "I crossed that off as coincidence."

"Pfui. It never struck you. You're slacking."

"Okay. I am not electronized."

"There is no such word."

"There is now. I've used it." I was getting indignant. "I mean I am not lightning. It was six weeks ago that Cramer showed us that list of names, and I gave it the merest glance. I know you did too, but look who you are. What if it were the other way around? What if I had remembered that name from one short glimpse of that list six weeks ago and you hadn't? I would be the owner of this house and the bank account, and you would be working for me. Would you like that? Or do you prefer it as it is? Take your pick."

He snorted. "Call Mr. Cramer."

"Right." I swiveled to the phone and dialed.

3

IF YOU like Anglo-Saxon, I belched. If you fancy
Latin, I eructed. No matter which, I had known that
Wolfe and Inspector Cramer would have to put up
with it that evening, because that is always a part of my
reaction to sauerkraut. I don't glory in it or go for a
record, but neither do I fight it back. I want to be liked
just for myself.

If either Cramer or Wolfe noticed it he gave no sign. I
was where I belonged during an evening session in the
office and, with Wolfe behind his desk and Cramer in
the red leather chair, I was to one side of the line of
fire. It had started off sociable enough, with Wolfe offering refreshment and Cramer choosing bourbon and
water, and Fritz bringing it, and Cramer giving it a go
and saying it was good whisky, which was true.

"You said on the phone," he told Wolfe, "you have
something I can use."

Wolfe put his beer glass down and nodded. "Yes, sir.
Unless you no longer need it. I've seen nothing in the
paper recently about the Leonard Dykes case—the body
fished out of the river nearly two months ago. Have you
got it in hand?"

"No."

"Any progress?"

"Nothing—no."

"Then I would like to consult you about something,
because it's a little ticklish." Wolfe leaned back and
adjusted himself for comfort. "I have to make a choice.
Seventeen days ago the body of a young woman named
Joan Wellman was found on a secluded road in Van
Cortlandt Park. She had been struck by an automobile.

Her father, from Peoria, Illinois, is dissatisfied with the way the police are handling the matter and has hired me to investigate. I saw him just this evening; he left only two hours ago, and I phoned you immediately. I have reason to think that Miss Wellman's death was not an accident and that there was an important connection between the two homicides—hers and Dykes's."

"That's interesting," Cramer conceded. "Something your client told you?"

"Yes. So I'm faced with an alternative. I can make a proposal to your colleague in the Bronx. I can offer to tell him of this link connecting the two deaths, which will surely be of great help to him, on the condition that he collaborates with me, within reason, to satisfy my client—when the case is solved—that I have earned my fee. Or I can make that proposal to you. Since the death of my client's daughter occurred in the Bronx and therefore is in your colleague's jurisdiction, perhaps I should go to him, but on the other hand Dykes was killed in Manhattan. What do you think?"

"I think," Cramer growled, "I expected something like this and here it is. You want me to pay for information about a murder by promising to help you collect a fee, and you threaten to take it to the Bronx if I won't buy. If he won't buy either, then you withhold it? Huh?"

"I have no information to withhold."

"Goddam it, you said you—"

"I said I have reason to think the two deaths are connected. It's based on information, of course, but I have none that the police do not have. The Police Department is a huge organization. If your staff and the Bronx staff get together on this it's likely that sooner or later they'll get where I am. I thought this would save you time and work. I can't be charged with withholding information when I know nothing that the police don't know—collectively."

Cramer snorted. "Some day," he said darkly, and snorted again.

"I offer this," Wolfe said, "because you might as well

have it, and because the case looks complex enough to need a lot of work and my resources are limited. I make the offer conditional because if with my hint you solve it in a hurry without further consultation with me, I don't want my client to refuse to pay my bill. I am willing to put it like this: if, when it's finished, you think it likely that the Wellman case would not have been solved if Mr. Wellman had not come to me, you tell him so, not for publication."

Wolfe levered himself forward to reach for his glass and drink.

"I'll take it that way," Cramer stated. "Let's have it."

Wolfe wiped his lips with his handkerchief. "Also Mr. Goodwin is to be permitted to look over the two files—on Dykes and on Miss Wellman."

"I don't have the Wellman file."

"When I explain the connection you'll get it."

"It's against Department regulations."

"Indeed? I beg your pardon. It would be mutually helpful to share information, and it would waste my time and my client's money to collect again the facts you already have, but of course a violation of regulations is unthinkable."

Cramer glared at him. "You know," he said, "one of the many reasons you're hard to take is that when you're being sarcastic you don't sound sarcastic. That's just one of your offensive habits. Okay, I'll see you get facts. What's this connection?"

"With the condition as stated."

"Hell yes. I'd hate to see you starve."

Wolfe turned to me. "Archie. That letter?"

I got it from under the paperweight and handed it to him.

"This," he told Cramer, "is a copy of a letter Miss Wellman wrote to her parents on Thursday, February first. She was killed the evening of the next day, Friday." He held it out, and Cramer got up to take it. "Read it all if you like, but the relevant part is the marked paragraph."

Cramer ran over it. He took his time, and then sat frowning at it. Looking up at Wolfe, he kept the frown. "I've seen that name somewhere. Baird Archer. Isn't that it?"

Wolfe nodded. "Shall we see how long it takes you to dig it up?"

"No. Where?"

"On the list of names written by Leonard Dykes which you came here to show me six weeks ago. It was seventh on the list, I think—possibly eighth. Not sixth."

"When did you first see this letter?"

"This evening. My client gave it to me."

"I'll be damned." Cramer gawked at him and at the relevant paragraph. He folded the letter with slow deliberate fingers and put it in his pocket.

"The original," Wolfe told him, "is in the possession of your colleague in the Bronx. That's my copy."

"Yeah. I'll borrow it." Cramer reached for his glass, took a swallow, and focused his eyes on a corner of Wolfe's arcwood desk. He took another swallow and went back to studying the desk. So alternating, two more swallows with intervals for desk study emptied the glass. He put it down on the little table.

"What else have you got?"

"Nothing."

"What have you done?"

"Nothing. Since I saw that letter, I have dined."

"I bet you have." Cramer came up out of his chair, still springy in spite of his years. "I'll be going. Damn it, I was going home."

He headed for the hall. I followed.

When I returned to the office after letting the law out, Wolfe was placidly opening a bottle of beer.

"What do you say," I suggested, "I get on the phone and call in Saul and Fred and Orrie, and you lay it out, and we set a deadline, sundown tomorrow would do, for solving *both* cases? Just to make a monkey out of Cramer?"

Wolfe scowled at me. "Confound it, don't bounce like

that. This will be no skirmish. Mr. Cramer's men have been looking, more or less, for a Baird Archer for seven weeks. The Bronx men have been looking for one for seventeen days. Now they'll get serious about it. What if there isn't one?"

"We know there was enough of one to date Joan Wellman for February second."

"We do not. We know only that she wrote her parents that a stranger on the telephone had said he was Baird Archer, and that a manuscript of a novel bearing that name had been submitted to her employers, read by her, and returned in the mail to a Baird Archer at General Delivery." Wolfe shook his head. "No, this will be more than a skirmish. Before we're through Mr. Wellman may indeed be a pauper unless his rancor wears thin. Let the police do their part."

Knowing him as I did, I didn't care for that. I sat down. "Sitzlust again?" I demanded offensively.

"No. I said let the police do their part. This will take work. We'll start with the assumption, not risky I think, that Miss Wellman's letter to her parents was straightforward. If so, it had something for us besides the name of Baird Archer. He asked her if anyone else had read his manuscript and she said no. It could have been an innocent question, but in the light of what happened to her it raises a point. Was she killed because she had read the manuscript? As a conjecture that is not inane. How many public stenographers are there in the city? Say in Manhattan?"

"I don't know. Five hundred. Five thousand."

"Not thousands surely. People who make presentable copies of documents or manuscripts from drafts."

"That's typing services, not public stenographers."

"Very well." Wolfe drank beer and leaned back. "I thought of suggesting this to Mr. Cramer, but if we're to spend some of Mr. Wellman's money this is as good a way to start as any. I would like to know what that novel was about. Baird Archer may have typed the manuscript himself, but he may not. We'll put Saul and

Fred and Orrie on a round of the typing services. Have them here at eight in the morning and I'll give them instructions. There is a possibility not only of learning about the novel, but also of getting a description of Baird Archer."

"Right." This was more like it. "It wouldn't hurt me to stretch my legs too."

"You will. There's a chance, though this may be slimmer, that the novel had previously been submitted to another publisher. It's worth trying. Start with the better firms, of the class of Scholl and Hanna. But not tomorrow. Tomorrow get all you can from the police files on both Miss Wellman and Dykes, covering everything. For instance, did Dykes have a typewriter in his apartment?"

I lifted a brow. "Do you think Dykes was Baird Archer?"

"I don't know. He wrote that list of names, obviously inventions. He certainly wasn't Baird Archer on February second, since he had been dead five weeks. You will also go to Scholl and Hanna. In spite of what Miss Wellman wrote her parents, it's possible that someone else read that manuscript, or at least glanced through it. Or Miss Wellman may have said something about it to one of her associates. Or, less likely, Baird Archer may have delivered the manuscript in person and be remembered—of course that was last fall, months ago."

Wolfe heaved a sigh and reached for his glass. "I suggest that you extend the deadline beyond sundown tomorrow."

"What the hell," I said generously, "I'll give you till Friday."

It was just as well I didn't say what Friday.

4

WHAT with getting Saul and Fred and Orrie sicked onto
the typing services, and dealing with the morning mail,
and going to the bank to deposit Wellman's check, it
was well after ten o'clock Tuesday when I got to
Cramer's office on Twentieth Street. He wasn't there but
had left instructions with Sergeant Purley Stebbins. I am
one of the few people Purley knows that he has not
completely made up his mind about. Since I'm a private
detective, the sooner I die, or at least get lost outside the
city limits, the better—of course that's basic, but he can't
quite get rid of the suspicion that I might have made a
good cop if I had been caught in time.

I not only got a look at the files, I even got to talk
with two of the help who had worked on Dykes and one
from the Bronx who had worked on Joan Wellman. By
the time I left, a little before three, I had a lot in my
notebook and more in my head.

For here I'll trim it down. Leonard Dykes, forty-one,
found banging up against a pile in the East River on
New Year's Day, had for eight years been a clerk, not a
member of the bar, in the office of the law firm of
Corrigan, Phelps, Kustin and Briggs. Up to a year ago
the firm's name had been O'Malley, Corrigan and
Phelps, but O'Malley had been disbarred and there had
been a reorganization. Dykes had been unmarried, sober,
trustworthy, and competent. He had played cards every
Tuesday evening with friends, for small stakes. He had
twelve thousand dollars in government bonds and a
savings account, and thirty shares of United States Steel,
which had been inherited by a married sister who lived
in California, his only close relative. No one discoverable

had hated or feared him or wished him ill. One sentence in one report said, "No women at all." There was a photograph of him after he had been hauled out of the river, not attractive, and one of him alive that had been taken from his apartment. To be objective, I'll put it that he had been less unattractive before drowning than after. He had had popeyes, and his chin had started backing up about a quarter of an inch below his mouth.

The other thousand or so facts in the file on Dykes had as little discernible bearing on his murder as those I have given for samples.

On Joan Wellman, the Bronx had not been as much in love with the hit-and-run theory as Wellman suspected, but it was just as well that her father did not have access to the police file. They didn't care much for Joan's version of her Friday date in her letter home, especially since they could find no one among her office associates to whom she had mentioned it. I gave them a low mark on that, knowing how full offices are of petty jealousies and being willing to give our client's daughter credit for enough sense to keep her mouth shut about her private affairs. Aside from the search for the car that had run over her, the Bronx had mostly concentrated on her boy friends. If you want to give the average dick a job he really likes, sit him down with a man who has been seen fairly recently in the company of a pretty girl who has just died a sudden and violent death. Think of the questions he can ask. Look at the ground he can cover, no matter who the man is, with no risk of a comeback that will cost him anything.

So the Bronx had done the boy friends up brown, especially an advertising copywriter named Atchison, apparently because his name began with "A" and had a "c" and an "h" in it, and it had dawned upon some eagle eye that Archer did too, and what more do you want? Luckily for Atchison, he had taken a four-thirty train Friday afternoon, February second, to spend the weekend with friends at Westport. Two dicks had worked like dogs trying to pry that alibi loose, with no success.

As far as I could tell from the file, it looked as if Joan had had not only beauty and intelligence but also good old-fashioned virtue. The three boy friends who had been flushed were unanimous on that. They had admired and respected her. One of them had been after her for a year to marry him and had had hopes. If any of them had had reason to prefer her dead, the Bronx had failed to dig up a hint of it.

I went back home and typed it all up for Wolfe, and got reports on the phone from Saul and Fred and Orrie.

I spent most of Wednesday at the office of Scholl and Hanna on Forty-fifth Street. What I got out of it was a respectful appreciation of the book-publishing business as a means of corralling jack. The office took up two whole floors, with nothing spared anywhere in the way of rugs and furniture. Scholl was in Florida, I was told, and Hanna never got in until ten-thirty. I was escorted down a hall to the room of a junior executive who needed a haircut and was chewing gum, and when I showed him the note I had from our client he said they would be glad to cooperate with the bereaved father of their late employee, and I could ask questions of any of the staff I cared to see, starting with him if I wanted to. But would I please tell him, had something new turned up? City detectives, three of them, had been there again yesterday, for hours, and now here was Nero Wolfe's Archie Goodwin. What was stirring? I told him something harmless and began on him.

The fact that Wolfe never leaves the office on business, unless there is an incentive more urgent than the prospect of a fee, such as saving his own skin, has a lot to do with the way I work. When I'm out on a case and get something helpful I like to recognize it before I deliver it to Wolfe, but as I left Scholl and Hanna's I couldn't see a crumb. It was hard to believe that I had spent nearly five hours in the office where Joan Wellman had worked, questioning everybody from the office boy to Hanna himself, without getting a single useful item, but that was how it looked. The one thing that tied in at all was an entry in the columns of a big book I had been shown. I give it with the column headings:

NUMBER: 16237
DATE: Oct. 2
NAME AND ADDRESS: Baird Archer, General Delivery, Clinton Station, N. Y. City
TITLE: Put Not Your Trust
DETAIL: Novel 246 pp.
POSTAGE ENCLOSED: 63¢
READ BY: Joan Wellman
DISPOSITION: Rejected ret'd. mail Oct. 27

That was my haul. The manuscript had been received by mail. No one had ever heard of Baird Archer, except for that entry. No one else had looked at the manuscript or remembered anything about it. If Joan had made any comment on it to anyone they had forgotten it. She had not mentioned the phone call from Baird Archer or her appointment with him. I could go on with negatives for a page.

When I reported to Wolfe that evening I told him, "It looks to me as if we're all set. Two hundred and forty-six sheets of typewriter paper weigh a lot more than twenty-one ounces. Either he wrote on both sides, or he used thin light paper, or he didn't enclose enough postage. All we have to do is find out which and we've got him."

"Harlequin," he growled.

"Have you a better suggestion? From what I've brought in?"

"No."

"Did I get anything at all?"

"No."

"Okay. That's what I mean. Two days of me, nothing. Two days of the boys calling on typing services, nothing. At two hundred bucks a day, four C's of Wellman's money already gone. This would be all right for an agency or the cops, that's how they work, but it's not your way. I'll bet you a week's pay you haven't turned your brain on it once during the forty-eight hours!"

"On what?" he demanded. "I can't grapple with a shadow. Get me something of him—a gesture, an odor, a word, a sound he made. Bring me something."

I had to admit, though of course not to him, that he had a point. You could say that Cramer had a trained army looking for Baird Archer, but it wouldn't mean much. They had no idea what he looked like. They had no evidence that anyone had ever known him, or even met him, by that name. There was no proof that Baird Archer had ever been anything *but* a name. It would be about the same if you just made up a name for a man, say Freetham Choade, and then tried to find him. After you look in the phone book, what do you do next?

I spent the rest of that week collecting some very interesting data about the quality and tone of publishers' offices. I learned that Simon and Schuster, in Rockefeller Center, had fallen hard for modern and didn't give a damn what it cost; that Harper and Brothers liked old desks and didn't care for ashtrays; that the Viking Press had a good eye for contours and comeliness when hiring female help; that The Macmillian Company had got itself confused with a Pullman car; and so on. I covered the whole trade, big and little, and the only concrete result was a dinner date with a young woman at Scribner's who struck me as worth following up on the chance that she might have something I would like to know about. No one anywhere knew anything about a Baird Archer. If he had submitted the manuscript of "Put Not Your Trust" to any other firm than Scholl and Hanna, there was no record or memory of it.

Over the weekend I had a couple of talks with Purley Stebbins. If we were getting nowhere fast, so were the cops. They had uncovered a Baird Archer somewhere down in Virginia, but he was over eighty and couldn't read or write. Their big idea was to find some link between Leonard Dykes and Joan Wellman, and three of Cramer's best men were clawing away at it. When I reported that to Wolfe Sunday evening he snorted.

"Jackassery. I gave them the link."

"Yes, sir," I said sympathetically. "That was what tired you out."

"I am not tired out. I am not even tired."

"Then I lied to our client. The second time he called today I told him that you were exhausted with overwork on his case. I had to tell him something drastic because he's getting impatient. What's wrong with the beer? Too cold?"

"No. I am considering you. Most of these typing services are run by women, aren't they?"

"Not most. All."

"Then you will start on that tomorrow morning. You may be luckier than Saul and Fred and Orrie, but they will continue at it too. We'll finish that job before we try something else. Some of the women are surely young and personable. Don't overwork."

"I won't." I gazed at him admiringly. "It's uncanny, these flashes of inspiration you get. Absolutely brilliant!"

He exploded. "Confound it, what have I got? Get me something! Will you get me something?"

"Certainly." I was composed. "Drink your beer."

So the next day, Monday, after finishing the morning office chores I took a geographical section of the list Saul and I had compiled, and went at it. The other three had covered downtown Manhattan up to Fourteenth Street, the Grand Central section, and the West Side from Fourteenth to Forty-second. That day Fred was in Brooklyn, Orrie in the Bronx, and Saul on the East Side. I took the West Side from Forty-second Street up.

At ten-thirty I was in bedlam, having entered through a door inscribed BROADWAY STENOGRAPHIC SERVICE. In a room big enough to accommodate comfortably five typewriter desks and typists, double that number were squeezed in, hitting the keys at about twice my normal speed. I was yelling at a dame with a frontage that would have made a good bookshelf.

"A woman like you should have a private room!"

"I have," she said haughtily, and led me through a door in a partition to a cubbyhole. Since the partition was only six feet high, the racket bounced down on us off the ceiling. Two minutes later the woman was telling me, "We don't give out any information about clients. Our business is strictly confidential."

I had given her my business card. "So is ours!" I shouted. "Look, it's quite simple. Our client is a reputable firm of book publishers. They have a manuscript of a novel that was submitted to them, and they're enthusiastic about it and want to publish it, but the page of the script that had the author's name and address got lost somehow and can't be found. They remember the author's name, Baird Archer, but not the address, and they want to get in touch with him. They might not be so anxious if they didn't want to publish the novel, but they do. His name is not in any phone book. The manuscript came in the mail, unsolicited. They've advertised and got no answer. All I want to know, did you type a manuscript of a novel for a man named Baird Archer, probably last September? Sometime around then? The title of the novel was 'Put Not Your Trust.'"

She stayed haughty. "Last September? They've waited long enough to inquire."

"They've been trying to find him."

"If we typed it a page couldn't have got lost. It would have been fastened into one of our folders."

The boys had told me of running into that one. I nodded. "Yes, but editors don't like to read fastened scripts. They take the folders off. If you typed it for him, you can bet he would want you to help us find him. Give the guy a break."

She had remained standing. "All right," she said, "I'll look it up as soon as I get something straightened out." She left me.

I waited for her twenty minutes, and then another ten while she fussed through a card file. The answer was no. They had never done any work for a Baird Archer. I took an elevator up to the eighteenth floor, to the office of the Raphael Typing Service.

Those first two calls took me nearly an hour, and at

that rate you can't cover much ground in a day. They were all kinds and sizes, from a big outfit in the Paramount Building called Metropolitan Stenographers, Inc., down to two girls with their office in their room-bath-and-kitchenette in the upper Forties. For lunch I had canneloni at Sardi's, on John R. Wellman, and then resumed.

It was warm for February, but it was trying to make up its mind whether to go in for a steady drizzle, and around three o'clock, as I dodged through the sidewalk traffic to enter a building on Broadway in the Fifties, I was wishing I had worn my raincoat instead of my brown topcoat. My quarry in that building was apparently one of the small ones, since its name on my list was just the name of a woman, Rachel Abrams. The building was an old one, nothing fancy, with Caroline, women's dresses, on the left of the entrance, and the Midtown Eatery on the right. After stopping in the lobby to remove my topcoat and give it a shake, and consulting the building directory, I took the elevator to the seventh floor. The elevator man told me to go left for 728.

I went left, rounded a corner to the right, continued, turned right again, and in ten paces was at Room 728. The door was wide open, and I stuck my head in to verify the number, 728, and to see the inscription:

RACHEL ABRAMS
*Stenography
and Typing*

I stepped into a room about ten by twelve, not more, with a typewriter desk, a little table, a couple of chairs, a clothes rack, and an old green metal filing cabinet. A woman's hat and cloth coat hung on the rack, and an umbrella, and at the back of the typewriter desk was a vase of yellow daffodils. On the floor were some sheets of paper, scattered around. That was accounted for by the fact that the one window was raised, way up, and a strong draft was whirling through.

Something else was coming through too: voices from down in the street that were shouts. Three steps took me to the window, and I looked out and down. People had stopped in the drizzle and were gawking. Three men, from different directions, were running across the street toward the building, and on this side a group was forming on the sidewalk. In the center of the group two men were bending over a figure of a woman prostrate on the sidewalk, with her skirt up, showing her bare legs, and her head twisted sideways. I have good eyes, but from seven floors up, in the dim light of the drizzle blown by the wind, things were blurred. Most of the group were looking at the huddled figure, but some were gazing straight up at me. Off to the left a hundred feet, a cop was trotting toward the group.

I assert that it took me not more than three seconds to realize what had happened. I assert it not to get a credit mark, since I can't prove it, but to account for what I did. Of course it was only a hunch, but I had never had one that felt like a better bet. Wolfe had told me to get him something, and I had missed getting it by three minutes or maybe only two. I was so sure of it that what I did was automatic. Pulling back from the window and straightening, I darted a glance at the desk and one at the filing cabinet. I started with the desk only because it was nearer.

That was probably the briefest search on record, or close to it. The shallow middle drawer was eliminated with one look. The top left drawer held paper and carbon and envelopes. The one below it had three compartments, with miscellaneous contents, and in the middle one was a notebook bound in brown imitation leather. At the top of the first page was written the word "Receipts," and the first entry was dated Aug. 7, 1944. I flipped the pages to 1950, began with July, ran my eye over the items, and there it was: "Sept. 12, Baird Archer, $60.00 dep." Six lines down another entry said: "Sept. 23, Baird Archer, $38.40 in full."

"Of all the goddam lousy luck," I said with feeling and, slipping the notebook in my pocket, made for the door. There was a bare chance that Rachel Abrams had enough life left in her to talk a little. As I rounded the second turn in the hall an elevator door opened and a flatfoot emerged. I was so engrossed that I didn't even glance at him, which was a mistake because cops can't bear not to be glanced at, especially when they're on something hot. He stopped in my path and demanded, "Who are you?"

"Governor Dewey," I told him. "How do you like me without the mustache?"

"Oh, a wag. Show me some identification."

I raised the brows. "How did I get behind the Iron Curtain without knowing it?"

"I'm in a hurry. What's your name?"

I shook my head. "Honest, officer, I don't like this. Take me to the nearest Kremlin and I'll tell the sergeant." I stepped and pushed the down button.

"Aw, nuts." He tramped down the hall.

An elevator stopped and I entered. The elevator man was telling his passengers about the excitement. The street lobby was deserted. Out on the sidewalk the crowd was thick now, ignoring the drizzle, and I had to get authoritative to elbow my way through to the front. A cop was there, commanding them to stand back. I had a line ready to hand him to get me an approach, but when I got close enough for an unobstructed view I saw I wouldn't need it. She was smashed good, and there would be no more talking from a head that had taken that angle to the shoulders. Nor did I have to ask her name, since I had heard everybody telling everybody else, Rachel Abrams, as I pushed my way through the mob. I pushed my way out again, went to the corner and grabbed a taxi, and gave the driver the number on West Thirty-fifth Street.

When I mounted the stoop and let myself in with my

key it was five minutes past four, so Wolfe had gone up for his afternoon conference with the orchids. Hanging my hat and topcoat in the hall, I ascended the three flights to the plant rooms on the roof. For all the thousands of times I have seen that display of show-offs, they still take my eye and slow me down whenever I go through, but that day I didn't even know they were there, not even in the warm room, though the Phalaenopsis were in top bloom and the Cattleyas were splashing color all around.

Wolfe was in the potting room with Theodore, transferring young Dendrobium chrysotoxums from fours to fives. As I approached he snapped at me, "Can't it wait?"

"I suppose so," I conceded. "She's dead. I just want permission to phone Cramer. I might as well, since I was seen by the elevator man who let me off at her floor, and a cop, and my fingerprints are on her desk."

"Who is dead?"

"The woman who typed that manuscript for Baird Archer."

"When and how?"

"Just now. She died while I was in the elevator going up to her office on the seventh floor. She was going down faster, out of her window. What killed her was hitting the sidewalk."

"How do you know she typed the manuscript?"

"I found this in her desk." I took the notebook from my pocket and showed him the entries. His hands were too dirty to touch it, and I held it before his eyes. I asked him, "Do you want details now?"

"Confound it. Yes."

As I reported in full he stood with the tips of his dirty fingers resting on the potting bench, his head turned to me, his lips tight, his brow creased with a frown. His yellow smock, some half an acre in area, was exactly the color of the daffodils on Rachel Abrams' desk.

When I had finished the story I inquired grimly, "Shall I expound?"

He grunted.

"I should have stuck around, but it wouldn't have done any good because I was too goddam mad to function. If I had been three minutes earlier I would have had her alive. Also, if she was pushed out of the window I would have had the pusher alive, and you told me to get you something, and it would have been a pleasure to get you that. The lucky bastard. He must have entered a down elevator, or passed down the hall on his way to the stairs, not more than thirty seconds before I stepped out on that floor. When I looked out of the window he was probably there on the sidewalk, walking away because he wasn't morbid."

Wolfe's eyes opened and half shut again.

"If you're thinking," I said aggressively, "that she wasn't pushed, one will get you ten. I do not believe that the woman who typed that manuscript picked today to jump out of the window or to fall out by accident."

"Nevertheless, it's possible."

"I deny it. It would be too goddam silly. Okay, you said to get you something, and at least I got you this." I tapped the notebook with a finger.

"It doesn't help much." Wolfe was glum. "It establishes that Miss Wellman was killed because she had read that manuscript, but we were already going on that assumption. I doubt if it would gratify Miss Abrams to know that her death validated an assumption for us. Most people expect more than that of death. Mr. Cramer will want that notebook."

"Yeah. I shouldn't have copped it, but you said to get you something and I wanted to produce it. Shall I take it to him or phone him to send for it?"

"Neither. Put it here on the bench. I'll wash my hands and phone him. You have work to do. It's possible that Miss Abrams told someone something about the contents of that novel she typed. Try it. See her family and friends. Get a list of them. Saul and Fred and Orrie will phone in at five-thirty. You will phone at five-twenty-

five, to tell me where I can tell them to join you. Divide
the list among you."

"My God," I protested, "we're stretching it thinner and
thinner. Next you'll be trying to get it by photo-offset
from her typewriter platen."

He ignored it and headed for the sink to wash his
hands. I went to my room, one flight down, for my
raincoat. Downstairs I stopped in the kitchen to tell
Fritz I wouldn't be home for dinner.

5

IT WAS more than I had bargained for. Having got the
home address of a Rachel Abrams from the Bronx phone
book, having learned by dialing the number and speaking briefly with a female voice that that was it, and
having hit the subway before the rush hour, I had con-
gratulated myself on a neat fast start. I entered the old
apartment building on 178th Street a block off the Grand
Concourse less than an hour after Wolfe had told me to
see her family and friends.

But now I realized that I had been too damn fast. The
woman who opened the door of 4E to me was meeting
my eyes straight and inquiring placidly, "You're the one
that phoned? What is with my Rachel?"

"Are you Rachel's mother?" I asked.

She nodded and smiled. "Since some years I am. I
have never been told the opposite. What is?"

I hadn't bargained for this. I had taken it for granted
that either a cop or a journalist would have relayed the
news before I got there, and had been ready to cope
with tears and wailing, but obviously I had beat them to
it. Of course the thing to do was spill it to her, but her
quiet self-satisfaction when she said "my Rachel" was

too much for me. Nor could I say excuse it please, wrong number, and fade, because I had a job to do, and if I muffed it merely because I didn't like it I was in the wrong line of business. So I tried my damnedest to grin at her, but I admit that for a couple of seconds I was no help to the conversation.

Her big dark friendly eyes stayed straight at mine.

"I will maybe ask you to come in and sit," she said, "when you tell me what you want."

"I don't think," I told her, "I need to take much of your time. I told you my name on the phone, Archie Goodwin. I'm getting some stuff together for an article on public stenographers. Does your daughter discuss her work with you?"

She frowned a little. "You could ask her. Couldn't you?"

"Sure I could, if there's some reason why I shouldn't ask you."

"Why should there be a reason?"

"I don't know any. For instance, say she types a story or an article for a man. Does she tell you about him—what he looked like and how he talked? Or does she tell you what the story or article was about?"

The frown had not gone. "Would that be not proper?"

"Not at all. It's not a question of being proper, it's just that I want to make it personal, talking with her family and friends."

"Is it there will be an article about her?"

"Yes." That was not a lie. Far from it.

"Is it her name will be printed?"

"Yes."

"My daughter never talks about her work to me or her father or her sisters, only one thing, the money she makes. She tells about that because she gives me a certain part, but not for me, for the family, and one sister is in college. She does not tell me what men look like or about her work. If her name is going to be printed everybody ought to know the truth."

"You're absolutely right, Mrs. Abrams. Do you know—"

"You said you will talk with her family and friends. Her father will be home at twenty minutes to seven. Her sister Deborah is here now, doing her homework, but she is only sixteen—too young? Her sister Nancy will not be here today, she is with a friend, but she will be here tomorrow at half-past four. Then you want friends. There is a young man named William Butterfield who wants to marry her, but he is—"

She stopped short, with a twinkle in her eye. "If you will pardon me, but that is maybe too personal. If you want his address?"

"Please."

She gave me a number on Seventy-sixth Street. "There is Hulda Greenberg, she lives downstairs on the second floor, Two C. There is Cynthia Free, only that is not her real name. You know about her."

"I'm sorry, I'm afraid I don't."

"She acts on the stage."

"Oh, sure. Cynthia Free."

"Yes. She went to high school with Rachel, but she quit. I will not speak against her. If my daughter is once a friend she is always a friend. I will be getting old now, but what will I have? I will have my husband and Deborah and Nancy, and enough friends I have, many friends, but I know I will always have my Rachel. If her name is to be printed that must be part of it. I will tell you more about her, Mr. Goodwin, if you will come in and sit—oy, the phone. Excuse me, please?"

She turned and trotted inside. I stayed put. In a moment I heard her voice, faintly.

"Hello. . . . This is Mrs. Abrams. . . . Yes. . . . Yes, Rachel is my daughter. . . . Who is it you say? . . ."

There was no doubt about its being my move. The only question was whether to leave the door standing open or close it. It seemed better to close it. I reached for the knob, pulled it to quickly but with no bang, and headed for the stairs.

Out on the sidewalk, glancing at my wrist and seeing

5:24, I went to the corner for a look, saw a drugstore down a block, walked there, found a phone booth, and dialed the number. Fritz answered and put me through to the plant rooms.

When Wolfe was on I told him, "I've had a talk with Rachel's mother. She says her daughter never discusses her work at home. We were using the present tense because she hadn't got the news yet. She wants to see her Rachel's name in print, and thanks to that son of a bitch I missed by three minutes, she will. I didn't tell her because it would have wasted time. Tomorrow, when she knows that discussing her daughter's work may help to find the guy that killed her, she might possibly remember something, though I doubt it. I have some names, but they're scattered around town. Tell the boys to call me at this number." I gave it to him.

He spoke. "Mr. Cramer insists on seeing you. I gave him the information, and he sent for the notebook, but he wants to see you. He is sour, of course. You might as well go down there. After all, we are collaborating."

"Yeah. On what? Okay, I'll go. Don't overdo."

I waited in the booth to corner it. When the calls came I gave William Butterfield to Saul, Hulda Greenberg to Fred, and Cynthia Free to Orrie, telling them all to collect additional names and keep going. Then I hiked to the subway.

Down at Homicide on West Twentieth Street I learned how sour Cramer was. Over the years my presence has been requested at that address many times. When it's a case of our having something he would like to get, or he thinks it is, I am taken inside at once to his own room. When it's only some routine matter, I am left to Sergeant Purley Stebbins or one of the bunch. When all that is really wanted or expected is a piece of my hide, I am assigned to Lieutenant Rowcliff. If and when I am offered a choice of going to heaven or hell it will be simple; I'll merely ask, "Where's Rowcliff?" We were fairly even—he set my teeth on edge about the same as I did his—until one day I got the notion of stut-

tering. When he gets worked up to a certain point he
starts to stutter. My idea was to wait till he was about
there and then stutter just once. It more than met expectations. It made him so mad he had to stutter, he
couldn't help it, and then I complained that he was
mimicking me. From that day on I have had the long
end and he knows it.

I was with him an hour or so, and it was burlesque all
the way, because Wolfe had already given them my
story and there was nothing I could add. Rowcliff's line
was that I had overstepped when I searched her desk
and took the notebook, which was true, and that I had
certainly taken something besides the notebook and was
holding out. We went all around that, and back and
forth, and he had a statement typed for me to sign, and
after I signed it he sat and studied it and thought up
more questions. Finally I got tired.

"Look," I told him, "this is a lot of bull and you know
it. What are you trying to do, b-b-b-break my spirit?"

He clamped his jaw. But he had to say something. "I'd
rather b-b-b-break your goddam neck," he stated. "Get
the hell out of here."

I went, but not out. I intended to have one word with
Cramer. Down the hall I took a left turn, strode to the
door at the end, and opened it without knocking. But
Cramer wasn't there, only Purley Stebbins, sitting at a
table working with papers.

"You lost?" he demanded.

"No. I'm giving myself up. I just c-c-c-cooked Rowcliff
and ate him. Aside from that, I thought someone here
might want to thank me. If I hadn't been there today,
the precinct boys would probably have called it a jump
or a fall, and no one would have ever gone through that
book and found those entries."

Purley nodded. "So you found the entries."

"So I did."

"And took the book home to Wolfe."

"And then, without delay, turned it over."

"By God, so you did. Thank you. Going?"

"Yes. But I could use a detail without waiting for the morning paper. What's in the lead on how Rachel Abrams got out of the window?"

"Homicide."

"By flipping a coin?"

"No. Finger marks on her throat. Preliminary, the M.E. says she was choked. He thinks not enough to kill her, but we won't know until they're through at the laboratory."

"And I missed him by three minutes."

Purley cocked his head. "Did you?"

I uttered a colorful word. "One Rowcliff on the squad is enough," I told him and beat it. Out in the anteroom I went to a phone booth, dialed, got Wolfe, and reported, "Excuse me for interrupting your dinner, but I need instructions. I'm at Homicide on Twentieth Street, without cuffs, after an hour with Rowcliff and a word with Purley. From marks on her throat the dope is that she was choked and tossed out the window. I told you so. I divided the three names Mrs. Abrams gave me among the help, and told them to get more and carry on. There should be another call on the family either tonight or tomorrow, but not by me. Mrs. Abrams might open up for Saul, but not for me, after today. So I need instructions."

"Have you had dinner?"

"No."

"Come home."

I went to Tenth Avenue and flagged a taxi. It was still drizzling.

6

WOLFE does not like conferences with clients. Many's the time he has told me not to let a client in. So when, that evening, following instructions, I phoned Wellman at his hotel and asked him to call at the office the next morning at eleven, I knew it looked as bad to Wolfe as it did to me.

Eight days had passed since we had seen our client, though we had had plenty of phone calls from him, some local and some from Peoria. Apparently the eight days hadn't done him any good. Either he was wearing the same gray suit or he had two of them, but at least the tie and shirt were different. His face was pasty. As I hung his coat on the rack I remarked that he had lost some weight. When he didn't reply I thought he hadn't heard me, but after we had entered the office and he and Wolfe had exchanged greetings and he was in the red leather chair, he apologized.

"Excuse me, what did you say about my weight?"

"I said you had lost some."

"I guess so. I haven't been eating much and I don't seem to sleep. I go back home and go to the office or the warehouse, but I'm no darned good, and I take a train back here, and I'm no good here either." He went to Wolfe. "He told me on the phone you didn't have any real news but you wanted to see me."

Wolfe nodded. "I didn't want to, I had to. I must put a question to you. In eight days I have spent—how much, Archie?"

"Around eighteen hundred bucks."

"Nearly two thousand dollars of your money. You said you were going through with this even if it pauperized you. A man should not be held to a position taken under stress. I like my clients to pay my bills without immoderate pangs. How do you feel now?"

Wellman looked uncomfortable. He swallowed. "I just said I don't eat much."

"I heard you. A man should eat." Wolfe gestured. "Perhaps I should first describe the situation. As you know, I regard it as established that your daughter was murdered by the man who, calling himself Baird Archer, phoned for an appointment with her. Also that he killed her because she had read the manuscript she told about in her letter to you. The police agree."

"I know they do." Wellman was concentrating. "That's something. You did that."

"I did more. Most of your money has been spent in an effort to find someone who could tell us something about either the manuscript or Baird Archer, or both. It missed success by a narrow margin. Yesterday afternoon a young woman named Rachel Abrams was murdered by being pushed from a window of her office. Mr. Goodwin entered her office three minutes later. This next detail is being withheld by the police and is not for publication. In a notebook in her desk Mr. Goodwin found entries showing that last September a Baird Archer paid her ninety-eight dollars and forty cents for typing a manuscript. Of course that clinches it that your daughter was killed because of her knowledge of the manuscript, but I was already acting on that assumption, so it doesn't help any. We are—"

"It proves that Baird Archer did it!" Wellman was excited. "It proves that he's still in New York! Surely the police can find him!" He came up out of the chair. "I'm going—"

"Please, Mr. Wellman." Wolfe patted the air with a palm. "It proves that the murderer was in that building yesterday afternoon, and that's all. Baird Archer is still nothing but a name, a will-o'-the-wisp. Having missed Rachel Abrams by the merest tick, we still have no one alive who has ever seen or heard him. As for finding his trail from yesterday, that's for the police and they do it well; we may be sure that the building employees and tenants and passers-by are being efficiently badgered. Sit down, sir."

"I'm going up there. To that building."

"When I have finished. Sit down, please?"

Wellman lowered himself, and nearly kept going to the floor when his fanny barely caught the edge of the leather. He recovered and slid back a few inches.

"I must make it plain," Wolfe said, "that the chance of

success is now minute. I have three men interviewing
Miss Abrams' family and friends, to learn if she spoke to
any of them about Baird Archer or his manuscript, but
they have already talked with the most likely ones and
have got nothing. Mr. Goodwin has seen everyone at the
office of Scholl and Hanna who could possibly have what
we're after, and he has also called on other publishers.
For a week the police, with far greater resources than
mine, have been doing their best to find a trace of either
Baird Archer or the manuscript. The outlook has never
been rosy; now it is forlorn."

Wellman's glasses had slipped down on his nose, and
he pushed them back. "I asked about you before I came
here," he protested. "I thought you never gave up."

"I'm not giving up."

"Excuse me. I thought you sounded like it."

"I'm merely describing the situation. Forlorn is not too
strong a word. It would indeed be desperate but for one
possibility. The name Baird Archer was first seen on a
sheet of paper in the handwriting of Leonard Dykes. It
would not be poopery to assume that when he wrote
that list of names, obviously invented, he was choosing a
pseudonym for a manuscript of a novel, whether written
by him or another. But it is a fact, not an assumption,
that he included that name in a list he compiled, and
that that was the name of Miss Abrams' client, and it
was also the name on the manuscript read by your
daughter, and the name given by the man who phoned
her for an appointment. If I make this too elaborate it is
because I must make sure that it is completely clear."

"I like it clear."

"Good." Wolfe sighed. He was not enjoying himself. "I
undertook to learn about that manuscript through your
daughter's associates or the person who typed it, and I
have met defeat. I've been licked. The only connection
with Baird Archer that has not been explored is that of
Leonard Dykes, and it is certainly flimsy, the bare fact
that he wrote that name down; but to explore it is our
only hope."

"Then go ahead."

Wolfe nodded. "That's why I needed to see you. This is February twenty-seventh. Dykes was fished out of the water on New Year's Day. He had been murdered. The police rarely skimp on a murder, and the law office where Dykes worked assuredly saw a great deal of them. Mr. Goodwin has been permitted to see the file. People there were even asked then about Baird Archer, along with the other names on that list Dykes had written. Dykes had few intimacies or interests outside the office where he worked. Then, eight days ago, I showed the police that the name of Baird Archer connected Dykes's death with that of your daughter, and of course they again went after the people in that law office and are still after them. All possible questions have probably been asked, not once but over and over, of those people. It would be useless for me to open an inquiry there in the conventional manner. They wouldn't even listen to my questions, let alone answer them."

Wellman was concentrating. "You're saying you can't do it."

"No. I'm saying the approach must be oblique. Young women work in law offices. Mr. Goodwin may have his equal in making the acquaintance of a young woman and developing it into intimacy, but I doubt it. We can try that. However, it will be expensive, it will probably be protracted, and it may be futile—for your purpose and mine. If there were only one young woman and we knew she had information for us, it would be simple, but there may be a dozen or more. There's no telling what it will cost, or how long it will take, or whether we'll get anything. That's why I had to ask you, shall we try it or do you want to quit?"

Wellman's reaction was peculiar. He had been concentrating on Wolfe, to be sure he got it clear, but now he had shifted to me, and his look was strange. He wasn't exactly studying me, but you might have thought I had suddenly grown an extra nose or had snakes in my hair. I sent my brows up. He turned to Wolfe.

"Do you mean—" He cleared his throat. "I guess it's a good thing you asked me. After what I said here that day you have a right to think I would stand for anything, but that's a little too—with my money—a dozen young women—first one.and then another like that—"

"What the devil are you suggesting?" Wolfe demanded.

I not only kept my face straight, I stepped in, for three good reasons: we needed the business, I wanted to get a look at Baird Archer, and I did not want John R. Wellman to go back and tell Peoria that New York detectives debauched stenographers wholesale on order.

"You misunderstand," I told Wellman. "Much obliged for the compliment, but by intimacy Mr. Wolfe meant holding hands. He's right that sometimes I seem to get along with young women, but it's because I'm shy and they like that. I like what you said about its being your money. You'll have to take my word for it. If things start developing beyond what I think you would approve, I'll either remember it's your money and back off or I'll take off of the expense account all items connected with that subject."

"I'm not a prude," Wellman protested.

"This is farcical!" Wolfe bellowed.

"I'm not a prude," Wellman insisted manfully, "but I don't know those young women. I know this is New York, but some of them may be virgins."

"Absolutely possible," I agreed. I reproved Wolfe. "Mr. Wellman and I understand each other. His money is not to be used beyond a certain point, and he'll take my word for it. That right, Mr. Wellman?"

"I guess that'll do," he conceded. Meeting my eyes, he decided his glasses needed cleaning, removed them, and wiped them with his handkerchief. "Yes, that'll do."

Wolfe snorted. "There is still my question. The expense, the time it will take, the slender prospect of success. Also it will be in effect an investigation of the death of Leonard Dykes, not of your daughter. The approach will be oblique in more ways than one. Well, sir? Do we proceed or quit?"

"We proceed." Our client, still our client, put his glasses back on. "If I might—I would like to be assured that our relations are confidential. I wouldn't want my wife or my pastor to know about this—uh—this development."

Wolfe was looking as if he might bellow again, so I put in fast, "They won't, not from us. No one will."

"That's good. Do you want another check?"

Wolfe said we didn't, not just yet. That seemed to dispose of all the issues, but Wellman wanted to ask some questions, chiefly about Rachel Abrams and the building where her office was. Apparently he intended to go up there and poke around, and I was all for it, anything to get him outside before he got to worrying again about virgins, or Wolfe's resentment at having to confer with a client got out of hand.

After showing Wellman out I returned to the office. Wolfe was leaning back, scowling, running a fingertip around a race track on the arm of his chair.

I stretched and yawned. "Well," I remarked, "I suppose I'd better go up and change my clothes. The light brown, you know. They like a soft material that doesn't scratch when they put their head on your shoulder. Meanwhile you can be thinking up my instructions."

"There will be no instructions," he growled. "Confound it, get me something, that's all." He leaned forward to ring for beer.

7

MY REMARK about changing my clothes had of course been a feeble gag. Starting contacts with the personnel

in the office of Corrigan, Phelps, Kustin and Briggs
would require more elaborate outfitting than a light
brown suit, though it was a good shade and a nice soft
fabric. As Wolfe had told Wellman, everyone there
would certainly be fed up with questions about Leonard
Dykes and the name of Baird Archer, and if I had
merely gone there and opened fire I would have been
bounced.

I did go up to my room though, to think it over away
from Wolfe and the phone. The approach was simple.
What did we have too much of that girls liked, besides
me? That was a cinch: orchids, especially at that time of
year, when there were thousands of blossoms and practically all of them would be left on the plants till they
wilted. In a quarter of an hour I went down again to the
office and announced to Wolfe, "I'm going to need a lot
of orchids."

"How many?"

"I don't know. Maybe four or five dozen to start with.
I want a free hand."

"You won't get it. Consult me. No Cypripedium Lord
Fisher, no Dendrobium Cybele, no—"

"Not gaudy enough anyway. I'll stick to Cattleyas,
Brassos, and Laelios."

"You know the rarities."

"Sure. I ought to."

I went out and took a taxi to Homicide on Twentieth
Street. There I hit a snag. Purley Stebbins was out to
lunch. It would have been useless to try to get what I
wanted from any of the riffraff, so I insisted on seeing
Cramer and got waved down the hall to his room. He
was at his desk, eating pickles and salami and drinking
buttermilk. When I told him I wanted to take a look at
the Dykes file and make a list of the employees at the
law office where he had worked, he said he was busy
and had no time to argue and would I please go away.

"Yes, sir," I said politely. "We give you all we have.
We connect Dykes and Wellman for you. We tie in
Abrams before she's even cold, and hand it over. You

still have nowhere to go, but neither have we. Now all I want is a list of names which I could get elsewhere by spending a couple of hours and maybe twenty bucks, but you're too busy. I think it's what you eat. It's your stomach. Good God, look at that lunch."

He swallowed a mixture of pickle and salami he had been chewing, pushed a button, and spoke to the intercom.

"Rossi? I'm sending Goodwin in, Archie Goodwin. Let him take the Leonard Dykes file and make a list of the employees in that law office. That's all he does. Stay with him. Got it?"

A metallic voice crackled, "Right, Inspector."

I got back to Thirty-fifth Street in time for lunch, having stopped at a stationery store for some plain gummed labels. The other things I would need were on hand.

After lunch I went to it. There were sixteen female names on my list. I might have been able to dig out of the file who was what, but it would have been a job, and anyhow I didn't want to discriminate. A filing clerk was just as apt to be my meat as the confidential secretary of James A. Corrigan, the senior partner. As a starter all I needed were the names, and I went to the office and typed a label for each of them. I also typed, on plain pieces of paper, sixteen times so as not to use carbons:

> These orchids are so rare that they
> cannot be bought. I picked them
> for you. If you care to know why,
> phone me at PE 3-1212.
> Archie Goodwin

With the labels and typed notes in an envelope in my pocket, I ascended to the plant rooms, got a basket and knife, went to the warm room, and started cutting. I needed forty-eight, three apiece, but took a few extra because some were not perfect, mostly Cattleyas Diony-

sius, Katadin and peetersi, Brassocattleyas Calypso, four-
nierae and Nestor, and Laeliocattleyas barbarossa, Car-
mencita and St. Gothard. It was quite a collection. Theodore had offered to help, and I had no objection. The
only one he tried to talk me out of was Calypso, because
they weren't blooming so well, but I was firm.

In the potting room we got out boxes and tissue and
ribbon, and Theodore packed them expertly and inserted the typed notes while I pasted on the labels and
fought with the ribbon. The damn ribbon was what took
time. Wolfe is better at it than either Theodore or me,
but this was my party. When the last bow was tied and
the sixteen boxes were carefully packed in a large carton, it was twenty minutes to four. Still time. I lugged
the carton downstairs, got my hat and coat, went out
and found a taxi, and gave the driver the address, on
Madison Avenue in the Fifties.

The office of Corrigan, Phelps, Kustin and Briggs was
on the eighteenth floor of one of those buildings that
think there is nothing like marble in big slabs if you
want real class, with double doors for an entrance at the
end of a wide corridor. The automatic door-closer was
strong enough to push a horse out, and my entry was a
little clumsy on account of the carton. In the long anteroom a couple of guys were on chairs, another one was
pacing up and down, and back of a rail a three-shades-
of-blond sourpuss was fighting it out with a switchboard.
Near her, inside the rail, was a table. I took the carton
there, put it on the floor by the rail, opened it, and
began removing the ribboned boxes and putting them
on the table.

She sent me a withering glance. "Mother's Day in
February?" she inquired wearily. "Or atom bombs, perhaps?"

I finished my unpacking and then stepped to her. "On
one of those boxes," I told her, "you will find your name.
On the others there are other names. They should be
delivered today. It may possibly make you take a
brighter view—"

I stopped because I had lost her. She had left the switchboard and made a beeline for the table. I don't know what it was that she was hoping life had in store for her, but it must have been something that could be put in a small box, the way she went for it. As she started her eye over the labels, I crossed to the door, pulled it open by getting a firm foothold, and departed.

If that was typical of the reaction of females in that office to ribboned boxes there was no telling how soon I would be getting a phone call, so I told the taxi driver it would be okay if he made it to Thirty-fifth Street in less than an hour, but with the midtown traffic at that time of day it made no difference.

When we had finally made it and I had mounted the stoop and let myself in, I went to the kitchen and asked Fritz, "Any calls?"

He said no. There was a gleam in his eyes. "If you need any help with all the ladies, Archie, for my age I am not to be ignored. A Swiss has a long usefulness."

"Thanks. I may need you. Theodore told you?"

"No. Mr. Wolfe told me."

"The hell he did."

I was supposed to report myself in whenever I returned from an errand, so I went to the office and buzzed the plant rooms, where Wolfe spent every afternoon from four to six, on the house phone.

"I'm back," I told him. "Delivered according to plan. By the way, I'll put them on Wellman's account at three dollars per. A bargain for him."

"No. I do not sell orchids."

"He's a client. They were a required item."

"I do not sell orchids," he said gruffly and hung up. I got out the work book and figured the time and expenses of Saul and Fred and Orrie, who had been called off, and made out their checks.

The first call came a little before six. I usually answer, "Nero Wolfe's office, Archie Goodwin speaking," but thought it advisable, temporarily, to make a cut, and said merely, "Archie Goodwin speaking."

A dry clipped voice, but still female, asked, "Is this Mr. Archie Goodwin?"

"Yes."

"My name is Charlotte Adams. I have received a box of orchids with a note from you inside. Thank you very much."

"You're welcome. They're nice, aren't they?"

"They're beautiful, only I don't wear orchids. Are they from Mr. Nero Wolfe's conservatory?"

"Yes, but he doesn't call it that. Go ahead and wear them, that's what they're for."

"I'm forty-eight years old, Mr. Goodwin, so the possible reasons for your sending me orchids are rather restricted. More so than with some of the other recipients. Why did you send them?"

"I'll be frank with you, Miss Adams. *Miss* Adams?"

"No. Mrs. Adams."

"I'll be frank anyway. Girls keep getting married and moving to Jackson Heights, and my list of phone numbers is getting pretty ragged. I asked myself what would girls like to see that I can offer, and the answer was ten thousand orchids. They're not mine, but I have access. So you're cordially invited to come tomorrow evening at six o'clock, nine-oh-two West Thirty-fifth Street, and look at the orchids, and then we'll all have dinner together, and I see no reason why we shouldn't have a good time. Have you got the address?"

"Am I supposed to swallow this rigmarole, Mr. Goodwin?"

"Don't bother to swallow it. Do your swallowing tomorrow at dinner. I promise it will be fit to swallow. Will you come?"

"I doubt it," she said, and hung up.

Wolfe had entered during the conversation and got established behind his desk. He was frowning at me and pulling at his lower lip with a finger and thumb.

I addressed him. "A bum start. Nearly fifty, married, and a wise guy. She had checked the number somehow and knew it was yours. However, I intended to tell them that anyhow. We've got—"

"Archie."

"Yes, sir."

"What was that flummery about dinner?"

"No flummery. I haven't told you, I've decided to ask them to stay to dinner. It will be much—"

"Stay to dinner *here?*"

"Certainly."

"No." It was his flattest no.

I flared. "That," I said, as flat as him, "is childish. You have a low opinion of women and—now let me finish—anyhow, you don't want them around. But because this case has completely dried up on you, you have dumped this in my lap, and I need all the play I can get, and besides, are you going to send a crowd of your fellow beings, regardless of sex, away from your house hungry at the dinner hour?"

His lips were tight. He parted them to speak. "Very well. You can take them to dinner at Rusterman's. I'll phone Marko and he'll give you a private room. When you know how many—"

The phone rang, and I swiveled and got it and told the transmitter, "Archie Goodwin speaking."

A feminine voice said, "Say something else."

"It's your turn," I stated.

"Was it you that brought the boxes?"

It was the switchboard misanthrope. "Right," I admitted. "Did they all get delivered?"

"Yes, all but one. One was home sick. Brother, did you stir up some hell around there! Is it true that you're the Archie Goodwin that works for Nero Wolfe?"

"I am. This is his number."

"Well, well! The note said to call it and ask why. Why?"

"I'm lonely and I'm giving a party. Tomorrow at six. Here at Nero Wolfe's place. The address is in the book. You will be in no danger if enough of you come. Plenty of orchids, plenty of drinks, a chance to know me better, and a dinner fit for Miss America. May I ask your name?"

"Sure, Blanche Duke. You say tomorrow at six?"

"That's right."

"Would you care to make a note of something?"

"I love to make notes."

"Put down Blanche Duke. Isn't that a hell of a name? Two jiggers of dry gin, one of dry vermouth, two dashes of grenadine, and two dashes of Pernod. Got it?"

"Yeah."

"I may come tomorrow, but if I don't, try that yourself. I never know what I'm going to do tomorrow."

I told her she'd better come, swiveled, and spoke to Wolfe. "That's better than Mrs. Adams, at least. Not so bad for the first hour after the office closed. About taking them to Rusterman's, they'd probably like going to the best restaurant in New York, but—"

"You won't take them to Rusterman's."

"No? You said?"

"I've reconsidered. You will give them dinner here. I'll arrange the menu with Fritz—perhaps Mondor patties, and duckling with cherries and grapes. For women, the Pasti Grey Riesling will be good enough; I'm glad to have a use for it."

"But you don't care for it."

"I won't be here. I shall leave at five minutes to six, dine with Marko, and spend the evening with him."

I have often stated, in these reports of Wolfe's activities, that he never leaves the house on business, but I suppose now I'll have to qualify it. Strictly speaking, I could say that his intention was not to leave the house *on* business, merely on account of business, but that would be quibbling.

I protested. "You ought to be here to look them over. They'll be expecting to see you. Mrs. Adams is forty-eight, about right for you, and she can't have a happy home life or she wouldn't be working. Besides, how do you—"

The phone rang. I got it and said who I was. A high soprano made me hold the receiver away from my ear.

"Mr. Goodwin, I simply had to call you! Of course it isn't proper, since I've never met you, but if I don't tell you my name and never see you I don't think it will be such a terrible misstep, do you? Those are the loveliest orchids I have ever seen! I'm going to a little party this evening, just a few of us at a friend's apartment, and I'm going to wear them, and can you imagine what they'll say? And can you imagine what I'll say when they ask me who gave them to me? I simply can't imagine! Of course I can say they're from an unknown admirer, but really I'm not the kind of girl who would dream of having unknown admirers, and I haven't the faintest idea what I'll say when they ask me, but I simply can't resist wearing them because . . ."

When I hung up, five minutes later, Wolfe muttered at me, "You didn't invite her."

"No," I assented. "She's a virgin. And as far as I'm concerned she always will be."

8

THAT was the first time in history that a bunch of outsiders had been let into the plant rooms with Wolfe not there. The awful responsibility damn near got Theodore down. Not only did he regard it as up to him to see that none of them toppled a bench over or snitched a blossom from one of the rare hybrids, but also I had arranged a fancy assortment of liquids on a table in the potting room, which was being freely patronized by some of the guests, and he was afraid one of them would spill a glass of 80-proof into a pot that he had been nursing for ten years. I was sorry to give him that added anxiety, but I wanted them relaxed.

I had done all right. I had got only seven phone calls, but apparently there had been talk at the office during Wednesday, for ten of them showed up, arriving in two groups. Also there had been two calls on Wednesday while I was out. My journey was necessary, a trip to the Bronx to call on Mrs. Abrams. She was anything but delighted to see me, but I wanted to ask her to do something and I rode it out. I finally talked her into it. I also had to sign up John R. Wellman, but that was comparatively easy and all it took was a phone call to his hotel.

From a purely personal standpoint they were above average as a job lot, and it would have been no ordeal to get acquainted and quench their thirst and tell them about orchids if I hadn't been so busy sorting them out for future reference. I might as well save you the bother of doing likewise if you don't want to take the trouble, for it won't make much difference. I can tell you that now, but there was no one to tell me that then.

But I was working like a dog getting their names and stations filed. By dinnertime I had them pretty well arranged. Charlotte Adams, 48, was the secretary of the senior partner, James A. Corrigan. She was bony and efficient and had not come for fun. The only other one her age was a stenographer, plump and pimply, with a name that made her giggle cheerfully when she told you: Helen Troy. Next, going down by ages, was Blanche Duke, the tri-shaded blonde. I had mixed a shaker of her formula. She had made two trips to the potting room for refills and then had decided to save steps and take the shaker around with her.

One or two of the other seven may have been crowding thirty, but most of them still had some twenties to cover. One was a little more than I had counted on. Her name was Dolly Harriton, and she was a member of the bar. She wasn't yet one of the firm, but judging from the set of her good-looking chin and the smooth quick take of her smart gray eyes, she soon would be or else. She had the air, as she moved along the aisles, of collecting points for cross-questioning an orchid-grower being sued by his wife for non-support.

Nina Perlman, a stenographer, was tall and straight with big slow-moving dark eyes. Mabel Moore, a typist, was a skinny little specimen wearing red-rimmed glasses. Sue Dondero, Emmett Phelps's secretary, with fine temples and no perceptible lipstick, came close from all angles to my idea of a girl to have around. Portia Liss, a filing clerk, should either have had something done to her teeth or quit laughing so much. Claire Burkhardt, a stenographer, was either just out of high school or was cheating. Eleanor Gruber, Louis Kustin's secretary, was probably the one I would have invited if I had invited only one. She was the kind you look at and think she should take off just one or two pounds, and then you ask where from and end by voting for the status quo. Her eyes didn't actually slant; it was the way the lids were drawn.

By the time we went down to dinner I had picked up a few little scraps, mostly from Blanche Duke, Sue Dondero, and Eleanor Gruber. Tuesday at quitting time Corrigan, the senior partner, had called them into his room to tell them that PE 3-1212 was Nero Wolfe's phone number, and Archie Goodwin was Wolfe's confidential assistant, and that Wolfe might have been engaged by an opposing interest in one of the firm's cases. He had suggested that it might be desirable to ignore the notes in the boxes of orchids, and had warned them to guard against any indiscretion. Today, Wednesday, when the idea of making a party of it had caught on (this from Blanche Duke after she had been toting the shaker around a while), Mabel Moore had spilled it to Mrs. Adams, and Mrs. Adams, presumably after consulting with Corrigan, had decided to come along. I got other scattered hints of personalities and quirks and frictions, but not enough to pay for the drinks.

At 7:25 I herded them into the potting room to tell them that wine had been chilled for dinner, but that if any of them preferred to continue as started they were welcome. Blanche Duke raised her shaker on high and said she was a one-drink woman. There was a chorus of approval, and they all loaded themselves with bottles and accessories. I led the way. Going through the intermediate room, Helen Troy caught her heel between the slats of the walk, teetered, waved a bottle, and down came two pots of Oncidium varicosum. There were gasps and shrieks.

I said grandly, "Good for her. She showed great presence of mind, she held onto the bottle. Follow me, walking on orchids."

When I had got them downstairs and into the dining room, which looked festive enough for anybody, with the gleaming white cloth and silver and glass and more orchids, and told them to leave the head of the table for me but otherwise sit as they chose, I excused myself, went to the kitchen, and asked Fritz, "Are they here?"

He nodded. "Up in the south room. Quite agreeable and comfortable."

"Good. They know they may have to wait a long while?"

"Yes, it's understood. How are you succeeding?"

"Not bad. Two of them don't drink, but on the whole we are on our way to gaiety. All set?"

"Certainly."

"Shoot."

Rejoining the party, I took the chair at the head, Wolfe's place, the first time I had ever sat there. Most of them lifted their glasses to welcome me back after a long absence. I was touched and thought an acknowledgment was called for. As Fritz entered with the soup tureen, I pushed my chair back and stood. Portia Liss kept on chattering, and Dolly Harriton, the member of the bar, shushed her.

"Oyez, oyez!" Helen Troy cried.

I spoke. "Ladies and no gentlemen thank God, I have a lot of speeches to make, and I might as well get one done. Thank you for coming to my party. There is only one thing I would rather look at than orchids, and you are it. [Applause.] In the absence of Mr. Wolfe I shall follow his custom and introduce to you the most important member of this household, Mr. Fritz Brenner, now dishing soup. Fritz, a bow, please. [Applause.] I am going to ask you to help me with a little problem. Yesterday I received a phone call from a lady, doubtless fair, who refused to tell me her name. I beg you to supply it. I shall repeat some, by no means all, of what she said to me, hoping it will give you a hint. I am not a good mimic but shall do my best.

"She said: 'Mr. Goodwin, I simply had to call you! Of course it isn't proper, since I've never met you, but if I don't tell you my name and never see you I don't think it will be such a terrible misstep, do you? Those are the loveliest orchids I have ever seen! I'm going to wear them to a little party this evening, and can you imagine what they'll say? And can you imagine what I'll say when they ask who gave them to me? I simply can't imagine! Of course I can say they're from an unknown admirer, but really—' "

There was no use going on because the shrieks and hoots were drowning me out. Even Mrs. Adams loosened up enough to smile. Claire Burkhardt, the high school girl, choked on a bite of roll. I sat down and started on my soup, flushed with triumph. When it was a little quieter I demanded, "Her name?"

So many shouted it together that I had to get it from Sue Dondero, on my right. It was Cora Barth. I did not file it.

With Fritz having eleven places to serve, I had told him to leave the liquids to me. An advantage of that arrangement was that I knew what each one was drinking and could keep the refills coming without asking any questions, and another was that Sue Dondero offered to help me. Not only was it nice to have her help, but also it gave me a chance to make a suggestion to her, while we were together at the side table, which I had wanted to make to someone upstairs but hadn't got around to.

She said yes, and it was agreed that for a signal I would pull at my right ear.

"I am pleased to see," I told her, "that you are sticking to vermouth and soda. A girl with temples like yours has an obligation to society. Keep 'em smooth."

"Not to society," she dissented. "To spelling. Whisky or gin gives me a hangover, and if I have a hangover I can't spell. Once I spelled lien l-e-a-n."

"Good God. No, that's for Nina Perlman."

Having done all right with the soup, they did even better with the Mondor patties, As for talk and associated noises, they kept it going without much help from me, except for filling in a few gaps. But I was glad Wolfe wasn't there to see how they treated the duckling, all but Eleanor Gruber and Helen Troy. The trouble was, they were full. I watched them pecking at it, or not even pecking, with two exceptions, and decided that something drastic was called for if I didn't want a letdown. I raised my voice to get attention.

"Ladies, I need advice. This is—"

"Speech, speech!" Claire Burkhardt squeaked.

"He's making one, you idiot!" somebody told her.

"Oyez, oyeth," said Helen Troy.

"This," I said, "is a democracy. No one can shove anything down people's throats, not even Fritz's salad. As your host and by no means unknown admirer, I want you to have a good time and go away from here saying, 'Archie Goodwin can be trusted. He had us at his mercy, but he gave us a chance to say yes or no.'"

"Yes!" Blanche Duke called.

"Thank you." I inclined my head. "I was about to ask, how many feel like eating salad? If you want it, Fritz will enjoy serving it. But what if you don't? Yes or no?"

There were six or seven noes.

"Do you still say yes, Miss Duke?"

"My God, no. I didn't know you meant salad."

"Then we'll skip it. However, I won't ask for a vote on the almond parfait. You should taste it, at least." I turned to Fritz, at my elbow. "That's how it is, Fritz."

"Yes, sir." He started removing plates still loaded with his duckling, one of his best dishes. I wasted no sympathy on him because I had warned him. I have had much more opportunity than he has to learn the eating habits of American females. At an affair of the Society of Gourmets that duckling would have drawn cheers.

Their reaction to the almond parfait made up for it some. In their relaxed condition they were more or less ignoring the code, and a couple of them took spoonfuls while Fritz was still serving. Portia Liss exclaimed, "Oh! It's absolutely heavenly! Isn't it, Mrs. Adams?"

"I can't say, Portia. I haven't any."

But a few minutes later she conceded grudgingly, "It's remarkable. Quite remarkable."

Others had extravagant comments. Helen Troy finished first. She arose and shoved her chair back and put her palms on the table to lean on. Her pimples were purple now instead of pink.

"Oyeth, oyeth," she said.

"Who's making a speech?" someone demanded.

"I am. This is my maiden effort."

Someone tittered.

"My *maiden* effort," she insisted, "at my age. I've been thinking what we can do for Mr. Goodwin and I'm standing up to put it in the form of a motion. I move that one of us goes and puts her arms around Mr. Goodwin's neck and kisses him and calls him Archie."

"Which one?" Mabel Moore demanded.

"We'll vote on it. I nominate me. I'm already up."

There were cries of dissent. Claire Burkhardt, at Helen Troy's left, got her elbow and pulled her back onto her chair. Nominations were made. Someone suggested they should draw lots. Half an hour earlier I would have let it slide, on the chance that Sue or Eleanor would get elected, which would have been a pleasant experience, but at this stage I didn't want to risk having a tone set that it might be hard to jostle them out of. So I spoke up.

"Don't you think you ought to consult me?"

"Don't butt in," Blanche Duke said rudely.

"I'm sorry, but I have to. This is dangerous. If a certain one of you came close to me right now and put her arms around me and kissed me, I might be able to remember I'm your host and I might not. Whereas—"

"Which one?" voices demanded.

I ignored them. "Whereas if any other one did it, I couldn't keep from showing my disappointment. You can't expect me to tell you her name. We'll forget it. Anyhow, nobody seconded the motion, so it would be illegal."

I pulled at my right ear. "Another thing, the motion was put wrong. Doing it that way, who would it please most? Not me. You. I would much rather kiss than be kissed. But don't misunderstand me, you're my guests, and I would be happy to do something to please you. I'd love to please you. If you have a suggestion?"

Sue Dondero came through fine. "I have two."

"Good. One at a time."

"First, let all of us call you Archie."

"Easy. If I may call you Charlotte and Blanche and Dolly and Mabel and Portia and Eleanor and Claire and Nina and Helen and Sue."

"Of course. Second, you're a detective. Tell us something about being a detective—something exciting."

"Well." I hesitated and looked around, left and right. "Maybe I should treat it like the salad. Yes or no?"

I wasn't sure all of them said yes, but plenty of them did. Fritz had the coffee cups in place and was pouring. I edged my chair back a little, crossed my legs, and worked my lips, considering.

"I'll tell you," I said finally, "what I think I'll do. I could tell you about some old case that was finished long ago, but it might be more interesting if I pick one that we're working on right now. I can skip the parts that we're keeping to ourselves, if any. Do you like that idea?"

They said they did. Except Mrs. Adams, whose lips had suddenly become a thin line, and Dolly Harriton, whose smart gray eyes might have been a little disconcerting if she had been closer.

I made it casual. "I'll have to hit only the high spots or it will take all night. It's a murder case. Three people have been murdered: a man named Leonard Dykes, who worked in the office where you are, a girl named Joan Wellman, an editor in a publishing firm, and a girl named Rachel Abrams, a public stenographer and typist."

There were murmurings, and looks were exchanged. Nina Perlman said emphatically, in a soft satin voice that five or six Manhattans had had no effect on, "I didn't do it."

"Three murders by one person?" Eleanor Gruber asked.

"I'll come to that. Our first connection with it, not much of one, a cop came and showed us a list of fifteen men's names which had been written on a piece of paper by Leonard Dykes. They had found it between the pages of a book in Dykes's room. Mr. Wolfe and I weren't much interested and barely glanced at it. Then—"

"Why did the cop show you the list?" Dolly Harriton put in.

"Because they hadn't found any men to fit any of the names, and he thought we might have a suggestion. We didn't. Then, six weeks later, a man named John R. Wellman called and wanted us to investigate the death of his daughter, whose body had been found in Van Cortlandt Park—run over by a car. He thought she had been murdered, not killed by accident. He told us all about it, and showed us a copy of a letter Joan, his daughter, had written home. In it she said she had had a phone call from a man who gave his name as Baird Archer, author of a novel which he had submitted to Joan's firm some months back."

"Oh, my God," Blanche Duke said morosely. "Baird Archer again."

"I don't want to bore you," I declared.

Most of them said I wasn't.

"Okay. Joan had read Archer's novel and rejected it with a letter signed by her. On the phone he offered to pay her twenty dollars an hour to discuss his novel with him and tell him how to improve it, and she made a date to meet him the next day after office hours. So she said in her letter home. It was the evening of the next day that she was killed."

I reached for my coffee cup, drank some, and leaned back. "Now hold on to your hats. It had been six weeks since the cop had shown us that list of names, and we had just glanced at it. But when Mr. Wolfe and I saw Joan's letter home we immediately recognized the name of Baird Archer as one of those on Dykes's list. That proved there was some kind of connection between Leonard Dykes and Joan Wellman, and since they had both died suddenly and violently, and Joan had a date with Archer the day she died, it made it likely that their deaths were connected too, and connected with Archer. When you asked for something exciting about being a detective, if you meant something like tailing a murderer in Central Park and getting shot at, okay, that has its attractions, but it's not half as exciting as our spotting that name. If we hadn't, there would be one cop working on Dykes's death in his spare time, and another one in the Bronx likewise on Joan Wellman, instead of the way it is, which you know something about. That's what I call exciting."

It didn't seem essential to give the precise circumstances of the recognition of Baird Archer's name. If Wolfe had been there he would have told it his way, but he wasn't, and I was. Glancing around to see that coffee refills were being attended to and that cigarettes and matches were at hand for everyone, I resumed.

"Next I'm going to spill something. If it gets printed the cops won't like it, and they sure won't like me, but they don't anyhow. A girl named Rachel Abrams was a public stenographer and typist with a little one-room office on the seventh floor of a building up on Broad-

way. Day before yesterday she went out the window
and smashed to death on the sidewalk. More excitement
for me as a detective, which is what I'm supposed to be
talking about. It would probably have been called
suicide or an accident if I hadn't happened to walk into
her office two or three minutes after she had gone out
the window. In a drawer of her desk I found a little
brown book in which she had kept a record of her
receipts and expenses. Under receipts there were two
entries showing that last September she had been paid
ninety-eight dollars and forty cents by a man named
Baird Archer."

"Ah," Dolly Harriton said. There were other reactions.

"I'll be dreaming about Baird Archer," Nina Perlman
muttered.

"I am already," I told her. "As you can see, here's a job
for a detective if there ever was one. I won't try to tell
you how the cops are going at it, of course one or more
of them has talked with all of you the past two days, but
here's how we see it, and how we'll go on seeing it
unless something shows we're wrong. We believe that
Dykes's death was somehow connected with the
manuscript of that novel. We believe that Joan Wellman
was killed because she had read that manuscript. We
believe that Rachel Abrams was killed because she had
typed that manuscript. So naturally we want Baird Archer, and we want the manuscript. We've got to find one or
both, or we're licked. Any suggestions?"

"Good lord," Sue Dondero said.

"Get a copy of the novel," Portia Liss offered.

Someone snickered.

"Look," I said impulsively, "unless you object I'm
going to do something. There are a couple of people
connected with this case upstairs now, waiting to see
Mr. Wolfe. I think it would be interesting if they came
down and told you about it." I pressed the floor button
with my toe. "Unless you've had enough?"

"Who are they?" Mrs. Adams wanted to know.

"The father of Joan Wellman and the mother of Rachel Abrams."

"It won't be very gay," Dolly Harriton commented.

"No, it won't. Things and people mixed up with detectives are seldom gay."

"I want to see 'em," Helen Troy said loudly. "It's human nature."

Fritz had entered, and I spoke to him. "Where are Mrs. Abrams and Mr. Wellman, Fritz? In the south room?"

"Yes, sir."

"Will you please ask them to be good enough to come down here?"

"Yes, sir."

He went. I inquired about drinks and got three orders.

9

BLANCHE DUKE darned near ruined it.

When Wellman and Mrs. Abrams were ushered in by Fritz, ten pairs of eyes were focused on them, though in two or three cases the focusing required a little effort. I arose, performed the introductions, and brought them to the two chairs I had placed, one on either side of me. Mrs. Abrams, in a black silk dress or maybe rayon, was tight-lipped and scared but dignified. Wellman, in the same gray suit or its twin, was trying to take in all their faces without seeming to. He sat straight, not touching the back of the chair. I had my mouth open to speak when Blanche beat me to it.

"You folks need a drink. What'll you have?"

"No, thanks," Wellman said politely. Mrs. Abrams shook her head.

"Now listen," Blanche insisted, "you're in trouble. I've been in trouble all my life, and I know. Have a drink. Two jiggers of dry gin, one jigger of dry vermouth—"

"Be quiet, Blanche," Mrs. Adams snapped.

"Go to hell," Blanche snapped back. "This is social. You can't get Corrigan to fire me, either, you old papoose."

I would have liked to toss her out a window. I cut in. "Did I mix that right, Blanche, or didn't I?"

"Sure you did."

"Call me Archie."

"Sure you did, Archie."

"Okay, and I'm doing this right too. I do everything right. Would I let Mrs. Abrams and Mr. Wellman go without drinks if they wanted them?"

"Certainly not."

"Then that settles it." I turned to my right, having promised Mrs. Abrams that Wellman would be called on first. "Mr. Wellman, I've been telling these ladies about the case that Mr. Wolfe and I are working on, and they're interested, partly because they work in the office where Leonard Dykes worked. I told them you and Mrs. Abrams were upstairs waiting to see Mr. Wolfe, and I thought you might be willing to tell them something about your daughter Joan. I hope you don't mind?"

"I don't mind."

"How old was Joan?"

"She was twenty-six. Her birthday was November nineteenth."

"Was she your only child?"

"Yes, the only one."

"Was she a good daughter?"

"She was the best daughter a man ever had."

There was an astonishing interruption—at least, astonishing to me. It was Mrs. Abrams' voice, not loud but clear. "She was no better than my Rachel."

Wellman smiled. I hadn't seen him smile before. "Mrs. Abrams and I have had quite a talk. We've been comparing notes. It's all right, we won't fight about it. Her Rachel was a good daughter too."

"No, there's nothing to fight about. What was Joan going to do, get married or go on with her career, or what?"

He was still a moment. "Well, I don't know about that. I told you she graduated from Smith College with honors."

"Yes."

"There was a young fellow from Dartmouth we thought maybe she was going to hitch up with, but she was too young and had sense enough to know it. Here in New York—she was here working for those publishers nearly four years—she wrote us back in Peoria about different—"

"Where's Peoria?" Blanche Duke demanded.

He frowned at her. "Peoria? That's a city out in Illinois. She wrote us about different fellows she met, but it didn't sound to us like she was ready to tie up. We got to thinking it was about time, anyway her mother did, but she thought she had a big future with those publishers. She was getting eighty dollars a week, pretty good for a girl of twenty-six, and Scholl told me just last August when I was here on a trip that they expected a great deal of her. I was thinking of that yesterday afternoon. I was thinking that we expected a great deal of her too, her mother and me, but that we had already had a great deal."

He ducked his head forward to glance at Mrs. Abrams and came back to me. "Mrs. Abrams and I were talking about that upstairs. We feel the same way about it, only with her it's only been two days, and she hasn't had so long to think it over. I was telling her that if you gave me a pad of paper and a pencil and asked me to put down all the different things I can remember about Joan, I'll bet there would be ten thousand different things, more than that—things she did and things she said, times she was like this and times she was like that. You haven't got a daughter."

"No. You have much to remember."

"Yes, I have. What got me to thinking like that, I was wondering if I deserved what happened because I was too proud of her. But I wasn't. I thought about it this way, I thought there had been lots of times she did something wrong, like when she was little and told lies, and even after she grew up she did things I didn't approve of, but I asked myself, can I point to a single thing she ever did and honestly say I wish she hadn't done that? And I couldn't."

His eyes left me and went to my guests. He took his time, apparently looking for something in each face.

"I couldn't do it," he said firmly.

"So she was perfect," Claire Burkhardt remarked. It wasn't really a sneer, but it enraged Blanche Duke. She blazed at Claire.

"Will you kindly get lost, you night-school wonder? The man's in trouble! His daughter's dead! Did you graduate from college with honors?"

"I never went to night school," Claire said indignantly. "I went to Oliphant Business Academy!"

"I didn't say she was perfect," Wellman protested. "She did quite a few things I didn't think were right when she did them. All I was trying to tell you ladies, she's dead now and it's different. I wouldn't change a thing about her if I could, not one single thing. Look at you here now, all this drinking—if your fathers were here or if they knew about it, would they like it? But if you got killed tonight and they had to take you home and have you buried, after they had had time to think it over, do you suppose they'd hold it against you that you'd been drinking? Certainly not! They'd remember how wonderful you'd been, that's all, they'd remember all the things you had done to be proud of!"

He ducked his head. "Wouldn't they, Mrs. Abrams? Isn't that how you feel about your Rachel?"

Mrs. Abrams lifted her chin. She spoke not to Wellman but to the gathering. "How I feel about my Rachel." She shook her head. "It's been only two days. I will be honest with you ladies. While Mr. Wellman was talking I was sitting here thinking. My Rachel never took a drink. If I had ever seen her take a drink I would have called her a bad daughter in strong words. I would have been so angry it would have been terrible. But if it could be that she was here now, sitting at that table with you, and she was drinking more than any of you, so that she was so drunk she would look at me and not know me, I would say to her, 'Drink, Rachel! Drink, drink, drink!'"

She made a little gesture. "I want to be honest, but maybe I'm not saying it right. Maybe you don't know what I mean."

"We know what you mean," Eleanor Gruber muttered.

"I mean only I want my Rachel. I'm not like Mr. Wellman. I have two more daughters. My Deborah is sixteen and she is smart in high school. My Nancy is twenty and she goes to college, like Mr. Wellman's Joan. They are both smarter than Rachel and they are more fashionable. Rachel did not make eighty dollars every week like Joan, with office rent to pay and other things, but she did good all the time and once she made one hundred and twelve dollars in one week, only she worked nights too. But you ladies must not think I put her nose down on it. Some of our friends thought that, but they were wrong. She was glad in her heart that Nancy and Deborah are smart, and she made Nancy go to college. If she got some dollars ahead I would say, 'Buy yourself a pretty dress or take a little trip,' and she would laugh and say, 'I'm a working girl, Mamma.' She called me Mamma, but Nancy and Deborah called me Mom, and that's the whole difference right there."

She gestured again. "You know she is only dead two days?" It sounded rhetorical, but she insisted, "You know that?"

There were murmurings. "Yes, we know."

"So I don't know how it will be when it is longer, like Mr. Wellman. He has thought about it a long time and he is spending money for Mr. Wolfe to find the man that killed his Joan. If I had money like him maybe I would spend it that way too, but I don't know. All I think about now is my Rachel. I try to see why it happened. She was a working girl. She did her work good and got paid for it the regular rates. She never hurt anybody. She never made any trouble. Now Mr. Goodwin tells me a man asked her to do work for him, and she did it good, and he paid her the regular rates, and then after some time goes by he comes back and kills her. I try to see why that happened, and I can't. I don't care how much explaining I get, I don't think I can ever see why any man had to kill my Rachel, because I know so well about her. I know there's not a man or woman anywhere that could stand up and say, 'Rachel Abrams did a bad thing to me.' You ladies know how hard that is, to be the kind of woman so that nobody can say that. I'm not that kind of woman."

She paused. She tightened her lips, and then released them to say, "I did a bad thing to my Rachel once." Her chin started to quiver. "Excuse me, please." She faltered, arose, and made for the door.

John R. Wellman forgot his manners. Without a word, he popped up, circled behind my chair, and followed Mrs. Abrams. His voice came from the hall, and then silence.

The guests were silent too. "There's more coffee," I told them. "Anybody want some?"

No takers. I spoke. "One thing Mrs. Abrams said wasn't strictly accurate. She said I told her that the man who paid Rachel for typing the script came back and killed her. What I told her was that Rachel was killed because she had typed the script, but not that it was the man who had paid her for typing it."

Three of them were dabbing at their eyes with their handkerchiefs. Two others should have been.

"You don't know that," Dolly Harriton challenged.

"To prove it, no. But we like it."

"You're crazy," Helen Troy asserted.

"Yeah? Why?"

"You said the death of Leonard Dykes was connected with these two. Did you mean the same man killed all of them?"

"I didn't say so, but I would for a nickel. That's what I think."

"Then you're crazy. Why should Con O'Malley kill those girls? He didn't—"

"Be quiet, Helen," Mrs. Adams said sharply.

She ignored it. "He didn't kill—"

"Helen, be quiet! You're drunk."

"I am not drunk! I was, but I'm not now. How could anybody be drunk after listening to those two?" To me: "Con O'Malley didn't kill Leonard Dykes on account of any manuscript. He killed him because it was Dykes that got him disbarred. Everybody—"

She was drowned out. Half of them spoke and the other half shouted. It may have been partly to relieve the feelings that had been piled up by Wellman and Mrs. Abrams, but there was more to it than that. Both Mrs. Adams and Dolly Harriton tried to shut them up, but nothing doing. Looking and listening, I caught enough scraps to gather that a long-standing feud had blazed into battle. As near as I could make out, Helen Troy, Nina Perlman, and Blanche Duke were arrayed against Portia Liss, Eleanor Gruber, and Mabel Moore, with Sue Dondero interested but not committed, and Claire Burkhardt, the night-school wonder, not qualified for combat. Mrs. Adams and Dolly Harriton were outside.

In one of those moments of comparative calm that even the hottest fracas will have, Blanche Duke tossed a grenade at Eleanor Gruber. "What were you wearing when O'Malley told you? Pajamas?"

That shocked them into silence, and Mrs. Adams took advantage of it. "This is disgraceful," she declared. "You ought to be ashamed of yourselves. Blanche, apologize to Eleanor."

"For what?" Blanche demanded.

"She won't," Eleanor said. She turned a white face to me. "We should all apologize to you, Mr. Goodwin."

"I don't think so," Dolly Harriton said dryly. "Since Mr. Goodwin staged this, I must admit cleverly and effectively, I hardly believe he has an apology coming. Congratulations, Mr. Goodwin."

"I must decline them, Miss Harriton. I haven't congratulations coming either."

"I don't care," Eleanor insisted to me, "what you have coming. I'm going to say this. After what Blanche said to me. And what you must have heard before. Do you know who Conroy O'Malley is?"

"Sure. I've been allowed to have a look at the police file on Leonard Dykes. A former member of the firm who got disbarred about a year ago."

She nodded. "He was the senior member. The name of the firm was O'Malley, Corrigan and Phelps. I was his secretary. Now I am Louis Kustin's secretary. Must I say that what Blanche said, her insinuation about my relations with Mr. O'Malley, that that was pure malice?"

"There's no must about it, Miss Gruber. Say it if you want to, or just skip it."

"I do say it. It's too bad because really I like Blanche, and she likes me. This was starting to die down, and then the police came back and stirred it up again, and now you say it was something you told them about these two girls being killed that made them come back. I'm not blaming you, but I wish you hadn't, because—well, you saw what happened here just now. Could you hear what we said?"

"Some."

"Anyway, you heard Helen say that Conroy O'Malley killed Dykes because Dykes got him disbarred. That isn't true. O'Malley was disbarred for bribing a foreman of a jury in a civil suit. I don't know who it was that informed the court, that never came out, but it was certainly someone connected with the other side. Of course it made a lot of talk in the office, all kinds of wild talk—that Louis Kustin had done the informing because

O'Malley didn't like him and wouldn't make him a member of the firm, and that—"

"Is this wise, Eleanor?" Dolly Harriton asked coldly.

"I think so," Eleanor said, not fazed. "He ought to understand." She went on to me. "—and that others had done it, Mr. Corrigan and Mr. Briggs among them, for similar reasons, and that Leonard Dykes had done it because O'Malley was going to fire him. I wouldn't even be surprised if there was talk that I had done it, I suppose because he wouldn't buy me some new pajamas. As the months went by there wasn't so much of it, and then Leonard Dykes got killed and it started up again. I don't know who began it that O'Malley had killed Dykes because he found out that Dykes had been the informer to the court, but someone did, and it was worse than ever. Just a lot of wild talk. No one really knew anything. You heard Blanche ask me if I was wearing pajamas when O'Malley told me something."

She seemed to think she had asked a question, so I grunted an affirmative.

"Well, what he told me, just a few weeks ago, was that he had heard that it was the jury foreman's wife who had written the anonymous letter to the judge telling about the bribing. It isn't likely that I was wearing pajamas because I don't wear them in the office, and it was in the office that he told me—of course he's no longer connected with the firm, but he comes there once in a while. The talk that O'Malley killed Dykes is simply ridiculous."

"Why don't you say what you think?" Helen Troy demanded. "You think Uncle Fred killed Dykes. Why don't you say so?"

"I've never said I think that, Helen."

"But you do."

"I do," Blanche Duke stated, still ready to tangle.

"Who is Uncle Fred?" I asked.

Helen answered. "He's my uncle, Frederick Briggs. They don't like him. They think he informed on O'Malley because he wouldn't make him a partner, and Dykes found out about it and threatened to tell O'Malley, and Uncle Fred killed Dykes to keep him from telling. You know perfectly well you think that, Eleanor."

"I do," Blanche repeated.

"You girls work in a law office," Dolly Harriton said warningly, "and you should realize that gabbing in the women's room is one thing, and talking like this to Mr. Goodwin is quite another. Didn't you ever hear of slander?"

"I'm not slandering anyone," Eleanor declared, and she wasn't. She looked at me. "The reason I tell you all this, I think you've wasted a lot of orchids and food and drink. Your client is Mr. Wellman, and you're investigating the death of his daughter, and you went to all this trouble and expense because you think there was a connection between her and Leonard Dykes. That list of names he wrote that was found in his room—what if some friend was there one evening and said he was trying to choose a name to use on something he had written, and Dykes and the friend made up some names and Dykes wrote them down? There are a dozen ways it could have happened. And from what you say, that name Baird Archer is absolutely the only thing that connects Dykes with Joan Wellman and Rachel Abrams."

"No," I contradicted her. "There's another. They were all three murdered."

"There are three hundred homicides in New York every year." Eleanor shook her head. "I'm just trying to put you straight. You got us all worked up, or Mrs. Abrams and Mr. Wellman did, and from that row we had you might think you have started something, but you haven't. That's why I told you all that. We all hope you find the man that killed those girls, I know I do, but I don't think you'll ever do it this way."

"Look," Nina Perlman said, "I've got an idea. Let's all chip in and hire him to find out who informed on O'Malley and who killed Dykes. Then we'd know."

"Nonsense!" Mrs. Adams snapped.

Portia Liss objected. "I'd rather hire him to catch the man that killed the girls."

"That's no good," Blanche told her. "Wellman has already hired him for that."

"How much do you charge?" Nina asked.

She got no reply, not that I resented it, but because I was busy. I had left my chair and gone to the side table, where there was a large celadon bowl, and, getting a couple of sheets from my pocket notebook and tearing them into pieces, was writing on the pieces. Blanche, asking what I was doing, got no reply either until I had finished writing, put the pieces of paper in the bowl, and, carrying the bowl, returned to the table and stood behind Mrs. Adams.

"Speech," I announced. Helen Troy did not say oyez.

"I admit," I said, "that I have ruined the party, and I offer my regrets. If you think that I am rudely sending you home I regret that too, but it must be faced that I have doused all hope of continued revelry. I do offer a little consolation, with the permission of Mr. Wolfe. For a period of one year from date each of you will be sent upon request three orchids each month. You may request three at one time or separately, as you prefer. Specifications of color will be met as far as possible."

There were appropriate noises and expressions. Claire Burkhardt wanted to know, "Can we come and pick them out?"

I said that might be arranged, by appointment only. "Earlier," I went on, "it was suggested that one of you be chosen to demonstrate on my person your appreciation for this occasion. Maybe you no longer feel like it, but if you do I have a proposal. In this bowl are ten pieces of paper, and on each piece I have written one of your names. I will ask Mrs. Adams to take one of the pieces from the bowl, and the one whose name is drawn will accompany me forthwith to the Bobolink, where we will dance and dally until one of us gets tired. I don't tire easily."

"If my name is in there you will please remove it,"
Mrs. Adams ultimatumed.

"If it's drawn," I told her, "you can draw another.
Does anyone else wish to be excused?"

Portia Liss said, "I promised to be home by midnight."

"Simple. Get tired at eleven-thirty." I held the bowl
above the level of Mrs. Adams' eyes. "Will you draw
one, please?"

She didn't like doing it, but it was a quick and easy
way of getting the party over and done with, so after a
second's hesitation she reached up over the rim of the
bowl, withdrew a slip, and put it on the table.

Mabel Moore, at her left, called out, "Sue!"

I removed the other slips and stuck them in a pocket.

Sue Dondero protested, "My lord, I can't go to the
Bobolink in these clothes!"

"It doesn't have to be the Bobolink," I assured her. "I
guess you're stuck, unless you want us to draw again."

"What for?" Blanche snorted. "What do you bet they
didn't all say Sue?"

I didn't dignify it with a denial. I merely took nine
slips from my right-hand pocket and tossed them on the
table. Later on in the evening there might be occasion to
show Sue the nine in my left-hand pocket, those I had
taken from the bowl.

10

ORDINARILY Fritz takes Wolfe's breakfast tray up to
him at eight o'clock, but that Thursday he phoned down
to say he wanted to see me before he went up to the
plant rooms at nine, and I thought I might as well save
Fritz a trip. So at 8:05, having catered, I pulled a chair
around and sat. Sometimes Wolfe breakfasted in bed

and sometimes at the table by the window. That morning the sun was shining in and he was at the table. Looking at the vast expanse of yellow pajamas in the bright sun made me blink. He never says a word if he can help it until his orange juice is down, and he will not gulp orange juice, so I gave a fair imitation of sitting patiently. Finally he put the empty glass down, cleared his throat explosively, and started spreading the half-melted butter on a hot griddle cake.

He spoke. "What time did you get home?"

"Two-twenty-four."

"Where did you go?"

"With a girl to a night club. She's the one. The wedding is set for Sunday. Her folks are in Brazil, and there's no one to give her away, so you'll have to give me away."

"Pfui." He took a bite of buttered griddle cake and ham. "What happened?"

"Outline or blow by blow?"

"Outline. We'll fill in later."

"Ten came, including a female lawyer, young and handsome but tough, and an old warhorse. They drank upstairs and wrecked only two Oncidiums. By the—"

"Forbesi?"

"No. Varicosum. By the time we descended they were genial. I sat at your place. I had warned Fritz that the soup and patties would fill them up and they would snoot the duckling, and they did. I made speeches, which were well received, but no mention of murder until coffee, when I was asked to tell them about detective work, as arranged, and obliged. I set forth our current problem. At an appropriate moment I sent for our client and Mrs. Abrams, and if you had been there you would have been stirred, though of course you wouldn't admit it. They admitted it by wiping their eyes. By the way, Wellman had a nerve to suspect me of going too far too fast. He never met Mrs. Abrams until last evening, and he took her home. Oh, yes, I told them about finding Baird Archer's name in Rachel Abrams' account book, because I had to tie her in to clear the track for Mrs. Abrams. If it gets printed Cramer will yap, but it was me that found the book, and he admits I talk too much."

"So do I." Wolfe took a sip of steaming black coffee. "You say they were stirred?"

"Yes. Their valves opened. But all they did was start a free-for-all about who informed on O'Malley, the former senior partner, and got him disbarred for bribing a jury foreman, and about who killed Dykes. They have assorted theories, but if they have any evidence worth buying they're saving it. One named Eleanor Gruber, who is a looker but too busy being clever—she was O'Malley's secretary and is now Louis Kustin's—she undertook to straighten me out. She hates to see us waste our time trying to clinch a link between Dykes and Joan and Rachel, because there isn't any. Nobody contradicted her. I decided to adjourn and try one at a time, having been introduced, selected one named Sue Dondero, Emmett Phelps's secretary, and took her to a night club and spent thirty-four of our client's dollars. The immediate objective was to get on a satisfactory personal basis, but I found an opportunity to let her know that we intend, if necessary, to blow the firm of Corrigan, Phelps, Kustin and Briggs into so many little pieces that the Department of Sanitation will have us up for cluttering the streets. As I said, the wedding is Sunday. I hope you'll like her."

I upturned a palm. "It all depends. If one or more of them has really got a finger caught, either a firm member or an employee, I may have made a start at least. If not, Miss Gruber is not only shapely but sensible, and I may ditch Sue for her. Time will tell, unless you want to tell me now."

Wolfe had finished with the ham, and the eggs done with black butter and sherry, and was starting the wind-up, a griddle cake with no butter but plenty of thyme honey. In the office he would have been scowling, but he would not allow himself to get into a scowling mood while eating.

"I dislike business with breakfast," he stated.

"Yeah, I know you do."

"You can fill in later. Get Saul and put him on the disbarment of Mr. O'Malley."

"That was covered fairly well in the police file on Dykes. I've told you about it."

"Nevertheless, put Saul on it. Put Fred and Orrie on Dykes's associations outside that law office."

"He didn't have any to speak of."

"Put them on it. We've made this assumption and we'll either validate it or void it. Pursue your acquaintance with those women. Take one of them to lunch."

"Lunch isn't a good time. They only have—"

"We'll argue later. I want to read the paper. Have you had breakfast?"

"No. I got up late."

"Go and eat."

"Glad to."

Before I did so, I called Saul and Fred and Orrie and told them to come in for briefing. After breakfast I had that to attend to and also various office chores I had got behind on. There was a phone call from Purley Stebbins, who wanted to know how I had made out with my dinner party, and I asked him which one or ones he was tailing, or, as an alternative, which one he had on a line, but he brushed me off. I made no attempt to arrange to buy a lunch. So fast a follow-up on Sue would have been bad strategy, and a midday fifty minutes with one of the others would have given me no scope. Besides, I had had less than five hours' sleep and hadn't shaved.

When Wolfe came down to the office at eleven he went over the morning mail, dictated a couple of letters, looked through a catalogue, and then requested a full report. To him a full report means every word and gesture and expression, and I have learned to fill the order not only to his satisfaction but to mine. It took more than an hour. When I was through, after asking a few questions, he issued a command.

"Phone Miss Troy and take her to lunch."

I remained calm. "I understand and sympathize," I told him, "but I can't oblige. You're desperate and therefore impulsive. I could present an overwhelming case against it, but will mention only two items: first, it's nearly one o'clock and that's too late, and second, I don't feel like it. There are some things I know more about than you do, and one of them is my extractive ability with women. Take it from me, it would be hard to conceive a lousier idea than for me to invite a middle-aged lawyer's niece with pimples to a quick bite in a crowded midtown beanery, especially since she is probably right now on a stool at a fountain lunch working on a maple-nut sundae."

He shivered.

"I'm sorry to upset you, but maple-nut sundaes are—"

"Shut up," he growled.

All the same, I was quite aware that it was up to me. True, Saul and Fred and Orrie were out collecting, but they were even farther away from Joan Wellman than I was, and that was some distance. If one of those ten females, or one of the other six whom I hadn't met, had just one measly little fact tucked away that would start Wolfe's lips pushing out and in, no one but me was going to dig it out, and if I didn't want it to drag on into the Christmas season, only ten months away, I had better pull something.

Back in the office after lunch, Wolfe was seated at his desk, reading a book of lyrics by Oscar Hammerstein, his mind a million miles from murder, and I was wandering around trying to think of something to pull, when the phone rang and I went to answer it.

A woman's voice told me, "Mr. Corrigan would like to speak to Mr. Wolfe. Put Mr. Wolfe on, please?"

I made a face. "Get home all right, Mrs. Adams?"

"Yes."

"Good. Mr. Wolfe is busy reading poetry. Put Corrigan on."

"Really, Mr. Goodwin."

"I'm stubborner than you are, and you made the call, I didn't. Put him on." I covered the transmitter and told Wolfe, "Mr. James A. Corrigan, the senior partner."

Wolfe put the book down and took his instrument. I stayed on, as always when I wasn't signaled to get off.

"This is Nero Wolfe."

"This is Jim Corrigan. I'd like to have a talk with you."

"Go ahead."

"Not on the phone, Mr. Wolfe. It would be better to meet, and some of my associates would like to sit in. Would it be convenient for you to call at our office, say around five-thirty? One of my associates is in court."

"I don't call at people's offices, Mr. Corrigan. I stay in my office. I won't be available at five-thirty, but six would do if you wish to come."

"Six would be all right, but it would be better to make it here. There will be four of us—perhaps five. Six o'clock here?"

"No, sir. If at all, here."

"Hold the wire a minute."

It was more like three minutes. Then he was on again. "Sorry to keep you waiting. All right, we'll be there at six or a little after."

Wolfe cradled his phone, and I did likewise.

"Well," I remarked, "at least we touched a sore spot somewhere. That's the first cheep we've got out of anybody in ten days."

Wolfe picked up his book.

11

THAT was the biggest array of legal talent ever gathered
in the office. Four counselors-at-law in good standing
and one disbarred.

James A Corrigan (secretary, Charlotte Adams) was
about the same age as his secretary, or maybe a little
younger. He had the jaw of a prizefighter and the frame
of a retired jockey and the hungriest pair of eyes I ever
saw—not hungry the way a dog looks at a bone you're
holding up but the way a cat looks at a bird in a cage.

Emmett Phelps (secretary, Sue Dondero) was a surprise to me. Sue had told me that he was the firm's
encyclopedia, the guy who knew all the precedents and
references and could turn to them with his eyes shut,
but he didn't look it. Something over fifty, and a couple
of inches over six feet, broad-shouldered and long-
armed, on him a general's or admiral's uniform would
have looked fine.

Louis Kustin (secretary, Eleanor Gruber) was the
youngster of the bunch, about my age. Instead of hungry
eyes he had sleepy ones, very dark, but that must have
been a cover because Sue had told me that he was their
trial man, and hot, having taken over the tougher courtroom assignments when O'Malley had been disbarred.
He looked smaller than he was on account of the way he
slumped.

Frederick Briggs, Helen Troy's Uncle Fred, had white
hair and a long bony face. If he had a secretary I hadn't
met her. From the way he blinked like a half-wit at
everyone who spoke, it seemed a wonder he had been
made a partner even in his seventh decade—or it could

have been his eighth—but it takes all kinds to make a
law firm. I wouldn't have hired him to change blotters.

Conroy O'Malley, who had been the senior partner
and the courtroom wizard until he got bounced off the
bar for bribing a juror, looked as bitter as you would
expect, with a sidewise twist to his mouth that seemed
to be permanent. With his mouth straightened and the
sag out of his cheeks and a flash in his eye, it wouldn't
have been hard to imagine him dominating a courtroom,
but as he was then he couldn't have dominated a phone
booth with him alone in it.

I had allotted the red leather chair to Corrigan, the
senior partner, with the others in an irregular arc facing
Wolfe's desk. Usually, when there are visitors, I don't get
out my notebook and pen until Wolfe says to, but there
was no law against my trying an experiment, so I had
them ready and when Corrigan opened up I began
scribbling. The reaction was instantaneous and unanimous. They all yapped at once, absolutely horrified and
outraged. I looked astonished.

Wolfe, who knows me fairly well, thought he was
going to slip me a caustic remark, but he had to chuckle.
The idea of getting the goats of four lawyers and one
ex-lawyer at one crack appealed to him too.

"I don't think," he told me mildly, "we'll need a record
of this."

I put the notebook on my desk in easy reach. They
didn't like it there so handy. Throughout the conference
they took turns darting glances at me to make sure I
wasn't sneaking in some symbols.

"This is a confidential private conversation," Corrigan
stated.

"Yes, sir," Wolfe conceded. "But not privileged. I am
not your client."

"Quite right." Corrigan smiled, but his eyes stayed
hungry. "We wouldn't mind if you were. We are not a
hijacking firm, Mr. Wolfe, but I don't need to say that if
you ever need our services it would be a pleasure and
an honor."

Wolfe inclined his head an eighth of an inch. I raised a brow the same distance. So they had brought butter along.

"I'll come straight to the point," Corrigan declared. "Last evening you got more than half of our office staff down here and tried to seduce them."

"Seduction in its statutory sense, Mr. Corrigan?"

"No, no, of course not. Orchids, liquors, exotic foods— not to tempt their chastity but their discretion. Administered by your Mr. Goodwin."

"I take the responsibility for Mr. Goodwin's actions on my premises as my agent. Are you charging me with a malum? In se or prohibitum?"

"Not at all. Neither. Perhaps I started badly. I'll describe the situation as we see it, and you correct me if I'm wrong. A man named Wellman has engaged you to investigate the death of his daughter. You have decided that there is a connection between her death and two others, those of Leonard Dykes and Rachel Abrams. In—"

"Not decided. Assumed as a working hypothesis."

"All right. And you're working on it. You have two reasons for the assumption: the appearance of the name Baird Archer in all three cases, and the fact that all three died violently. The second is merely coincidental and would have no significance without the first. Looked at objectively, it doesn't seem like a very good reason. We suspect you're concentrating on this assumption because you can't find anything else to concentrate on, but of course we may be wrong."

"No. You're quite right."

They exchanged glances. Phelps, the six-foot-plus encyclopedia, muttered something I didn't catch. O'Malley, the ex, was the only one who didn't react at all. He was too busy being bitter.

"Naturally," Corrigan said reasonably, "we can't expect you to spread your cards out. We didn't come here to question you, we came to let you question us."

"About what?"

"Any and all relevant matters. We're willing to spread our cards out, Mr. Wolfe; we have to. Frankly, our firm is in a highly vulnerable position. We've had all the scandal we can absorb. Only a little over a year ago our senior partner was disbarred and narrowly escaped a felony conviction. That was a major blow to the firm. We reorganized, months passed, we were regaining lost ground, and then our chief confidential clerk, Leonard Dykes, was murdered, and it was all reopened. There was never a shred of evidence that there was any connection between O'Malley's disbarment and Dykes's death, but it doesn't take evidence to make scandal. It affected us even more seriously than the first blow; the effect was cumulative. Weeks went by, and Dykes's murder was still unsolved, and it was beginning to die down a little, when suddenly it came back on us through the death of someone we had never heard of, a young woman named Joan Wellman. However, that was much less violent and damaging. It was confined mostly to an effort by the police to find some trace, through us or our staff, of a man who was named Baird Archer, or who had used that name, and the effort was completely unsuccessful. After a week of that it was petering out too, and then here they came again, we didn't know why at the time, but now we know it was because of the death of another young woman we had never heard of, named Rachel Abrams. At that point don't you think we had a right to feel a little persecuted?"

Wolfe shrugged. "I doubt if it matters what I think. You did feel persecuted."

"We certainly did. We do. We have had enough. As you know, the Abrams girl died three days ago. Again what the police are after is a trace of a Baird Archer, though God knows if there were any trace of such a man or such a name at our office they should have dug it up long ago. Anyhow, there's nothing we can do except hope they find their damned Baird Archer, and wait for this to begin to die down too. That's how we felt yesterday. Do you know what happened in court this afternoon? Louis Kustin was trying an important case for us, and during a recess opposing counsel came up to him and said—what did he say, Louis?"

Kustin stirred in his chair. "He asked me what I was doing about a new connection when our firm dissolves." His voice had a sharp edge, not at all sleepy like his eyes. "He was trying to get me sore to spoil my style. He didn't succeed."

"You see," Corrigan told Wolfe. "Well, that's how we felt yesterday. Then those boxes of orchids came with notes from your man Goodwin. Then today we learn what happened last night. We learn what happened here, and we also learn that Goodwin told one of our staff that you have an idea that a trail to the murderer of the Wellman girl can be picked up at our office, that he never saw you more bullheaded about an idea, and that your client and you both intend to go the limit. We know enough about you and your methods to know what that means. As long as you've got that idea you'll never let go. The police and the talk may die down and even die out, but you won't, and God knows what you'll do to our staff. You've damn near got them scratching and pulling hair already."

"Nuts," I cut in. "They've been at it for months."

"They were cooling off. You got 'em tight and then brought in a bereaved father and mother to work on their nerves. God only knows what you'll do next." Corrigan returned to Wolfe. "So here we are. Ask us anything you want to. You say that idea is a working hypothesis, go ahead and work on it. You're investigating the murder of Joan Wellman, and you think one of us has something for you, maybe all of us. Here we are. Get it over with."

Corrigan looked at me and asked politely, "Could I have a drink of water?"

I took it for granted that he meant with something in it and asked him what, meanwhile pushing a button for Fritz, since I wasn't supposed to leave a conference unless I had to. Also I broadened the invitation. Two of them liked Scotch, two bourbon, and one rye. They exchanged remarks. Briggs, the blinking half-wit, got up to stretch and crossed the room for a look at the big globe, probably with the notion of trying to find out where he was. I noticed that Wolfe did not order beer, which seemed to be stretching things pretty thin. I had nothing against his habit of using reasonable precaution not to take refreshment with a murderer, but he had never seen any of those birds before and he had absolutely nothing to point at them with. Bullheaded was putting it mildly.

Corrigan put his half-empty glass down and said, "Go ahead."

Wolfe grunted. "As I understand it, sir, you invite me to ask questions and satisfy myself that my assumption is not valid. That could take all night. I'm sorry, but my dinner dish this evening is not elastic."

"We'll go out and come back."

"And I can't commit myself to satisfaction by an hour or even a day."

"We don't expect a commitment. We just want to get you off our necks as soon as possible without having our organization and our reputation hurt worse than they are already."

"Very well. Here's a question. Which one of you first suggested this meeting with me?"

"What difference does that make?"

"I'm asking the questions, Mr. Corrigan."

"So you are. It was—" The senior partner hesitated. "Yes, It was Phelps."

"No," Phelps contradicted him. "You came to my room and asked me what I thought of it."

"Then it was you, Fred?"

Briggs blinked. "I really couldn't say, Jim. I make so many suggestions, I may well have made this one. I know Louis phoned in at his lunch recess to ask for some figures, and we were discussing it."

"That's right," Kustin agreed. "You said it was being considered."

"You're having a hell of a time answering a simple question," a biting voice told them. It was Conroy O'Malley, the ex. "The suggestion came from me. I phoned you around eleven o'clock, Jim, and you told me about Nero Wolfe smashing in, and I said the only thing to do was have a talk with him."

Corrigan screwed up his lips. "That's right. Then I went in to get Emmett's opinion."

Wolfe went at O'Malley. "You phoned Mr. Corrigan around eleven this morning?"

"Yes."

"What about?"

"To get the news. I had been out of town for a week, and the minute I returned the police had got at me again about Baird Archer. I wondered why."

"What were you doing out of town?"

"I was in Atlanta, Georgia, getting facts about the delivery of steel for a bridge."

"On behalf of whom?"

"This firm." O'Malley's mouth twisted until it was distorted almost to a diagonal. "You don't think my old associates would let me starve, do you? No indeed. I eat every day. Not only do I get a share of the income from unfinished business when I left, I am also given work to do outside the office. Do you know what is the outstanding characteristic of my former associates? Love for their fellow man." He tapped his chest with a forefinger. "I am their fellow man."

"Goddam it, Con," Phelps blurted, "where does that get you? What do you want? What do you expect?"

A gleam had come and gone in Kustin's sleepy eyes as O'Malley spoke. He said dryly, "We're here to answer Wolfe's questions. Let's keep the answers responsive."

"No," Wolfe said, "this isn't a courtroom. Sometimes an unresponsive answer is the most revealing, almost as good as a lie. But I hope you will resort to lies as little as possible, since they will be of use to me only when exposed and that's a lot of work. For instance, I am going to ask each of you if you have ever tried your hand at writing fiction or had a marked and sustained desire to write fiction. If you all say no, and if later, through interviews with friends and acquaintances, I find that one of you lied, that will be of some value to me, but it will save trouble if you'll tell the truth short of serious embarrassment. Have you ever tried writing fiction, Mr. O'Malley? Or wanted to, beyond a mere whim?"

"No."

"Mr. Briggs?"

"No."

He got five noes.

Wolfe leaned back and surveyed them. "Of course," he said, "it is clearly essential to my assumption that either Leonard Dykes or someone he knew wrote a piece of fiction long enough to be called a novel—Dykes himself by preference, since he was killed. Doubtless the police have touched on this in questioning you, and you have disclaimed any knowledge of such an activity by Dykes, but I like things firsthand. Mr. Corrigan, have you ever had any information or hint, from any source, that Dykes had written, was writing, or wanted or intended to write, a work of fiction?"

"No."

"Mr. Phelps?"

Five noes again.

Wolfe nodded. "That shows why, even if you put up with this for a solid week, I can't engage not to harass your staff. For that kind of operation Mr. Goodwin is highly qualified. If you admonish those young women not to see him, I doubt if it will work. If they disobey and you fire them, you will merely make them riper for him. If you warn them specifically that any knowledge they may have, however slight, of Dykes's literary performances or ambitions is not to be disclosed, sooner or later Mr. Goodwin will know it, and I shall ask why you don't want me to get facts. And if any of them does innocently have such knowledge, perhaps from some remark once heard, we'll get it."

They didn't care for that. Louis Kustin was displaying a bored smile. "We're not schoolboys, Wolfe. We graduated long ago. Speaking for myself, you're welcome to any fact you can get, no matter what, that's conceivably connected with your case. I don't know any. I'm here— all of us are— to satisfy you on that point."

"Then tell me this, Mr. Kustin." Wolfe was placid. "I gather that although the disbarment of Mr. O'Malley was a blow to the firm's reputation, you personally benefited from it by being made a partner and by replacing Mr. O'Malley as chief trial counsel. Is that correct?"

Kustin's eyes woke up. They gleamed. "I deny that that has any connection with your case."

"We're proceeding on my assumption. Of course you may decline to answer, but if you do, what are you here for?"

"Answer him, Louis," O'Malley said jeeringly. "Just say yes."

They looked at each other. I doubt if either of them had ever regarded opposing counsel with just that kind of hostility. Then Kustin's eyes, anything but sleepy now, returned to Wolfe and he said, "Yes."

"And naturally your share of the firm's profits was increased?"

"Yes."

"Substantially?"

"Yes."

Wolfe's glance went left. "You too benefited, Mr. Corrigan? You became the senior partner with an increased share?"

Corrigan's prizefighter's jaw was jutting. "I became the senior in a firm that was damn near on the rocks. My percentage of the profits went up, but the profits went down. I would have done better to cut loose."

"Was there anything to stop you?" O'Malley inquired. From his tone I would have guessed that he hated Corrigan about one-fifth as much as he did Kustin.

"Yes, Con, there was. I had my associates to think of.

My name was on the door with theirs. There was loyalty to stop me."

Suddenly, totally without warning, O'Malley bounded to his feet. I suppose he had done it a thousand times in a courtroom, to object to a question or dramatize a motion to dismiss, but it startled the others as much as it did me. He flung up an arm and called out in a ringing voice, "Loyalty!" Then he dropped back into his chair, picked up his glass and raised it, said, "To loyalty," and drank.

The four firm members glanced at one another. I changed my mind about O'Malley's ability to dominate a phone booth.

Wolfe spoke. "And you, Mr. Briggs? You also moved up when Mr. O'Malley was out?"

Briggs blinked violently. "I resent this," he said stiffly. "I am opposed to this whole procedure. I know something of you, Mr. Wolfe, and I regard your methods as unethical and reprehensible. I am here under protest."

"Frederick," O'Malley said gravely, "should be on the bench. He should have been appointed to the bench as soon as he was out of law school. He would be an ideal judge. He has the kind of daring mind that glories in deciding an issue without understanding it."

Phelps, the encyclopedia, protested, "Everybody can't be brilliant like you, Con. Maybe it's just as well they can't."

O'Malley nodded at him. "You're dead right, Emmett. But you're always right. I've never resented it, you know, your always being right, I don't know why. Not because you're the only one who didn't profit by my downfall; I never resented it."

"I did profit. I moved up one and I get a bigger cut." Phelps went to Wolfe. "We all profited by our partner's misfortune, or we will, if this doesn't ruin us altogether. Even I. Strictly speaking, I am not an attorney-at-law; I am a scholar. To a lawyer the most interesting case is the one he is currently engaged in. To me the most interesting case is one that was tried in Vienna in 1568.

I inject this only to explain why this case of yours is to me unutterably dull. It might not be if I had myself killed Dykes and those two young women, but I doubt it. I would be attentive, naturally, but not interested. You will forgive me, I hope."

That, I thought, might be useful in future conversations with Sue Dondero, Phelps's secretary. From her scanty remarks about her boss I hadn't got that slant on him, and surely she would like to know more about him if she didn't already. Girls feel that it's their duty to know all about their bosses.

Wolfe was cocking his head at the encyclopedia. "Murders bore you, Mr. Phelps?"

"I didn't say that. 'Bore' is an active verb. I am merely indifferent."

"But isn't your livelihood involved?"

"Yes. That's why I'm here. I came and I'll talk, but don't expect to arouse me."

"Then I won't try." Wolfe's eyes moved. "By the way, Mr. O'Malley, why are you here?"

"Loyalty." I had refilled O'Malley's glass, and he lifted it. "To loyalty!"

"To whom? Your former associates? I was getting the impression that you are not too well disposed toward them."

"That just shows"—O'Malley put his glass down—"how wrong appearances can be. My old friends Jim and Emmett and Louis and Fred? I'd go through hell for them—in fact I have. Isn't that acceptable as my motive for coming?"

"I'd prefer something a little less moot."

"Then try this. I was a man of extraordinary talent and not without ambition. My talent had been developed and my faculties trained to one end: to enter a courtroom with a briefcase, confront a judge and jury, and so manipulate their thoughts and emotions that I got the verdict I wanted. I hadn't lost a case for four years when one day I found myself faced by certain defeat; there was no question about it. Under that pressure I did something foolish: I bribed a juror, the first and only time. I got a hung jury, and a few weeks later got a settlement out of court, and I thought I was safely out of it, when suddenly it hit me. Someone informed the court, they got the juror in and worked on him and broke him, and there I was. Insufficient evidence saved me from a felony conviction, the jury was divided six to six, but I was disbarred."

"Who informed the court?"

"I didn't know at the time. Now I have reason to believe it was the juror's wife."

"Were any of your associates privy to your act?"

"No. They wouldn't have stood for it. They were shocked—the shock of righteous men—meaning by 'righteous men' those who have not been caught. They were also loyal, they helped me fight it, but it was hopeless. So here I am, a man with an extraordinary talent that can't be used. I can use it only in one place and I am not allowed to go there. Moreover, I am stigmatized. People who could use my talents outside of courtrooms don't want them. And I'm broke. I'm in no position to postulate that I should go on living; there seems no point in it; but through perversity I'm going to. My only source of income is this firm, payments on account of business that was unfinished when I left, and they give me errands to do. So it is to my interest for the firm to prosper. I offer that as my reason for coming here with them. If you don't like it either, I have still another alternative. Would you like to hear it?"

"If it isn't too fanciful."

"It's not fanciful at all. I am embittered against my former associates because they let me down. I think it quite possible that one of them killed Dykes and the two women, though I have no idea why, and that you're going to hang on until you get it, and I want to see it happen. Do you like that better?"

"It has attractions."

"Or here's another. I myself killed Dykes and the women, though again I have no idea why, and I think you're more dangerous than the police and want to keep an eye on you." O'Malley picked up his glass. "That's four, that should be enough."

"It'll do for the time being," Wolfe concurred. "Of course they're mutually exclusive. In one your associates helped you fight and in another they let you down. Which was it actually?"

"They fought like tigers to save me."

"Goddam it, Con," Phelps exploded, "we did! We let everything else go! We did our damnedest!"

O'Malley was unmoved. "Then you'd better take that one," he told Wolfe. "Number Two. It has corroboration, which is always a help."

"I prefer it anyway." Wolfe glanced up at the clock on the wall. "I want all you can tell me about Dykes, gentlemen, but it's my dinnertime. As I said, I'm sorry we're not prepared for guests."

They left their chairs. Corrigan asked, "What time do you want us back?"

Wolfe made a face. He hated the prospect of work during digestion. "Nine o'clock?" he suggested. "Will that suit?"

They said it would.

12

WHEN, an hour after midnight, Wolfe finally called it a day and let them go, it looked as if I would be seeing a lot of the girls. Not that they had balked at answering questions. We had at least four thousand facts, an average of a thousand an hour, but if anyone had offered me a dime for the lot it would have been a deal. We were full of information to the gills, but not a glimmer of Baird Archer or fiction writing or anything pertaining thereto. Wolfe had even sunk so low as to ask where and how they had spent the evening of February second and the afternoon of February twenty-sixth, though the cops had of course covered that and double-checked it.

Especially we knew enough about Leonard Dykes to write his biography, either straight or in novel form. Having started in as office boy, by industry, application, loyalty, and a satisfactory amount of intelligence, he had worked up to office manager and confidential clerk. He was not married. He had smoked a pipe, and had once got pickled on two glasses of punch at an office party, proving that he was not a drinker. He had had no known interest in anything outside his work except baseball in summer and professional hockey games in winter. And so forth and so on. None of the five had any notion about who had killed him or why.

They kept getting into squabbles about anything and everything. For instance, when Wolfe was asking about Dykes's reaction to the disbarment of O'Malley, and was told by Corrigan that Dykes had written him a letter of resignation, Wolfe wanted to know when. Sometime in the summer, Corrigan said, he didn't remember exactly, probably in July. Wolfe asked what the letter had said.

"I forget how he put it," Corrigan replied, "but he was just being scrupulous. He said he had heard that there was talk among the staff that he was responsible for O'Malley's trouble, that it was baseless, but that we might feel it would be harmful to the firm for him to continue. He also said that it was under O'Malley as senior that he had been made office manager, and that the new regime might want to make a change, and that therefore he was offering his resignation."

Wolfe grunted. "Was it accepted?"

"Certainly not. I called him in and told him that we were completely satisfied with him, and that he should ignore the office gossip."

"I'd like to see his letter. You have it?"

"I suppose it was filed—" Corrigan stopped. "No, it wasn't. I sent it to Con O'Malley. He may have it."

"I returned it to you," O'Malley asserted.

"If you did I don't remember it."

"He must have it," Phelps declared, "because when you showed it to me—no, that was another letter. When you showed me Dykes's resignation you said you were going to send it to Con."

"He did," O'Malley said. "And I returned it—wait a minute, I'm wrong. I returned it to Fred, in person. I stopped in at the office, and Jim wasn't there, and I gave it to Fred."

Briggs was blinking at him. "That," he said stiffly, "is absolutely false. Emmett showed me that letter." He blinked around. "I resent it, but I'm not surprised. We all know that Con is irresponsible and a liar."

"Goddam it, Fred," Phelps objected, "why should he lie about a thing like that? He didn't say he showed it to you, he said he gave it to you."

"It's a lie! It's absolutely false!"

"I don't believe," Wolfe interposed, "that the issue merits such heat. I would like to see not only that letter but also anything else that Dykes wrote—letters, memoranda, reports—or copies of them. I want to know how he used words. I would like that letter to be included if it is available. I don't need a stack of material—half a dozen items will do. May I have them?"

They said he might.

When they had gone I stretched, yawned, and inquired, "Do we discuss it now or wait till morning?"

"What the devil is there to discuss?" Wolfe shoved his chair back and arose. "Go to bed." He marched out to his elevator.

Next day, Friday, I had either bum luck or a double brush-off, I wasn't sure which. Phoning Sue Dondero to propose some kind of joint enterprise, I was told that she was leaving town that afternoon for the weekend and wouldn't return until late Sunday evening. Phoning Eleanor Gruber as the best alternative, I was told that she was already booked. I looked over the list, trying to be objective about it, and settled on Blanche Duke.

When I got her I must admit she didn't sound enthusiastic, but probably she never did at the switchboard. She couldn't make it Friday but signed up for Saturday at seven.

We were getting reports by phone from Saul and Fred and Orrie, and Friday a little before six Saul came in person. The only reason I wouldn't vote for Saul Panzer for President of the United States is that he would never dress the part. How he goes around New York, almost anywhere, in that faded brown cap and old brown suit, without attracting attention as not belonging, I will never understand. Wolfe has never given him an assignment that he didn't fill better than anyone else could except me, and my argument is why not elect him President, buy him a suit and hat, and see what happens?

He sat on the edge of one of the yellow chairs and asked, "Anything fresh?"

"No," I told him. "As you know, it is usually impossible to tell just when a case will end, but this time it's a cinch. When our client's last buck is spent we'll quit."

"As bad as that? Is Mr. Wolfe concentrating?"

"You mean is he working or loafing? He's loafing. He has started asking people where they were at three-fifteen Monday afternoon, February twenty-sixth. That's a hell of a way for a genius to perform."

Wolfe entered, greeted Saul, and got behind his desk. Saul reported. Wolfe wanted full details as usual, and got them: the names of the judge, jury foreman, and others, the nature of the case that O'Malley had been losing, including the names of the litigants, and so forth. The information had gone to the court by mail in an unsigned typewritten letter, and had been detailed enough for them to go for the juror after a few hours' checkup. Efforts to trace the informing letter had failed. After an extended session with city employees, the juror had admitted getting three thousand dollars in cash from O'Malley, and more than half of it had been recovered. Louis Kustin had been defense attorney at the trials of both the juror and O'Malley, and by brilliant performances had got hung juries in both cases. Saul had spent a day trying to get the archives for a look at the unsigned typewritten informing letter, but had failed.

The bribed juror was a shoe salesman named Anderson. Saul had had two sessions with him and his wife. The wife's position stood on four legs: one, she had not written the letter; two, she had not known that her husband had taken a bribe; three, if she had known he had taken a bribe she certainly wouldn't have told on him; and four, she didn't know how to typewrite. Apparently her husband believed her. That didn't prove anything, since the talent of some husbands for believing their wives is unbounded, but when Saul too voted for her that was enough for Wolfe and me. Saul can smell a liar through a concrete wall. He offered to bring the Andersons in for Wolfe to judge for himself, but Wolfe said no. Saul was told to join Fred and Orrie in the check of Dykes's friends and acquaintances outside the office.

Saturday morning a large envelope arrived by messenger. Inside was a note from Emmett Phelps, the six-foot scholar who was indifferent to murder, typed on the firm's letterhead:

Dear Mr. Wolfe:

I am sending herewith, as you requested, some material written by Leonard Dykes.

Included is his letter of resignation dated July 19, 1950, which you said you would like to see. Evidently Mr. O'Malley's statement that he had returned the letter to Mr. Briggs was correct, since it was here in our files. Mr. O'Malley was in the office yesterday and I told him the letter had been found.

Kindly return the material when you have finished with it.

Sincerely,
Emmett Phelps

Dykes's letter of resignation was a full page, single-spaced, but all it said was what Corrigan had told us—that on account of the staff gossip that he had informed on O'Malley and so damaged the firm's reputation, and, further, because the new regime might want to make a change, he respectfully submitted his resignation. He had used three times as many words as he needed. As for the rest of the material—memoranda, reports, and copies of letters—it may have shown Wolfe how Dykes used words, but aside from that it was as irrelevant as last year's box score. Wolfe waded through it, passing each item to me as he finished, and I read every word, not wanting to leave an opening for another remark about my powers of observation like the time I had muffed the name of Baird Archer. When I had finished I handed the lot back to him, with some casual comment, and got at my typewriter to do some letters he had dictated.

I was banging away when he suddenly demanded, "What does this stand for?"

I got up to go and look. In his hand was Dykes's letter of resignation. He slid it across to me. "That notation in pencil in the corner. What is it?"

I looked at it, a pencil scribble like this:

$$Ps146\text{-}3$$

I nodded. "Yeah, I noticed it. Search me. Public School 146, Third Grade?"

"The S is lower case."

"So it is. Am I supposed to pop it out?"

"No. It's probably frivolous, but its oddity stirs curiosity. Does it suggest anything to you?"

I pursed my lips to look thoughtful. "Not offhand. Does it to you?"

He reached for it and frowned at it. "It invites speculation. With a capital P and a small S, it is presumably not initials. I know of only one word or name in the language for which 'Ps' is commonly used as an abbreviation. The figures following the 'Ps' increase the likelihood. Still no suggestion?"

"Well, 'Ps' stands for postscript, and the figures—"

"No. Get the Bible."

I crossed to the bookshelves, got it, and returned.

"Turn to Psalm One-forty-six and read the third verse."

I admit I had to use the index. Having done so, I turned the pages, found it, and gave it a glance.

"I'll be damned," I muttered.

"Read it!" Wolfe bellowed.

I read aloud. " 'Put not your trust in princes, nor in the son of man, in whom there is no help.' "

"Ah," Wolfe said, and sighed clear to his middle.

"Okay," I conceded. " 'Put Not Your Trust' was the title of Baird Archer's novel. At last you've got a man on base, but by a fluke. I hereby enter it for the record in coincidences that the item you specially requested had that notation on it and you spotted it. If that's how—"

"Pfui," Wolfe snorted. "There was nothing coincidental about it, and any lummox could have interpreted that notation."

"I'm a superlummox."

"No." He was so pleased he felt magnanimous. "You got it for us. You got those women here and scared them. You scared them so badly that one or more of them felt it necessary to concede a connection between Baird Archer and someone in that office."

"One of whom? The women?"

"I think not. I prefer a man, and it was the men I asked for material written by Dykes. You scared a man or men. I want to know which one or ones. You have an engagement for this evening?"

"Yes. With a blond switchboard operator. Three shades of blond on one head."

"Very well. Find out who made that notation on Dykes's letter in that square distinctive hand. I hope to heaven it wasn't Dykes himself." Wolfe frowned and shook his head. "I must correct myself. All I expect you to learn is whose hand that notation resembles. It would be better not to show the letter and the notation itself."

"Sure. Make it as tough as you can."

But it wasn't as tough as it sounded because the handwriting was so easy to imitate. During the afternoon I practiced it plenty before I prepared my bait. When I left for my date at 6:40 I had with me, in the breast pocket of my newest lightweight blue suit, one of the items that had been sent us—a typewritten memorandum from Leonard Dykes—with a penciled notation in the margin made by me:

CO3-4620

13

BLANCHE DUKE surprised me that evening. She had two shots of her special formula—gin, vermouth, grenadine, and Pernod—before dinner, and then quit. No more. Also she wore a nice simple blue dress and went easy with cosmetics. Also, most important, she could dance much better than Sue Dondero. On the whole, while she was not something for the Bobolink to stare at, she certainly needed no excuses, and she made the Bobolink band seem even better than it was. By ten o'clock I would have been perfectly willing to split the check with our client. But I was there on business.

When we went back to our table after I had fancied up a samba all I could and she had kept with me as though we had done it a hundred times, and I insisted that with dinner only a memory it was time for a drink, she refused.

"Look," I objected, "this isn't going right. All I'm getting out of it is a good time, when I'm supposed to be working. The idea was to get you lit enough to loosen up, and you're drinking water. How can I get you babbling if you won't drink?"

"I like to dance," she stated.

"No wonder, the way you do it. So do I, but I've got a problem. I've got to quit enjoying myself and drag something out of you."

She shook her head. "I don't drink when I'm dancing because I like to dance. Try me tomorrow afternoon while I'm washing my hair. I hate washing my damn hair. What makes you think there's something in me to drag out?"

Our waiter was hovering, and I appeased him with an order for something.

"Well," I told her, "there ought to be, since you think O'Malley killed Dykes. You must have some reason—"

"I don't think that."

"You said you did Wednesday evening."

She waved a hand. "It gets Eleanor Gruber's goat. She's crazy about O'Malley. I don't think that at all. I think Len Dykes committed suicide."

"Oh. Whose goat does that get?"

"Nobody's. It might get Sue's, but I like her, so I don't say it, I just think it."

"Sue Dondero? Why her?"

"Well—" Blanche frowned. "Of course you didn't know Len Dykes."

"No."

"He was a funny duck. He was a nice guy in a way, but he was funny. He had inhibitions about women, but he carried a picture of one in his wallet, and who do you think it was? His sister, for God's sake! Then one day I saw him—"

She stopped abruptly. The band had struck up a conga. Her shoulders moved to the beat. There was only one thing to do. I stood up and extended a hand, and she came, and we edged through to the floor. A quarter

of an hour later we returned to the table, sat, and
exchanged glances of unqualified approval.

"Let's get the dragging over with," I suggested, "and
then we can do some serious dancing. You were saying
that one day you saw Dykes—doing what?"

She looked blank a moment, then nodded. "Oh, yes.
Do we really have to go on with this?"

"I do."

"Okay. I saw him looking at Sue. Brother, that was a
look! I kidded him about it, which was a mistake, because it made him decide to pick me to tell about it. It
was the first time—"

"When was this?"

"A year ago, maybe more. It was the first time he had
ever put an eye on a woman, at his age! And he had
fallen for her so hard he might as well have had an
ulcer. He kept it covered all right, except with me, but I
certainly got it. He tried to date her, but nothing doing.
He asked me what to do, and I had to tell him something, so I told him Sue was the kind of girl who was
looking for glamour, and he ought to get famous somehow, like getting elected senator or pitching for the
Yankees or writing a book. So he wrote a book, and the
publishers wouldn't take it, and he killed himself."

I showed no excitement. "He told you he wrote a
book?"

"No, he never mentioned it. Along about then he
stopped talking about her, and I never brought it up
because I didn't want to get him started again. But it
was one of the things I suggested, and there's all this
racket about a book that got rejected, so why can't I put
two and two together?"

I could have objected that suicide by Dykes in December wouldn't help to explain the murder of Joan
Wellman and Rachel Abrams in February, but I wanted
to get to the point before the band started up again. I
took a sip of my drink.

I smiled at her to keep it friendly. "Even if you're

right about the suicide, what if you're shifting the cast? What if it was you instead of Sue he put his eye on?"

She snorted. "Me? If you mean that for a compliment, try again."

"I don't." My hand went to my breast pocket and came out with a folded paper. "This is a memorandum on office expenses prepared by Dykes, dated last May." I unfolded it. "I was going to ask you why he scribbled your home phone number on it, but now you can just say it was while he was telling you about Sue and asking your advice, so what's the use." I started to refold it.

"*My* phone number?" she demanded.

"Yep. Columbus three, four-six-two-oh."

"Let me see it."

I handed it to her, and she took a look. She held it to her right to get more light and looked again. "Len didn't write that," she declared.

"Why not?"

"It's not his writing."

"Whose is it? Yours?"

"No. It's Corrigan's. He writes square like that." She was frowning at me. "What is this, anyhow? Why should Corrigan be putting my phone number on this old memo?"

"Oh, forget it." I reached and took the paper from her fingers. "I thought maybe Dykes had written it and just thought I'd ask. Corrigan may have wanted to phone you about something after office hours." A rattle came from the drum, and the band slid into a trot. I put the memo in my pocket and stood up. "Skip it. Let's see how we like this."

We liked it fine.

When I got home, around two, Wolfe had gone up to bed. I slid the bolts on the front and back doors, twirled the knob of the safe, and drank a glass of milk before ascending. People are never satisfied. What was on my mind as I pulled the covers up was the contrariness of life. Why couldn't it have been Sue who danced like that instead of Blanche? If a man could figure out some way of combining...

The Sunday schedule at Wolfe's house was different since Marko Vukcic, his closest friend and the owner of Rusterman's Restaurant, had talked him into installing a pool table in the basement. It was now routine for Wolfe to spend Sunday morning in the kitchen with Fritz, preparing something special. At one-thirty Marko would arrive to help appreciate it, after which they would go to the basement for a five-hour session with the cues. I rarely took part, even when I was around, because it made Wolfe grumpy when I got lucky and piled up a big run.

That Sunday I fully expected to upset the schedule when Wolfe, having breakfasted in his room, entered the kitchen and I told him, "That notation on that letter is in the handwriting of James A. Corrigan, the senior partner."

He scowled at me a moment, then turned to Fritz. "I have decided," he said aggressively, "not to use the goose fat."

I raised my voice. "That notation on that let—"

"I heard you! Take the letter to Mr. Cramer and tell him about it."

It would have done no good to scream, not when he used that tone, so I controlled myself. "You have trained me," I said stiffly, "to remember conversations verbatim, including yours. Yesterday you said you wanted to know who we had scared and whose hand that notation resembles. I spent a whole evening and a wad of Wellman's dough finding out. To hand it to Cramer, for God's sake? What if it is Sunday? If they're scared they'll come. May I use the phone?"

His lips had tightened. "What else did you get?"

"Nothing. That's what you asked for."

"Very well. Satisfactory. Fritz and I are going to do a guinea hen, and there is barely time. If you get Mr. Corrigan down here, or even all of them, what will happen? I will show him that notation and he will deny all knowledge of it. I will ask where that letter has been, and will be told that it has been easily accessible to all of them. That will take perhaps five minutes. Then what?"

"Nuts. If you insist on playing pool instead of working on Sunday, wait till tomorrow. Why hand it to Cramer?"

"Because for its one purpose he is as good as I am—even better. It validates for them, if not for me, my assumption that someone in that firm has a guilty connection with the murder of three people. We have already scared him into this; with that letter a police inspector may scare him into something else. Take it to Mr. Cramer and don't bother me. You know quite well that for me pool is not play; it is exercise."

He strode to the refrigerator.

I had a notion to spend a couple of hours with the Sunday papers before going downtown, but decided there was no point in my being childish just because Wolfe was. Besides, with him I never knew. It could be that he merely wanted to cook and eat and play pool instead of working, but it could also be that he was pulling something fancy. He often got subtle without letting me in on it, and it wasn't impossible that there was something about that notation, or the way we got it, that made him figure it would be better to turn it over to Cramer than spring it himself. Walking the fifteen blocks to Twentieth Street with a cold March wind whipping at me from the right, I considered the matter and concluded that it might either rain or snow.

Cramer wasn't in, but Sergeant Purley Stebbins was. He gave me the chair at the end of his desk and listened to my tale. I gave it all to him except the detail of how we had learned it was Corrigan's handwriting, seeing no necessity of dragging Blanche into it. I merely told him that we had good reason to believe that it looked like Corrigan's writing. Of course he knew that Baird Archer's novel had been titled "Put Not Your Trust." He looked around for a Bible to check on the third verse of the 146th Psalm, but couldn't find one.

He was skeptical, but not about that. "You say Wolfe got this letter yesterday?" he demanded.

"Right."

"And he's done nothing about it?"

"Right."

"He hasn't asked Corrigan about it, or any of the others?"

"Right."

"Then what the hell's wrong with it?"

"Nothing that I know of. We're cooperating."

Purley snorted. "Nero Wolfe passing us a juicy item like this without first squeezing it for himself? Poop."

"If you don't like it," I said with dignity, "I'll take it back and see if I can get something better. Would you accept a signed confession with dates and places?"

"I'll accept a signed statement from you, telling how you got this."

"Glad to, if you'll give me a decent typewriter."

What I got was what I expected, an Underwood about my age. I demanded a new ribbon, and they finally dug one up.

Back at home I did a few chores in the office and then got comfortable with the Sunday papers. Wolfe came in now and then for a section to take to the kitchen. Around noon he entered, sat behind his desk, and requested a full report of my evening with Miss Duke. Evidently the guinea hen was under control. I obliged, thinking he might let me in on the strategy if that was what it was, but all I got was a nod.

That was all for Sunday, except that after dinner I got invited to the pool game and made a run of twenty-nine, and after supper I was instructed to tell Saul and Fred and Orrie to report in at eleven in the morning.

They were there when Wolfe came down from the plant rooms: Saul Panzer, small and wiry, in his old brown suit; Fred Durkin, with his round red face and spreading bald spot, in the red leather chair by right of seniority; and Orrie Cather, with his square jaw and crew cut, looking young enough to still be playing pro football. Wolfe took Fred first, then Orrie, and Saul last.

Adding what they told us to what we already knew from the police file and the girls and the firm members, including Blanche's little contribution Saturday evening, we were certainly up on Leonard Dykes. I could give you fifty pages on him, but it would leave you just where we were, so what's the use? If anyone who had known him had any idea who had killed him or why, they weren't saying. Saul and Fred and Orrie were three good men, and they hadn't got the faintest glimmer, though they had covered every possible source except Dykes's sister, who was in California. Wolfe kept them till lunchtime and then cut them loose. Saul, who hated to turn in an empty bag even more than I did, offered to spend another day or two at it on his own, but Wolfe said no.

When they had gone Wolfe sat and stared across the room at nothing a full three minutes before he pushed back his chair, though Fritz had announced lunch. Then he heaved a deep sigh, got himself up, and growled at me to come on.

We had just returned to the office after a silent meal that was anything but convivial when the doorbell rang and I went to answer it. Not many times has it given me pleasure to see a cop on that stoop, but that was one of them. Even a humble dick would have been a sign that something had happened or might be ready to happen, and this was Inspector Cramer himself. I opened up and invited him to cross the sill, took his hat and coat, and escorted him to the office without bothering to announce him.

He grunted at Wolfe, and Wolfe grunted back. He sat, got a cigar from his vest pocket, inspected it, stuck it between his teeth, moved his jaw to try it at various angles, and took it out again.

"I'm deciding how to start this," he muttered.

"Can I help?" Wolfe asked politely.

"Yes. But you won't. One thing, I'm not going to get

sore. It wouldn't do any good, because I doubt if I've got anything on you that would stick. Is that deal we made still on?"

"Of course. Why not?"

"Then you will kindly fill me in. When you decided to trick us into taking a jab at someone, why did you pick Corrigan?"

Wolfe shook his head. "You had better start over, Mr. Cramer. That's the worst possible way. There was no trick—"

Cramer cut in rudely and emphatically with a vulgar word. He went on. "I said I'm not going to get sore, and I'm not, but look at it. You get hold of that letter with that notation on it, the first real evidence anyone has seen that links someone in that office with Baird Archer and therefore with the murders. A real hot find. There were several ways you could have used it, but you pass them all up and send the letter down to me. I sent Lieutenant Rowcliff up there this morning. Corrigan admits the notation resembles his handwriting, but absolutely denies that he made it or ever saw it or has any idea what it stands for. The others all make the same denials."

Cramer cocked his head. "I've sat here many a time and listened to you making an assumption on poorer ground than what I've made this one on. I don't know how you got hold of a sample of Corrigan's handwriting, but that would have been easy. And I don't know whether it was you or Goodwin who made that notation on that letter, and I don't care. One of you did. All I want to know is, why? You're too smart and too lazy to play a trick like that just for the hell of it. That's why I'm not sore and I'm not going to get sore. You expected it to get you something. What?"

He put the cigar in his mouth and sank his teeth in it.

Wolfe regarded him. "Confound it," he said regretfully, "we're not going to get anywhere."

"Why not? I'm being goddam reasonable."

"You are indeed. But we can't meet. You will listen to

me only if I concede your assumption that Mr. Goodwin or I made the notation on the letter, imitating Corrigan's hand. You will not listen to me if I deny that and substitute my own assumption, that the notation was in fact a trick but not mine. Will you?"

"Try it."

"Very well. Someone wanted to provide me with evidence that would support the line I was taking, but of such a nature and in such a manner that I would be left exactly where I was. Its pointing at Corrigan may have been deliberate or merely adventitious; it had to point at someone, and it may be that Corrigan was selected because he is somehow invulnerable. I preferred not to make an ass of myself by acting on it. All I would have got was a collection of denials. As it now stands, Lieutenant Rowcliff got the denials, and I am uncommitted. They don't know—*he* doesn't know—how I took it. For my part, I don't know who he is or what is moving him or why he wants to prod me, but I would like to know. If he acts again I may find out."

Wolfe upturned a palm. "That's all."

"I don't believe it."

"I didn't expect you to."

"Okay. I've listened to it on your assumption, now try mine. You made the notation on the letter yourself and made me a present of it. Why?"

"No, Mr. Cramer. I'm sorry, but that's beyond my powers. Unless you also assume that I've lost my senses, and in that case why waste time on me?"

"I won't." Cramer left his chair, and as he did so his determination not to get sore suddenly went up the flue. He hurled his unlit cigar at my wastebasket, missed by a yard, and hit me on the ankle. "Fat bloated lousy liar," he rasped, and turned and tramped out.

Thinking that under the circumstances it was just as well to let him wriggle into his coat unaided, I stayed put. But also thinking that he might take a notion to try a simple little trick himself, when the front door slammed I got up and moseyed to the hall for a look through the one-way glass panel, and saw him cross to the sidewalk and get into his car, the door of which had been opened for an inspector.

When I returned to the office Wolfe was leaning back with his eyes closed and his brow creased. I sat. I hoped to God he didn't feel as helpless and useless as I did, but from the expression on his face I had another hope coming. I looked at my wrist and saw 2:52. When I looked again it said 3:06. I wanted to yawn but thought I didn't deserve to, and choked it.

Wolfe's voice blurted, "Where's Mr. Wellman?"

"In Peoria. He went Friday."

He had opened his eyes and straightened up. "How long does it take an airplane to get to Los Angeles?"

"Ten or eleven hours. Some of them more."

"When does the next one go?"

"I don't know."

"Find out. Wait. Have we ever before been driven to extremities as now?"

"No."

"I agree. His gambit of that notation on that letter—what for? Confound him! Nothing but denials. You have the name and address of Dykes's sister in California."

"Yes, sir."

"Phone Mr. Wellman and tell him that I propose to send you to see her. Tell him it is either that or abandon the case. If he approves the expenditure, reserve a seat on the next plane and get packed. By then I shall have instructions ready for you. Is there plenty of cash in the safe?"

"Yes."

"Take enough. You are willing to cross the continent in an airplane?"

"I'll risk it."

He shuddered. He regards a twenty-block taxi ride as a reckless gamble.

14

I HADN'T been to the West Coast for several years. I slept most of the night but woke up when the stewardess brought morning coffee and then kept my eyes open for a look down at the country. There is no question that a desert landscape is neater than where things have simply got to grow, and of course they don't have the weed problem, but from up above I saw stretches where even a few good big weeds would have been a help.

My watch said 11:10 as the plane taxied to a stop on the concrete of the Los Angeles airport, and I set it back to ten past eight before I arose and filed out to the gangway and off. It was warm and muggy, with no sign of the sun. By the time I got my suitcase and found a taxi I had to use a handkerchief on my face and neck. Then the breeze through the open window came at me, and, not wanting to get pneumonia in a foreign country, I shut the window. The people didn't look as foreign as some of the architecture and most of the vegetation. Before we got to the hotel it started to rain.

I had a regulation breakfast and then went up and had a regulation bath. My room—it was the Riviera—had too many colors scattered around but was okay. It smelled swampy, but I couldn't open a window on account of the rain. When I was through bathing and shaving and dressing and unpacking it was after eleven, and I got at the phone and asked Information for the number of Clarence O. Potter, 2819 Whitecrest Avenue, Glendale.

I called the number, and after three whirs a female voice told my ear hello.

I was friendly but not sugary. "May I speak to Mrs. Clarence Potter, please?"

"This is Mrs. Potter." Her voice was high but not squeaky.

"Mrs. Potter, my name is Thompson, George Thompson. I'm from New York, and you never heard of me. I'm here on a business trip, and I would like to see you to discuss an important matter. Any time that will suit you will suit me, but the sooner the better. I'm talking from the Riviera Hotel and I can come out now if that will be convenient."

"Did you say Thompson?"

"That's right, George Thompson."

"But why do you—what's it about?"

"It's a personal matter. I'm not selling anything. It's something I need to know about your deceased brother, Leonard Dykes, and it will be to your advantage if it affects you at all. I'd appreciate it if I could see you today."

"What do you want to know about my brother?"

"It's a little too complicated for the telephone. Why not let me come and tell you about it?"

"Well, I suppose—all right. I'll be home until three o'clock."

"Fine. I'll leave right away."

I did so. All I had to do was grab my hat and raincoat and go. But down in the lobby I was delayed. As I was heading for the front a voice called Mr. Thompson, and with my mind on my errand I nearly muffed it. Then I reined and turned and saw the clerk handing a bellboy a yellow envelope.

"Telegram for you, Mr. Thompson."

I crossed and got it and tore it open. It said, "CONFOUND IT DID YOU ARRIVE SAFELY OR NOT." I went out and climbed into a taxi and told the driver we were bound for Glendale but the first stop would be a drugstore. When he pulled up in front of one I went into a phone booth and sent a wire: "Arrived intact am on my way to appointment with subject."

During the thirty-minute drive to Glendale it rained approximately three-quarters of an inch. Whitecrest Avenue was so new it hadn't been paved yet, and Number 2819 was out almost at the end, with some giant sagebrush just beyond, hanging on the edge of a gully, only I suppose it wasn't sagebrush. There were two saggy palms and another sort of a tree in the front yard. The driver stopped at the edge of the road in front, with the right wheels in four inches of rushing water in the gutter, and announced, "Here we are."

"Yeah," I agreed, "but I'm not a Seabee. If you don't mind turning in?"

He muttered something, backed up for an approach, swung into the ruts of what was intended for a driveway, and came to a stop some twenty paces from the front door of the big pink box with maroon piping. Having already told him he wasn't expected to wait, I paid him, got out, and made a dive for the door, which was protected from the elements by an overhang about the size of a card table. As I pushed the button a three-by-six panel a little below the level of my eyes slid aside, leaving an opening through which a voice came.

"Mr. George Thompson?"

"That's me. Mrs. Potter?"

"Yes. I'm sorry, Mr. Thompson, but I phoned my husband what you said, and he said I shouldn't let a stranger in, you see it's so remote here, so if you'll just tell me what you want . . ."

Outside the raincoat the pouring rain was slanting in at me, amused at the card-table cover. Inside the raincoat there was almost as much dampness as outside, from sweat. I wouldn't have called the situation desperate, but it did need attention. I inquired, "Can you see me through that hole?"

"Oh, yes. That's what it's for."

"How do I look?"

There was a noise that could have been a giggle. "You look wet."

"I mean do I look depraved?"

"No. No, you really don't."

Actually I was pleased. I had come three thousand miles to pull a fast one on this Mrs. Potter, and if she had received me with open arms I would have had to swallow scruples. Now, being kept standing out in that cloudburst on a husband's orders, I felt no qualms.

"Look," I offered, "here's a suggestion. I'm a literary agent from New York, and this will take us at least twenty minutes and maybe more. Go to the phone and call up some friend, preferably nearby. Tell her to hold the wire, come and unlock the door, and run back to the phone. Tell the friend to hang on. I'll enter and sit across the room from you. If I make a move you'll have your friend right there on the phone. How will that do?"

"Well—we just moved here a month ago and my nearest friend is miles away."

"Okay. Have you got a kitchen stool?"

"A kitchen stool? Certainly."

"Go get it to sit on and we'll talk through the hole."

The noise that could have been a giggle was repeated. Then came the sound of a turned lock, and the door swung open.

"This is silly," she said defiantly. "Come on in."

I crossed the threshold and was in a small foyer. She stood holding the door, looking brave. I took my raincoat off. She closed the door, opened a closet door and got a hanger, draped the dripping coat on it, and hooked it on the corner of the closet door. I hung my hat on the same corner.

"In that way," she said, nodding to the right, and I turned a corner into a big room that was mostly glass on one side, with glass doors, closed, to the outdoors at the far end. At the other end was a phony fireplace with phony logs glowing. The red and white and yellow rugs were matched by the cushions on the wicker furniture, and a table with books and magazines had a glass top.

She invited me to sit, and I did so. She stood far enough off so that I would have had to make three good bounds to grab her, and it is only fair to say that it might have been worth the effort. She was three inches shorter, some years older, and at least ten pounds plumper than my ideal for grabbing, but with her dark twinkling eyes in her round little face she was by no means homely.

"If you're wet," she said, "move over by the fire."

"Thanks, this is all right. This ought to be a nice room when the sun's shining."

"Yes, we think we'll like it very much." She sat down on the edge of a chair with her feet drawn back, maintaining her distance. "Do you know why I let you in? Your ears. I go by ears. Did you know my brother Len?"

"No, I never met him." I crossed my legs and leaned back, as evidence that I wasn't gathered for a pounce. "I'm much obliged to my ears for getting me in out of the rain. I believe I told you I'm a literary agent, didn't I?"

"Yes."

"The reason I had to see you, I understand you were your brother's only heir. He left everything to you?"

"Yes." She moved back in her chair a little. "That's how we bought this place. It's all paid for, cash, no mortgage."

"That's fine. Or it will be when it stops raining and the sun comes out. The idea is this, Mrs. Potter, since you were the sole legatee under your brother's will everything he had belongs to you. And I'm interested in something that I think he had—no, don't be alarmed, it's nothing that you've already used. Possibly you've never even heard of it. When did you last see your brother?"

"Why, six years ago. I never saw him after nineteen forty-five, when I got married and came to California." She flushed a little. "I didn't go back when he died, to the funeral, because we couldn't afford it. I would have gone if I had known he had left me all that money and bonds, but I didn't know that until afterwards."

"Did you correspond? Did you get letters from him?"

She nodded. "We always wrote once a month, sometimes oftener."

"Did he ever mention that he had written a book, a novel? Or that he was writing one?"

"Why, no." Suddenly she frowned. "Wait a minute, now maybe he did." She hesitated. "You see, Len was always thinking he was going to do something important, but I don't think he ever told anyone but me. After father and mother died I was all he had, and I was younger than him. He didn't want me to get married, and for a while he didn't write, he didn't answer my letters, but then he did, and he wrote long letters, pages and pages. Why, did he write a book?"

"Have you kept his letters?"

"Yes, I—I kept them."

"Have you still got them?"

"Yes. But I think you ought to tell me what you want."

"So do I." I folded my arms and regarded her, her round little honest face. In out of the rain, I was feeling a qualm, and this was the moment when I had to decide whether to trick her or let her in on it—a vital point, which Wolfe had left to my own judgment after meeting her. I looked at her face, with the twinkle gone from her eyes, and decided. If it came out wrong I could kick myself back to New York instead of taking a plane.

"Listen, Mrs. Potter. Will you listen carefully, please?"

"Of course I will."

"Okay. This is what I was going to tell you. It's not what I *am* telling you, only what I *intended* to. I'm George Thompson, a literary agent. I have in my possession a copy of a manuscript of a novel entitled 'Put Not Your Trust,' written by Baird Archer. But I have reason to believe that Baird Archer was a pen name used by your brother, that your brother wrote the novel—but I'm not sure about it. I also have reason to believe that I can sell the novel to one of the big movie companies for a good price, around fifty thousand dollars. You are your brother's sole heir. I want, with you, to go through the letters your brother wrote you, looking for evidence that he wrote or was writing the novel. Whether we find such evidence or not, I want to deposit the manuscript in the vault of a local bank for safekeeping, and I want you to write a letter to a certain law firm in New York, the firm your brother worked for. In the letter I want you to say that you have a copy of the manuscript of a novel written by your brother under the name of Baird Archer, giving the title of the novel, that an agent named Thompson thinks he can sell it to the movies for fifty thousand dollars, and that you want their legal advice in the matter because you don't know how such things should be done. I also want you to say that Thompson has read the manuscript but you have not. Get that?"

"But if you can sell it—" She was wide-eyed. It didn't alter my opinion of her. A prospect of fifty thousand unexpected bucks is enough to open eyes, no matter how honest they are. She added, "If it's my property I can just tell you to sell it, can't I?"

"You see," I reproached her, "you didn't listen."

"I did—too! I lis—"

"No. You did not. I warned you that that was only what I *intended* to tell you. There was some truth in it, but darned little. I do think that your brother wrote a novel of that title under the name of Baird Archer, and I would like to go through his letters to see if he mentioned it, but I have no copy of the manuscript, there is no prospect of selling it to the movies, I am not a literary agent, and my name is not George Thompson. Now, having—"

"Then it was all lies!"

"No. It would have—"

She was out of her chair. "Who are you? What's your name?"

"Have my ears changed any?" I demanded.

"What do you want?"

"I want you to listen. It wasn't a lie if I didn't say it, even if I intended to. Now here's what I do say, and it's the truth. You might as well sit down, because this is even longer."

She sat, but on about a third of the chair seat.

"My name," I said, "is Archie Goodwin. I'm a private detective, and I work for Nero Wolfe, also a private detec—"

"Nero Wolfe!"

"Right. It will please him to know that you had heard of him, and I'll be sure to tell him. He has been hired by a man named Wellman to find out who murdered his daughter. And another girl has been murdered, one named Rachel Abrams. Also, before that, your brother was murdered. We have reason to believe that the same person committed all three murders. It's a long and complicated reason, and I'll skip it. If you want the details later you can have them. I'll just say that our theory is that your brother was killed because he wrote that novel, Joan Wellman was killed because she had read it, and Rachel Abrams was killed because she had typed it."

"The novel—Len wrote?"

"Yes. Don't ask me what was in it, because we don't know. If we did, I wouldn't have had to come out here to see you. I came to get you to help us catch a man that murdered three people, and one of them was your brother."

"But I can't—" She gulped. "How can I help?"

"I'm telling you. I could have tricked you into helping. I've just proved it. You would have come along for a chance at fifty thousand dollars, you know darned well you would. You'd have let me go through your brother's letters for evidence, and whether we found it or not you'd have written the letter to the law firm. That's all I'm asking you to do, only now I'm giving it to you straight and asking you to do it not for a pile of dough but to help catch the man that killed your brother. If you would have done it for money, and you would, don't you think you ought to do it to bring a murderer to justice?"

She was frowning, concentrating. "But I don't see—You only want me to write a letter?"

"That's right. It's like this. We think your brother wrote that novel, and it was a vital element in the murders. We think that someone in that law office is involved and either committed the murders or knows who did. We think that someone is desperately determined that the contents of that manuscript shall not be known to any living person. If we're right, and you send the kind of letter I described, he'll have to move and move quick, and that's all we need, to start him moving. If we're wrong, your sending the letter will do nobody any harm."

She was keeping the frown. "What did you say you wanted me to say in the letter?"

I repeated it, with fuller detail. Toward the end she began slowly shaking her head. When I stopped she spoke.

"But that would be a lie—saying you have a copy of the manuscript when you haven't. I couldn't tell them a deliberate lie!"

"Maybe not," I said regretfully. "If you're the kind of person who has never told a lie in all your life, I can't expect you to tell one just to help find the man who killed your brother—and who also killed two young women, ran a car over one of them and pushed the other one out of a window. Even if it couldn't possibly hurt any innocent person, I wouldn't want to urge you to tell your very first lie."

"You don't have to be sarcastic." Her face had turned a mild pink. "I didn't say I never told a lie. I'm no angel. You're perfectly right, I would have done it for the money, only then I wouldn't have known it was a lie." Suddenly her eyes twinkled. "Why don't we start over and do it the other way?"

I would have liked to give her a good hug. "Listen," I suggested, "let's take things in order. We've got to go through his letters first anyhow, there's no objection to that, then we can decide on the next step. You get the letters, huh?"

"I guess so." She arose. "They're in a box in the garage."

"Can I help?"

She said no, thanks, and left me. I got up and crossed to a window to look out at the California climate. I would have thought it was beautiful if I had been a seal. It would be beautiful anyway if one of Dykes's letters had what I was after. I wasn't asking for anything elaborate like an outline of the plot; just one little sentence would do.

When she came back, sooner than I expected, she had two bundles of white envelopes in her hands, tied with string. She put them down on the glass-topped table, sat, and pulled the end of a bowknot.

I approached. "Start about a year ago. Say March of last year." I pulled a chair up. "Here, give me some."

She shook her head. "I'll do it."

"You might miss it. It might be just a vague reference."

"I won't miss it. I couldn't let you read my brother's letters, Mr. Thompson."

"Goodwin. Archie Goodwin."

"Excuse me. Mr. Goodwin." She was looking at postmarks.

Evidently she meant it, and I decided to table my motion, at least temporarily. Meanwhile I could do a job. I got out my notebook and pen and started writing at the top of a sheet:

Corrigan, Phelps, Kustin & Briggs
522 Madison Avenue
New York, N. Y.
Gentlemen:
          I am writing to ask your advice because my brother worked for you for many years up to the time of his death. His name was Leonard Dykes. I am his sister and in his will he left everything to me, but I suppose you know that.

> A man named Walter Finch has just been
to see me. He says he is a literary agent. He says that last
year my brother wrote a novel.

I stopped to consider. Mrs. Potter was reading a letter, with her teeth clamped on her lower lip. Well, I
thought, I can put it in, and it will be easy enough to
take it out if we have to. I resumed with my pen:

> I already knew that
because my brother mentioned it once in a letter, but
that was all I knew about it. Mr. Finch says he has a
copy of the manuscript and its title is "Put Not Your
Trust," and my brother put the name of Baird Archer
on it as the author, but my brother really wrote it. He
says he thinks he can sell it to the movies for $50,000.00,
and he says since my brother left everything to me I am
the legal owner of it and he wants me to sign a paper
that he is my agent and I will pay him 10 per cent of
what he gets for it from the movies.
>
> I am writing to you air mail because it is a
big sum of money and I know you will give me good
advice. I don't know any lawyer here that I know I can
trust. I want to know if the 10 per cent is all right and
should I sign the paper. Another thing I want to know is
that I haven't seen the manuscript except just the envelope he has it in and he won't leave it with me, and it
seems to me I ought to see it and read it if I am going to
sell it because I ought to know what I am selling.
>
> Please answer by air mail because Mr.
Finch says it is urgent and we must act quick. Thanking
you very much.
>
>   Sincerely yours,

It didn't come out that way all at once. I did a lot of
crossing out and changing, and the preceding was the
final result, of which I made a clear copy. I read it over
and passed it. There was the one sentence that might
have to come out, but I hoped to God it wouldn't.

My accomplice was reading steadily, and I had kept
an eye on her progress. There were four envelopes in a
little stack at her right, finished, and if she had started

with March and he had written one a month, she was up to July. My fingers itched to reach for the next one. I sat and controlled them until she finished another one and began folding it for return to the envelope, and then got up to take a walk. She was reading so damn slow. I crossed to the glass doors at the far end of the room and looked out. In the rain a newly planted tree about twice my height was slanting to one side, and I decided to worry about that but couldn't get my mind on it. I got stubborn and determined that I damn well was going to worry about that tree, and was fighting it out when suddenly her voice came.

"I knew there was something! Here it is. Listen!"

I wheeled and strode. She read it out.

"Here is something just for you, Peggy dear. So many things have been just for you all my life. I wasn't going to tell even you about this, but now it's finished and I have to. I have written a novel! Its title is "Put Not Your Trust." For a certain reason it can't be published under my name and I have to use a nom de plume, but that won't matter much if you know, so I'm telling you. I have every confidence that it will be published, since I am by no means a duffer when it comes to using the English language. But this is strictly for you alone. You mustn't even tell your husband about it."

Mrs. Potter looked up at me, at her elbow. "There! I had forgotten that he mentioned the title, but I knew—no! What are you—"

She made a quick grab, but not quick enough. I had finally pounced. With my left hand I had snatched the letter from her fingers, and with my right the envelope from the table, and then backed off out of reach.

"Take it easy," I told her. "I'd go through fire for you and I've already gone through water, but this letter goes home with me. It's the only evidence on earth that your brother wrote that novel. I'd rather have this letter than one from Elizabeth Taylor begging me to let her hold my hand. If there's anything in it that you don't want read in a courtroom that part won't be read, but I need it all, including the envelope. If I had to I would knock you down and walk on you to get out of here with it. You'd better take another look at my ears."

She was indignant. "You didn't have to grab it like that."

"Okay, I was impulsive and I apologize. I'll give it back, and you can hand it to me, with the understanding that if you refuse I'll take it by force."

Her eyes twinkled, and she knew it, and flushed a little. She extended a hand. I folded the letter, put it in the envelope, and handed it to her. She looked at it, glanced at me, held it out, and I took it.

"I'm doing this," she said gravely, "because I think my brother would want me to. Poor Len. You think he was killed because he wrote that novel?"

"Yes. Now I know it. It's up to you whether we get the guy that killed him." I got out my notebook, tore out a sheet, and handed it to her. "All you have to do is write that letter on your own paper. Maybe not quite all. I'll tell you the rest."

She started to read it. I sat down. She looked beautiful. The phony logs in the phony fireplace looked beautiful. Even the pouring rain—but no, I won't overdo it.

15

I PHONED Wolfe at 3:23 from a booth in a drugstore somewhere in Glendale. It is always a pleasure to hear him say "Satisfactory" when I have reported on an errand. This time he did better. When I had given him all of it that he needed, including the letter written by Dykes that I had in my pocket and the one written by Mrs. Potter that I had just put an air-mail stamp on and dropped in the slot at the Glendale Post Office, there was a five-second silence and then an emphatic "Very satisfactory." After another five bucks' worth of discussion of plans for the future, covering contingencies as well as possible, I dove through the rain to my waiting taxi and gave the driver an address in downtown Los Angeles. It rained all the way. At an intersection we missed colliding with a truck by an eighth of an inch, and the driver apologized, saying he wasn't used to driving in the rain. I said he soon would be, and he resented it.

The office of the Southwest Agency was on the ninth floor of a dingy old building with elevators that groaned and creaked. It occupied half the floor. I had been there once before, years back, and, having phoned that morning from the hotel that I would probably be dropping in, I was more or less expected. In a corner room a guy named Ferdinand Dolman, with two chins, and fourteen long brown hairs deployed across a bald top, arose to shake hands and exclaim heartily, "Well, well! Nice to see you again! How's the old fatty?"

Few people know Nero Wolfe well enough to call him the old fatty, and this Dolman was not one of them, but it wasn't worth the trouble to try to teach him manners, so I skipped it. I exchanged words with him enough to make it sociable and then told him what I wanted.

"I've got just the man for you," he declared. "He happens to be here right now, just finished a very difficult job. This is a break for you, it really is." He picked up a phone and told it, "Send Gibson in."

In a minute the door opened and a man entered and approached. I gave him one look, and one was enough. He had a cauliflower ear, and his eyes were trying to penetrate a haze that was too thick for them.

Dolman started to speak, but I beat him to it. "No," I said emphatically, "not the type. Not a chance."

Gibson grinned. Dolman told him he could go, and he did so. When the door had closed behind him I got candid. "You've got a nerve, trotting in that self-made

ape. If he just did a difficult job I'd hate to see who does
your easy ones. I want a man who is educated or can
talk like it, not too young and not too old, sharp and
quick, able to take on a bushel of new facts and have
them ready for use."

"Jesus." Dolman clasped his hands behind his head. "J.
Edgar Hoover maybe?"

"I don't care what his name is, but if you haven't got
one like that, say so, and I'll go shopping."

"Certainly we've got one. With over fifty men on the
payroll? Certainly we've got one."

"Show him to me."

He finally did, I admit that, but not until after I had
hung around for more than five hours and had inter-
viewed a dozen prospects. I also admit I was being
finicky, especially since there was a good chance that all
he would ever do was collect his twenty a day and
expenses, but after getting it set up as I had I didn't
want to run a risk of having it bitched up by some little
stumble. The one I picked was about my age, named
Nathan Harris. His face was all bones and his fingers
were all knuckles, and if I knew anything about eyes he
would do. I didn't go by ears, like Peggy Potter.

I took him to my room at the Riviera. We ate in the
room, and I kept him there, briefing him, until two in
the morning. He was to go home and get some luggage
and register at the South Seas Hotel under the name of
Walter Finch, and get a room that met the specifications
I gave him. I let him make notes all he wanted, with the
understanding that he was to have it all in his head by
the time it might be needed, which could be never. One
decision I made was to tell him only what Walter Finch,
the literary agent, might be expected to know, not to
hold out on him but to keep from cluttering his mind, so
when he left he had never heard the names of Joan
Wellman or Rachel Abrams, or Corrigan, Phelps, Kustin
and Briggs.

Going to bed, I opened the window three inches at
the bottom, and in the morning there was a pool that

reached to the edge of the rug. I got my wristwatch
from the bedstand and saw 9:20, which meant 12:20 in
New York. At the Glendale Post Office they had told me
that the letter would make a plane which would land at
La Guardia at eight in the morning New York time, so it
should be delivered at Madison Avenue any time now,
possibly right this minute as I stretched and yawned.

One of my worries was Mr. Clarence Potter. Mrs.
Potter had assured me that her husband wouldn't try to
interfere, whether he approved or not, but it tied a knot
in me, especially with an empty stomach, to think of the
damage he could do with a telegram to Corrigan,
Phelps, Kustin and Briggs. It was too much for me.
Before I even shut the window or went to the bathroom
I called the Glendale number. Her voice answered.

"Good morning, Mrs. Potter. This is Archie Goodwin. I
was just wondering—did you tell your husband about
it?"

"Yes, of course. I told you I was going to."

"I know you did. How did he take it? Should I see
him?"

"No, I don't think so. He doesn't quite understand it. I
explained that you have no copy of the manuscript and
there doesn't seem to be one anywhere, but he thinks we
should try to find one and perhaps it can be sold to a
movie studio. I told him we should wait for an answer to
my letter, and he agreed. I'm sure he'll understand when
he thinks it over."

"Of course he will. Now about Walter Finch. I've got
him, and he's in his room at the South Seas. He's a little
taller than average, and you'd probably guess him at
thirty-five. He has a bony face, and bony hands with
long fingers, and dark brown eyes that you might call
black. He looks straight at you when he talks, and his
voice is a medium baritone, you'd like it. Do you want to
write that down?"

"I don't need to."

"Sure you've got it?"

"Yes."

"I believe you. I'll be in my room at the Riviera all day. Call me any time if anything happens."

"All right, I will."

There's a loyal little woman with twinkles, I thought, hanging up. She knows damn well she's married to a dumbbell, but by gum she'll never say so. I phoned down for breakfast and newspapers, washed and brushed my teeth, and ate in my pajamas. Then I called the South Seas Hotel and asked for Walter Finch. He was there in his room, 1216, and said he was getting along fine with his homework. I told him to stay put until further notice.

When I showered and shaved and dressed, and finished with the newspapers and looked out at the rain some, I phoned down for magazines. I refused to let myself start listening for the phone to ring because it might be all day and night and into another day before there was a peep, and it wouldn't help to wear my nerves out. However, I did look at my watch fairly often, translating it into New York time, as I gave the magazines a play. Eleven-fifty meant two-fifty. Twelve-twenty-five meant three-twenty-five. Four minutes after one meant four minutes after four. One-forty-five meant a quarter to five, nearing the end of the office day. I tossed a magazine aside and went to a window to admire the rain again, then called room service and ordered lunch.

I was chewing a bite of albacore steak when the phone rang. To show how composed I was, I finished chewing and swallowing before I picked it up. It was Mrs. Potter.

"Mr. Goodwin! I just had a phone call! From Mr. Corrigan!"

I was glad I had finished swallowing. "Fine! What did he say?"

"He wanted to know all about Mr. Finch. I said just what you told me to." She was talking too fast, but I didn't interrupt. "He asked where the manuscript is, and I told him Mr. Finch has it. He asked if I had seen it or

read it, and I said no. He told me not to sign any paper
or agree to anything until he has seen me. He's taking a
plane in New York and he'll get to Los Angeles at eight
in the morning and he's coming right here to see me."

It was a funny thing. I was swallowing albacore, although I would have sworn that it was already down. It
tasted good.

"Did he sound as if he suspected anything?"

"He did not! I did it perfectly!"

"I'm sure you did. If I was there I'd pat you on the
head. I might even go further than that, so it's just as
well I'm not there. Do you want me to come out and go
over it again? What you'll say to him?"

"I don't think it's necessary. I remember everything."

"Okay. He'll want to get to Finch as soon as possible,
but he may ask you a lot of questions. What do you say
if he asks to see the letter from your brother in which he
mentioned writing a novel?"

"I say I haven't got it. That I didn't keep it."

"Right. He'll probably get to your place around nine
o'clock. What time does your husband leave?"

"Twenty minutes past seven."

"Well. It's a million to one that you'll be in no danger,
even if he's a killer, since he knows you have never seen
the manuscript, but we can't take a chance. I can't be
there myself because I have to be in Finch's room before
he gets there. Now listen. At eight in the morning a man
will come and show you his credentials from the Southwest Agency, a detective agency. Hide him where he can
hear what goes on, but be darned sure he's well hid.
Keep him—"

"No, that's silly! Nothing's going to happen to me!"

"You bet it isn't. Three murders is enough for one
manuscript. He'll be there, and you—"

"My husband can take the morning off and stay
home."

"No. I'm sorry, but that's out. Your talk with Corrigan
is going to be ticklish to handle, and we don't want
anyone joining in, not even your husband. A man will

come with credentials, and you'll let him in and hide him and keep him there until an hour after Corrigan has left. Either that or I come myself, and that would ball it up. What hotel is Finch at?"

"The South Seas."

"Describe him."

"He's rather tall, in his thirties, with a bony face and hands and dark eyes, and he looks straight at you when he talks."

"Right. For God's sake don't get careless and describe me. Remember it was Finch who came to see you—"

"Really, Mr. Goodwin! If you have no confidence in me!"

"I have. I sure have."

"Well, you'd better!"

"I had indeed better. I'll be out part of the afternoon. If you need me, leave word. Good luck, Mrs. Potter."

"Good luck to you too."

The albacore had cooled off some, but it was good, and I finished it. I felt wonderful. I called Finch at the South Seas and told him we had had a bite and had a fish on the hook, and it might be the big one, and I would drop in on him at eight in the morning. He said he was all set. I lifted the receiver to put in a call to New York, then replaced it. It was goofy to suppose there could be any risk in George Thompson's calling Nero Wolfe's number, but I'd rather be goofy than sorry. Taking my raincoat and hat, I went down to the lobby, out into the rain, and to a drugstore in the next block. There I made the call from a booth. When I got Wolfe and reported the development, he grunted across the continent, and that was all. He had no additional instructions or suggestions. I got the impression that I had interrupted him at something important like a crossword puzzle.

I only half drowned finding a taxi to take me to the address of the Southwest Agency. With Dolman I didn't have to be as choosy as the day before, since any mug should be able to keep a man from killing a woman right under his nose, but even so I didn't want any part of Gibson or one like him. He produced a fairly good specimen, and I gave him careful and fully detailed instructions and made him repeat them. From there I went to the South Seas Hotel for a surprise call on Finch, thinking it just as well to check him and also to have a look at the room. He was lying on the bed, reading a book entitled *Twilight of the Absolute*, which seemed a deep dive for a dick, but then, as Finch, he was a literary agent, so I refrained from comment. The room was perfect, of medium size, with the door to the bathroom in the far corner and one to a good big closet off to one side. I didn't stay long because my nerves were jumpy away from the phone in my room at the Riviera. If anything happened I wanted to know it quick. For instance, Clarence Potter would soon be home from work, or was already. What if he didn't understand it some more and decided to take a hand?

But at bedtime the phone hadn't let out a tinkle.

16

AT 8:02 Thursday morning I entered Finch's room at the South Seas. He was up and dressed but hadn't had breakfast, and I had only had orange juice before leaving the Riviera. Hanging my hat and raincoat, which had been sprinkled again, in the rear of the big closet, I gave him my order: griddle cakes, ham and eggs, a jar of honey, and coffee. He relayed it to room service, his own requirements being prunes and toast and coffee, which made me dart a glance at him, but he looked okay. When he was through I went to the phone and called the Glendale number and got an answer after four whirrs.

"Archie Goodwin, Mrs. Potter. Good morning. Did the man come?"

"Yes, he got here ten minutes ago. He'll hide in the kitchen. You know I'm all excited?"

"Sure, that's all right. It won't matter if it shows; Corrigan will think it's the prospect of fifty thousand bucks. Just take it easy. Do you want to ask anything?"

"No, not a thing."

"Good for you. I'm in Finch's room at the South Seas. Ring me if you need to, and of course when he leaves."

She said she would. I hung up and called the airport. The plane from New York, due at eight o'clock, had landed at 7:50, ten minutes early.

The cuisine at the South Seas wasn't as good as the Riviera, but I cleaned up my share. When we had finished we wheeled the breakfast table into the hall, and then had a discussion whether to make the bed. Harris, Finch to you, wanted to make it, but my point was that it would be unrealistic because no literary agent would have got up early enough to leave the room free for the chambermaid at that hour, and he had to concede it. He raised the question of whether I would stand in the closet or sit, and I said I would stand because no chair can be trusted not to squeak with a shift of weight. We had just got that settled when the phone rang. I was seated by it, but told Finch to take it and moved. He went and got it.

"Hello. . . . This is Walter Finch speaking. . . . Yes, I talked with Mrs. Potter. . . . That's right. . . . No, I didn't know she had written you, Mr. Corrigan, I only knew she had written for advice. . . . Yes, but may I speak to her, please?"

Pause.

"Yes, this is Finch, Mrs. Potter. Mr. Corrigan says he wants to see me, representing you about that manuscript. . . . Oh, I see. . . . Yes, I understand. . . . Certainly, I'll consult you before any agreement is made. . . . Please put him on."

Pause.

"Yes, I understand, Mr. Corrigan. . . . No, that's all right, I'm perfectly willing to discuss it. . . . Yes, if you come right away. I have an appointment at eleven. . . . Room Twelve-sixteen, the South Seas. . . . All right, I'll be here."

He hung up and turned to me with a grin. "Got a landing net?"

"No, a gaff. What was the hitch?"

"Nothing serious. He seemed to think he had a client, but she didn't agree. He's coming on his own, to protect the lowly, without prejudice to her."

"If you want me to," I offered, "I'll tell you what's wrong with our civilization."

"I want you to. What?"

"We've quit drinking champagne from ladies' slippers. I would like to drink some from hers."

I sat, bent and untied my laces and took off my shoes, took them to the closet, and put them on the floor out of the way. In my socks I hopped around on the spot where I would be standing, and heard no squeaks.

As I rejoined Finch the phone rang. He got it, spoke, covered the transmitter, and told me, "Mrs. Potter. She wants to know what color slippers you prefer."

I went and took it. "Yes, Mrs. Potter? Archie Goodwin."

"Why, he wasn't here more than ten minutes! He hardly asked me anything! He asked about Mr. Finch, and the letter from my brother, and then he wanted me to say he could represent me as my attorney, and I said what you told me to, but when he spoke to Mr. Finch he tried to make it that he was representing me. I was hoping he would ask more things, the things you said he might ask, but he didn't. There's really nothing to tell you, but I'm calling because I said I would."

"He's gone?"

"Yes, he had his taxi wait for him."

"Well, your part is probably finished, and you can let your bodyguard go if you want to. I was just telling Mr.

Finch that I would like to drink champagne from your slipper."

"You what? What did you say?"

"You heard me. Too late. I'll let you know what happens, and you let me know if you hear from him again—immediately."

"I will."

I hung up and turned to Finch. "We've got about twenty minutes. What do you want refreshed?"

"Nothing. I've got it."

"I hope to God you have." I sat. "I could fill you in on Corrigan now, but I still think it's better not to. I'll say this, I am now offering three to one that he's a killer, and if so he's in a damn tight corner with his teeth showing. I don't see how he can possibly jump you under the circumstances, but if he does don't count on me. I won't leave that closet for anything short of murder. If he actually kills you, yell."

"Thanks." He grinned at me. But he slipped his hand inside his coat to his armpit, came out with a gun, and dropped it into his side pocket.

Finch had given Corrigan the room number, and he might phone up from the lobby and might not. Also there was no telling how fast his driver was, and it would be too bad if Corrigan arrived sooner than expected, came straight up to the room, paused at the door, and heard voices. So we stopped talking well ahead of time. I was leaning back, studying the ceiling, when the knock came, and it didn't sound like a chambermaid. I straightened up and left the chair in one motion, and Finch started for the door. Before he reached it I was in the closet, with the door pulled to enough to leave no crack, but unlatched.

The sound of the voice answered one question: it wasn't a ringer, it was the senior partner himself. I heard the door closing and the footsteps passing the closet door, and Finch inviting the visitor to take the armchair. Then Corrigan's voice.

"You understand why I'm here, Mr. Finch. My firm

received a letter from Mrs. Potter requesting professional advice."

Finch: "Yes, I understand that."

Corrigan: "According to her, you state that you have
in your possession a manuscript of a novel entitled 'Put
Not Your Trust,' by Baird Archer, and that the author of
it was her deceased brother, Leonard Dykes, who used
'Baird Archer' as a pen name."

I held my breath. Here, right off the bat, was one of
the tricky little points I had briefed him on.

Finch: "That's not quite right. I didn't say that I know
Dykes was the author. I said I have reason to think he
was."

I breathed, not noisily.

Corrigan: "May I ask what reason?"

Finch: "A pretty good one. But frankly, Mr. Corrigan,
I don't see why I should let you cross-examine me.
You're not representing Mrs. Potter. You heard what she
told me on the phone. Naturally I'll tell her anything she
wants to know, but why you?"

Corrigan: "Well." A pause. "Other interests than Mrs.
Potter's may be involved. I suppose you know that
Dykes was an employee of my law firm?"

Finch: "Yes, I know that."

That was a fumble. He did not know that. I bit my lip.

Corrigan: "Just as you have reason to think that Dykes
was the author, I have reason to think that other interests are involved. Perhaps we can take a short cut and
save time. Let me see the manuscript. Let me go over it
now, in your presence. That will settle it."

Finch: "I'm afraid I can't do that. I don't own it, you
know."

Corrigan: "But you have it. How did you get it?"

Finch: "Properly and legitimately, in the course of my
business as a literary agent."

Corrigan: "You're not listed in the New York phone
book. Two agents who were asked have never heard of
you."

Finch: "Then you shouldn't be wasting time on me.

Really, Mr. Corrigan, this isn't Russia and you're not the MVD. Are you?"

Corrigan: "No. What harm could it possibly do anyone for you to let me look over that manuscript?"

Finch: "It's not a question of harm. It's ordinary business ethics. An agent doesn't show his clients' manuscripts to just anybody who would like to see them. Of course I'd gladly show it to you, in fact I'd be obliged to, if you were representing Mrs. Potter, whom I believe to be the owner of it. But as it is, nothing doing. That's final."

Corrigan: "In effect I *am* representing Mrs. Potter. She wrote my firm for advice. She has complete confidence in me. She refuses to engage me as her attorney only because she fears that a New York law firm would charge her a big fee. We wouldn't. We would charge her nothing."

Finch: "You should tell her that."

Corrigan: "I tried to. People here on the Coast, especially women of her class, have an ingrained suspicion of New Yorkers, you know that. It's a stupid prejudice, and Mrs. Potter is a stupid woman."

I thought to myself, brother, you couldn't be wronger. He was going on. "You may wonder why I'm making so much of this little matter, flying out here, and I'll tell you. I said other interests may be involved, and I have good reason to think they are—important interests. I warn you now, for the record, that you may dangerously compromise both yourself and Mrs. Potter. On reliable information I believe that that manuscript is libelous. I believe that even in submitting it for sale you are risking severe penalties. I strongly advise you to get competent legal advice on it, and I assure you that I am qualified to give it. I offer it without charge, not through an impulse of benevolence, but to protect the interests I mentioned. Let me see that manuscript!"

Finch: "If I decide I need legal advice I know where to get it. I never saw you before. I've never heard of you. How do I know what or who you are?"

Corrigan: "You don't. Naturally." Sounds indicated that he was leaving his chair. "Here. This may satisfy you. Here are—What's the matter?"

More sounds. Finch: "I'm polite, that's all. When a visitor stands, I stand. Keep your credentials, Mr. Corrigan. I don't care how good they are. As far as I'm concerned you're a stranger trying to stick his nose into my business, and I'm not having any. Flying out here because you think a manuscript may be libelous—that sounds pretty damn fishy. You'll see no manuscript that's in my care. You'll have to—uuhie!"

That's the best I can do at spelling the sound he made. Other immediate sounds were not spellable at all, though fairly interpretable. One was surely a chair toppling. Another was feet moving heavily and swiftly. Others were grunts. Then came three in a row that were unmistakable: a fist or fists landing, and, right after, something that was heavier than a chair hitting the floor.

Finch: "Get up and try again."

A pause with sound effects.

Corrigan: "I lost my head."

Finch: "Not yet. You may next time. Going?"

That ended the dialogue. Corrigan had no exit line that he cared to use. The only sounds that came were footsteps and the opening and closing of the door, then more footsteps and another opening of the door, and, after a wait, its closing and the lock being turned. I stayed put until the closet door swung open without my touching it.

Finch stood grinning. "Well?" he demanded.

"You're on the honors list," I told him. "This is my lucky week, first Mrs. Potter and now you. Where did you plug him?"

"Two body jabs and one on the side of the neck."

"How did he invite it?"

"He swung first and then tried to lock me. That wasn't much, but the strain of that talk, with you listening—I'm hungry. I want some lunch."

"You won't get any, not now, unless it's a sandwich in a taxi. It's your move. He'll see that manuscript or bust, and one will get you ten he's on his way to Mrs. Potter, who he thinks is stupid. You will get there first, if you step on it, and stay there. The address is twenty-eight-nineteen Whitecrest Avenue, Glendale. I'll phone her. Get going!"

"But what—"

"Scoot, damn it! Write me a letter."

He moved. He got hat and raincoat from the closet and was gone. I uprighted the chair that had toppled, straightened a rug, went to the closet for my shoes, and put them on. Then I sat in the armchair by the phone and called the Glendale number.

"Mrs. Potter? Archie Goo—"

"Did he come?"

"He did. I hid in the closet while Finch talked with him. He would give his diploma from law school to see that manuscript. When he saw there was nothing doing he tried to lay Finch out and got knocked down. He left in a hurry, and I'm giving ten to one that he's on his way to you, so I sent Finch and I'm hoping he'll get there before Corrigan does. What—"

"Really, Mr. Goodwin, I'm not afraid!"

"Don't I know it. But Corrigan will bear down hard for you to name him your counsel, and it will take most of the pressure off if Finch is there. Anyway, I think you'll like Finch, he's not coarse and crude like me. You may have to give him some lunch. If you make Corrigan your attorney, no matter what he says, I'll come and throw rocks through your windows."

"That would be coarse and crude, wouldn't it? I honestly think you have no confidence in me at all."

"Little you know. If Corrigan gets there first, stall him until Finch comes, and don't forget Finch has been there before."

"I won't."

We hung up.

Going to a window and seeing with pleasure that it

was raining only about half as hard as it had been, I
opened it a good four inches to get some air. I raised the
question whether to phone Wolfe and decided to await
further developments. Having had no opportunity for a
look at the morning papers, I phoned down for some,
and, when they came, got comfortable. The papers were
no damn good, except the sports pages, but I gave them
enough of a play to make sure that nothing had happened which required my immediate attention and then
picked up Finch's book, *Twilight of the Absolute,* and
gave it a try. I got the impression that it probably made
sense, but I ran across nothing that convinced me that I
had been wrong in trying to get along without it.

The phone rang. It was Finch. He was calling from
Mrs. Potter's. He began reminding me that he had not
accepted my offer of ten to one. I agreed. "I know you
didn't. He came, did he?"

"Yes. I was in ahead by five minutes. He was surprised
to see me and not delighted. He insisted on talking with
Mrs. Potter alone, but I listened in from the kitchen with
her knowledge and consent. He poured it on about the
danger of libel and how it wouldn't cost her anything for
him to read the manuscript and give her his professional
advice, and the way he put it, it was hard for her to
handle. She couldn't brush him off as a stranger, as I
had. You should have heard her."

"I would have liked to. What was her line?"

"Simple. She said if there was libel in the manuscript
she didn't want to know it and didn't want me to,
because then it wouldn't be right to sell it to the movies,
but if we just go ahead and sell it, it will be up to the
movie people and surely they have good lawyers. He
couldn't get it into her head that even so she would be
responsible."

"I'll bet he couldn't. Kiss her for me."

"I wouldn't mind a bit. She is sitting here. Frankly, it
was a waste of taxi fare to send me out here."

"No. Of course Corrigan has left?"

"Yes. He kept his taxi."

"He may be back. He came to get his hands on that manuscript and he intends to. If he does go back there's no telling what he'll try. Stick around. Stay until you hear from me."

"I think Mrs. Potter feels that her husband doesn't like the idea of men in the house while he's away, especially one at a time."

"He wouldn't, the bubblehead. You stay and do the housework for her. While you're at it, straighten up that tree that's just been planted in the back. It's crooked. I'll see that you get away before Bubblehead gets home."

He said I'd better.

I stretched out my legs, clasped my hands behind my head, and frowned at my toes. It seemed that a call to Wolfe was in order. As far as I could see it was Corrigan's move, but Wolfe might have something to suggest besides sitting on my prat waiting for it. On the other hand, I still had room within the framework of my instructions, and if I could think up one that would be worthy of Mrs. Potter I ought to do it. So I sat and invented bright ideas, but none that really shone, and was working away at the fourth or fifth when I became aware of a noise at the door. A key had been inserted and was being turned. As I was shaping the thought that chambermaids should be trained always to knock before entering a room, the door swung open, and there, facing me, was James A. Corrigan.

He saw me, of course, but I wasn't quick-witted enough to realize instantly that with the light from the window at my back he hadn't recognized me, so when he said something like, "Oh, I beg your pardon, the wrong room," I thought he was showing enough presence of mind for both of us, with some left over. But then he did recognize me and he goggled. Also he gaped.

I arose and spoke. "No, this is it. Come on in."

He stood, frozen.

"Shut the door and come on in," I insisted. "You might as well. I was expecting you. Did you think Finch would

be fool enough to run off to Glendale and leave the
manuscript here in a drawer unguarded?" He moved,
and I added quickly, "If you dash off I won't chase you.
I'll call downstairs, and if necessary I'll call the cops, and
we'll not only find you but also find out how you got that
key. I don't think it's breaking and entering, but by God
it's something, and I'll hang it on you."

He hooked his elbow on the edge of the door and
swung it. It didn't quite close, and he backed against it
until it did. Then he walked on in and stopped at arm's
length.

"So you followed me here," he stated. He was a little
hoarse. With his jockey's physique and prizefighter's jaw
and hungry eyes, he was certainly not imposing. The top
of his head was a good inch below my eye level.

He repeated it, this time as a question. "You followed
me here?"

I shook my head. "I can't think of a single question
you could ask that I would feel like answering. Nor do I
want to ask any, except maybe one: why don't you call
Nero Wolfe and talk it over with him? Reverse the
charge. There's a phone."

He sat down, not to be sociable. It was probably his
knees.

"This is persecution," he said.

"Not in the statutes," I objected. "But what you just
did is, getting a key to another man's hotel room, whether by bribery or just asking for it. Have you anything to
say?"

"No."

"Absolutely nothing?"

"No."

"Are you going to call Mr. Wolfe?"

"No."

"Then I'll use the phone myself. Excuse me." I got the
phone book, looked up a number, lifted the receiver, and
asked for it. A female voice answered, and I gave my
name and asked to speak to Mr. Dolman. In a moment
he was on.

"Dolman? Archie Goodwin. I'm in Room Twelve-sixteen at the South Seas Hotel. A man named James A. Corrigan is here with me, but will soon be leaving, and I want him tailed right. Send me three good men at once, and have three more ready to take over as required. He'll prob—"

"What the hell, is he there hearing you?"

"Yes, so don't send Gibson. He'll probably be moving around, so they should have a car. Step on it, will you?"

I hung up, because I was through and also because Corrigan had already started to move around. He was heading for the door. I got to him, gripped a shoulder and hauled him back, and faced him.

He didn't lose his head. "This is assault," he stated.

"Persecution *and* assault," I agreed. "How can I prove you entered this room illegally if I let you leave it? Shall I get the house dick up here?"

He stood, breathing, his hungry eyes on me. I was between him and the door. He turned, went to a chair, and sat. I stayed on my feet.

"They can't get here in less than a quarter of an hour," I told him. "Why not say something?"

Not a word. His big jaw was clamped. I leaned against the closet door and contemplated him.

It was nearer half an hour than a quarter before there was a knock on the door. I went and opened it and invited them to enter, and they filed in past me, and I'll be damned if the third of the trio wasn't Gibson. He grinned at me as he went by. Leaving the door open, I detoured around them and took a look. One of them, a wiry little guy with a crooked nose, spoke.

"I'm Phil Buratti. I'm in charge."

"Good," I told him. "It's a straight tailing job." I jerked a thumb. "This is James A. Corrigan, a lawyer from New York. He'll be leaving any minute. Since he knows you, keep as close as you like. Report direct to me, here."

Buratti stared at me. "He's the subject?"

"Right. Don't lose him."

Gibson let out a guffaw that rattled the windows.

Corrigan got up and marched. His direct route to the door was between the trio and me, and he took it. He went on out. The trio didn't move.

"Are you," I demanded, "waiting for the hounds?"

"Loony," Buratti said. "Come on, boys."

He led the way, and they followed.

I shut the door and went to the armchair and sat. Before I phoned Wolfe I wanted to make up my mind how thick I had been to sit there and let Corrigan walk in on me. I looked at my watch and saw 12:20, which meant 3:20 in New York. I decided that I had probably not been brilliant but there was no point in advertising it, and put in a call. The circuits were busy. Of course it was the worst time of day for it, with Los Angeles and Hollywood wanting to get New York before lunch and New York wanting to get the coast on returning from lunch. I sat, walked back and forth, and sat some more. Every ten or fifteen minutes the operator called to say the circuits were still busy. One o'clock came, and a quarter after. Finally my call got through, and I had Wolfe's voice.

I reported with details. I told him about Corrigan's visit with Mrs. Potter, his call on Finch at the hotel ending in a little mild violence, his second trip to Glendale, finding Finch there ahead of him, and Finch's phone call to me. I continued, "When Finch phoned me that Corrigan had left, licked, naturally I figured him to come back to the hotel to get into Finch's room to look for the manuscript. Covering the door of the room from the outside wasn't feasible, since he knew me. I decided to sit tight and welcome him if he came. He did so, with a key. His seeing me here jolted him, as expected. I invited him to talk, but he wanted to be alone, and nothing was said that would help you any. I phoned Dolman, and he sent two men and an ape with a sense of humor, and when Corrigan left, an hour and ten minutes ago, the three were on his tail. That's the status quo."

"There's a man with Mrs. Potter?"

"Yes, I thought I said so. Finch."

"Then there are no new instructions. Stay there."

"I would like to stick another pin in him."

"You have none to stick. How is the albacore?"

"Marvelous."

"It should be. Call me as necessary."

"Yes, sir."

He hung up. That shows that everything is relative. If I had admitted that Corrigan's walking in on me had been a surprise he might have made remarks. Going to the window for a look at the rain, I was reflecting on that point when the phone rang.

It was Buratti. "We're at the airport," he reported. "He came straight here. You said we could keep close, so I was standing right by him when he asked for a seat on the first plane to New York. The best he could do was the TWA that leaves at five o'clock, and he bought a ticket. He's in a phone booth now, making a call. Do we go to New York with him?"

"No, I guess not. I'd like to take Gibson along, but he's probably needed here. Get me a seat on the same plane and wait there for me. I have some errands to do, so don't get impatient. There's a faint chance he's pulling something, so keep an eye on him."

I hung up and then called the Glendale number. Apparently I wouldn't get to see Mrs. Potter again, but at least I could chat with her on the phone.

17

SOMEWHERE over New Mexico, or maybe Oklahoma, I decided it hadn't been too brainy to take the same plane as Corrigan. A later one would have done just as well. As it was, with me in Seat Five and him back of me in Fourteen, I would get no sleep. In such a situation logic is not enough. It certainly wouldn't have been logical for him to wander by in that crowded plane and jab a knife in me, especially as I had no briefcase or other receptacle big enough to hold the manuscript of a novel, but I wasn't going to sleep, and I didn't like his being at my rear. I had a notion to ask him to trade seats but voted it down.

It was a long and weary night.

At La Guardia Airport, where we landed in the morning on schedule, he was in a bigger hurry than me. He grabbed his bag and trotted out to a taxi. Before getting my suitcase I went to a booth and phoned Fritz to expect me for breakfast in thirty minutes and mix plenty of batter. As my taxi crossed Queensboro Bridge I saw the sun for the first time in four days.

Wolfe never came downstairs in the morning until after he finished in the plant rooms at eleven o'clock, but Fritz welcomed me home as if I had been gone a year. He met me at the front door, took my suitcase, hung up my hat and coat, escorted me to the kitchen, and put the griddle on. I was perched on a stool drinking orange juice when I heard the elevator, and a moment later Wolfe entered. He was actually breaking a rule. I thought it deserved some recognition and accepted his offer of a handshake. We made appropriate remarks. He sat. The kitchen is the only place on earth where he doesn't mind a chair that lets his fanny lap over the sides. I went to my seat at my breakfast table as Fritz flapped the first cake onto my hot plate.

"He looks skinny," Fritz told Wolfe. Fritz is convinced that without him we would both starve to death in a week.

Wolfe nodded in agreement and told me, "Two flowers are open on a Cypripedium Minos."

"Wonderful," I said with my mouth full. When the bite was down, "I assume you want a report. There's—"

"Eat your breakfast."

"I am. Unlike you, I don't mind business with meals. There's nothing but fill-in to add to what you already know, except that I came on the same plane as Corrigan, as arranged. At the airport he took his bag and scooted. I presume that with what you've collected here we're about ready to jump?"

He snorted. "Where? On whom?"

"I don't know."

"Neither do I. When Mr. Wellman first came to see me, eighteen days ago, I assumed that Dykes had written that novel, that he and two women were killed on account of their knowledge of it, and that someone in that law office was involved. We have validated that assumption, and that's all. We know nothing new."

I swallowed food. "Then my trip to rainy California was a washout."

"By no means. All we could do was force him or them to become visible by movement. All we can do now is continue the process. We'll contrive it."

"Right after breakfast? I've had no sleep."

"We'll see. Movement once started is hard to stop." He glanced at the wall clock. "I'm late. We'll see. It is satisfactory to have you back." He got up and went.

I finished breakfast and looked through the morning paper and went to·the office. I wouldn't have been surprised to see a stack of unopened mail, but apparently he had worked his head off during my absence. Bills and other items, out of their envelopes, were neatly arranged on my desk, and the exposed sheet of my desk calendar said March ninth, today. I was touched. I looked over things a little and then took my suitcase and mounted to my room. It was glad to see me back. When I'm up there I always turn the phone extension on, but that time I forgot to. I had unpacked and stripped and showered, and was using my electric shaver, when Fritz appeared at the bathroom door, panting.

"The phone," he said. "Mr. Corrigan wants to speak to Mr. Wolfe."

"Okay. I forgot to turn it on. I'll get it."

I went and flipped the switch and lifted the receiver. "This is Archie Goodwin."

I expected Mrs. Adams, but it was Corrigan himself. He said curtly that he wished to speak to Wolfe, and I told him Wolfe wouldn't be available until eleven. He said they wanted an appointment with him, and I asked who wanted it.

"I and my associates."

"Would eleven o'clock suit you? Or it could be eleven-thirty."

"We would prefer eleven o'clock. We'll be there."

Before I went to finish shaving I buzzed Wolfe on the house phone and told him, "Right you were. Movement once started is hard to stop. The law firm will be here at eleven."

"Ah," he said. "Contrivance may not be needed."

It was only ten-thirty, and I took my time completing my personal chores. I can dress fast, but I don't like to have to. When I went downstairs I was ready for anything, including a two-hour nap, but that would have to wait.

They were ten minutes late, so Wolfe was in the office when they arrived. Before any conversation got started I noticed an interesting little item. Off the end of Wolfe's desk, facing it, the big red leather chair is the most convenient spot for a visitor, and when there are two or more visitors that is obviously the seat for whoever has priority. When that group had been there before, Corrigan, the senior partner, had occupied it, but this time who should pop into it but the white-haired blinking Briggs, Helen Troy's Uncle Fred. Apparently no one remarked it but me, and that was equally interesting. As they sat, Emmett Phelps, the long-armed six-foot encyclopedia, was nearest me; Corrigan was next; then the sleepy-eyed slumpy Louis Kustin, successor to Conroy O'Malley as the firm's trial man; and then the disbarred O'Malley with a bitter twist to his mouth.

Wolfe's eyes went from left to right and back again. "Well, gentlemen?"

Three of them spoke at once.

"I can't converse with bedlam," Wolfe said testily.

Frederick Briggs, in the red leather chair, blinking, took the ball. "At our previous visit," he said slowly and distinctly, "I came with my associates under protest. On that occasion you were invited to question us. This time we have questions to ask you. You may remember that I characterized your methods as unethical and reprehensible, and you justified that criticism when you fabricated a notation on Dykes's letter of resignation, imitating the handwriting of one of us, and gave it to the police. What defense do you offer for that action?"

Wolfe's brows were up. "None, Mr. Briggs."

Briggs blinked furiously. "That is not acceptable. I insist—we insist—on an answer."

"Then I'll give you one." Wolfe was not aroused. "As you say, the notation was in Mr. Corrigan's hand. There are three possible explanations of how it was made. One, by Mr. Corrigan himself some time ago. Two, by me recently. Three, by any one of you, including Mr. Corrigan, either before or after I asked to see the letter. The letter was easily accessible, there in your office files. You, sir, can't possibly know which explanation is correct, unless you made the notation yourself. Questioned by the police, all of you have denied making it. I deny making it." Wolfe flipped a hand. "Surely you don't credit me with a monopoly in mendacity?"

"That's evasive. I insist—"

"Forget it, Fred," Kustin cut in irritably. His sleepy eyes were awake. "I told you, you won't get anywhere with that, and there's no jury to work on even if you knew how to do it. Get to the point."

"He won't." Phelps, the indifferent scholar, was irritated too. "Let Con do it."

O'Malley shook his head. His mouth kept its twist even when he spoke. "Thanks, Emmett, but I'm disbarred. You forget?"

"Go on, Fred," Corrigan told his junior—not in years.

"In my opinion," Briggs maintained, "we should demand an answer on that, but I defer under protest." He blinked at Wolfe. "To proceed. All five of us, including

Mr. O'Malley, have a mutual and common interest, to protect the reputation and welfare of our firm. In that interest we are indissolubly joined. Your position, openly stated, has been that a major factor in the death of Leonard Dykes was the manuscript of a novel, presumably written by him under an assumed name; that the manuscript was also a major factor in the deaths of two women; and that one or more members of this firm have guilty knowledge of the manuscript and therefore, inferentially, of the deaths. Is that correct?"

Wolfe nodded. "It's badly put, but I'll pass it."

"Tell your man to take his notebook, and I'll restate it."

"Damn it, Fred," Kustin objected, "he accepted it. What more do you want? Get on."

Briggs blinked at him. "I want to proceed as agreed, without unnecessary interruptions." He went to Wolfe. "Very well, you accept it. Then the contents of that manuscript are a vital element in your investigation. Is that true?"

"Yes."

"And therefore the contents of the manuscript are of vital importance to us, the members of the firm, and Mr. O'Malley. Is that true?"

"Yes."

"And therefore, if we were presented with an opportunity to learn the contents of the manuscript it would be natural and proper for us to make every effort to take advantage of it. Is that true?"

Wolfe rubbed his nose. "I don't want to quibble, but though it would indeed be natural, its propriety might be questioned. If to protect legitimate interests, yes. If to shield a criminal, no."

"There is no question of shielding a criminal."

Wolfe shrugged. "If that is stipulated, what you said is true."

"Very well. It was in furtherance of that effort that Mr. Corrigan went to California. It is in furtherance of that effort that we are here now. We don't know how you managed to anticipate Mr. Corrigan's effort, but you did. Your man not only got there but got inside of him. Since he succeeded in preventing Mr. Corrigan from seeing the manuscript, it may fairly be assumed that he himself did see it, and that therefore you and he are now acquainted with its contents. It was you who involved our firm in this affair. It was you who persuaded the police that we were involved. It was you who forged a notation on a letter we sent you—"

"Withdraw that," Wolfe snapped.

"That won't help, Fred," O'Malley advised him. "Don't drag it in."

Briggs blinked at him and then at Wolfe. "On consideration I withdraw that remark pro tempore, without prejudice. But that doesn't affect my conclusion, that our demand is justified, to be told the substance of that manuscript. You involved us. We demand that you warrant that involvement."

Briggs blinked around. "Well?" he challenged. "Is that clear and cogent?"

They agreed that it was.

Wolfe grunted. "Clear enough," he assented, "but it took you long enough to say it. You gentlemen are making an extraordinary pother, coming here in a body like this. Why the devil didn't one of you merely phone me and ask me to tell you what's in that manuscript? It would have taken you five seconds to ask it and me two seconds to answer it."

"What would you have answered?" Kustin demanded.

"That I'm not quite ready."

"Not quite ready for what?"

"To act."

To appreciate the full effect of those two little words you would have had to hear Wolfe pronounce them. He didn't snarl them or snap them, his voice kept its normal pitch, but if anyone present had anything to fear the full menace of it was in those two calm, precise syllables. They looked at one another.

Briggs asked indignantly, "Do you mean you refuse to tell us anything about it?"

Wolfe nodded. "At the moment, yes. I'm not quite ready. As practicing attorneys, you gentlemen know that the potency of knowledge depends on how and when it is used. I went to some trouble to get this and I intend to get full value from it."

Emmett Phelps stood up. "I told you fellows, didn't I? We're wasting time on him."

"Mr. Phelps is bored," Wolfe said dryly.

"Buy it from him," O'Malley suggested. "Make him an offer. It can be deducted as a legitimate expense, can't it, Emmett?" He left his chair. "Only don't expect me to contribute. I'm broke."

Wolfe spoke up. "I would like to anticipate any future charge of willful malevolence. I take no pleasure in prolonging suspense, either my own or another's. I'm being completely candid when I say that I still need a fact or two before I can act. To move not fully prepared, to disclose myself prematurely, would be folly, and I'm not a fool."

Kustin got to his feet, stepped to the desk, put his hands on it, and leaned forward at Wolfe. "I'll tell you what I think: I think it's a ten-cent bluff. I don't think you know any more about that manuscript than we do. I think you're exactly where you were when we came here a week ago yesterday." He straightened up. "Come on, fellows. He's a goddam fourflusher." He whirled to me. "You too, Goodwin. I wish I'd gone to California instead of Jim Corrigan. You'd have been called."

He marched out. Phelps and O'Malley were at his heels. Corrigan, who had said practically nothing, thought he would speak now, took a step toward the desk, but changed his mind and, with a glance at me, headed for the door. Briggs lifted himself out of the red leather chair, blinked at Wolfe, said, "My appraisal of your methods and tactics has certainly been reinforced here today," and turned and went.

I moseyed to the door to the hall, stood on the sill,

and watched them wriggling into their coats. I was perfectly willing to go and let them out, but Phelps got the door open before I moved, and held it for them, so I was saved the trouble. He banged it hard enough to leave no doubt of its closing, and I wheeled, returned to my desk, and permitted myself an all-out yawn. Wolfe was leaning back with his eyes shut.

"Will there be more movement?" I inquired. "Or is it time for a contrivance?"

No reply. I yawned again. "Once in a while," I observed, "you go right to the heart of things and tell a plain unvarnished truth. Like when you said that you still need a fact or two before you can act. It might be objected that you need more than one or two, but that isn't so. The one fact that Phelps, the scholar, is a lover of literature and bumped them off because it was a lousy novel and he couldn't bear it, would do the trick."

No word or sign. Suddenly I blew up. I sprang to my feet and roared, "Goddam it, go to work! Think of something! Do something!"

Without opening his eyes, he muttered, "And I said it was satisfactory to have you back."

18

THAT was an afternoon I wouldn't care to live through again, not even if I knew what the evening was going to bring. To begin with, Wolfe was totally unbearable. After lunch he got behind his desk with a book, and after a dozen assorted attempts to get a conversation started I quit. Then Saul Panzer phoned in, and he growled at me to get off the line. I had already suspected that he had Saul on a trail, since a check of the cash box and book had informed me that he had given Saul three hundred bucks, and that confirmed it. I always resent it when he sees fit to give one of the boys a chore that he thinks I don't need to know about, and that time it was more offensive than usual, since I couldn't very well blab anything, sitting there on my tail, yawning.

Worse than him, though, was me. He had told me twice to take a nap, so naturally I wasn't going to. I wanted to be there if the phone rang. I wanted to be there if Mrs. Adams came to confess to the three murders. But I did not want to make out checks or work on the germination records or go through catalogues. My problem was to stay awake without having anything to keep my eyes open, and it was even tougher after Wolfe went up to the plant rooms at four o'clock. For two solid hours only one notion occurred to me that had any attraction at all, to phone Mrs. Potter in Glendale and tell her I had got home safely, and I vetoed that because it might prove to be habit-forming. But by gum I stayed awake, if you can call it that.

There was another call from Saul just before dinner, and again I was told to get off the line. Wolfe's end of the chat was nothing but grunts. After dinner he told me to go to bed, and God knows I would have liked to, but I got stubborn and went for a walk instead. I dropped in at a movie, found myself getting fascinated with the idea of resting my head on the soft fat female shoulder next to me, jerked away, and got up and went home. It was a little after ten.

Wolfe was at his desk, going through the stack of germination slips that had accumulated while I was away. I asked him, "Any more movement?"

"No."

I gave up. "I might as well go up and lie down a while." I went and twirled the knob of the safe. "I put the bolt on in front and I'll check the back. Good night."

"Good night."

The phone rang. I stepped to my desk and got it.

"Nero Wolfe's residence, Archie Goodwin speaking."

"I want to speak to Wolfe."

"Who is it, please?"

"James A. Corrigan."

I covered the transmitter and told Wolfe, "Corrigan. He sounds hoarse and harassed. Do you care to speak to him?"

Wolfe took his instrument, and I put mine back at my ear.

"This is Nero Wolfe. Mr. Corrigan?"

"Yes. I've mailed you a letter, but you're responsible for this, so I think you ought to hear it. I hope you'll hear it in your dreams the rest of your life. This is it. Are you listening?"

"Yes, but—"

"Here it goes."

It busted my eardrum, or felt like it. It was a combination of a roar and a smack. By reflex my wrist moved the receiver away, then I moved it back. There was a confused clatter and a sort of thump, then nothing. I told the transmitter, "Hello hello!"

Nothing. I cradled it and turned. Wolfe was sitting with the instrument dangling from his hand, scowling at me.

"Well?" he demanded.

"Well yourself. How do I know? I suppose he shot himself."

"Where was he?"

I sneered. "Do you think I staged it?"

"There was a radio going."

"I heard it. 'The Life of Riley.' WNBC."

He replaced the phone, slow motion, and regarded me. "This is preposterous. I don't believe it. Get Mr. Cramer."

I swiveled and dialed and got a voice. I asked for Cramer, and he wasn't there. Neither was Stebbins. I got a sergeant named Auerbach, informed Wolfe, and he took it.

"Mr. Auerbach? This is Nero Wolfe. Are you familiar with the Dykes-Wellman-Abrams case?"

"Yes."

"And with the name James A. Corrigan?"

"Yes, I know the name."

"I just had a phone call. The voice said it was James A. Corrigan, but it was husky and agitated and I can't vouch for it. It said—I think you should put this down. Have you pencil and paper?"

"In a second—okay, shoot."

"He said it was Corrigan, and then, quote, 'You're responsible for this, so I think you ought to hear it. I hope you'll hear it in your dreams the rest of your life. This is it. Are you listening? Here it goes.' Unquote. There came immediately the sound of an explosion, resembling a gunshot, and other confused noises, followed by silence except for the sound of a radio, which had been audible throughout. That's all."

"Did he say where he was phoning from?"

"I've told you all I know. As I said, that's all."

"Where are you now?"

"At my home."

"You'll be there if we want you?"

"Yes."

"Okay." He hung up. So did Wolfe. So did I.

"So your memory's failing," I observed. "You forgot that he said he had mailed you a letter."

"I like to see my mail first, without interference. Where does Mr. Corrigan live?"

I got the Manhattan phone book, turned the pages, and found it. Then, to check, I went and unlocked the filing cabinet, got out the Wellman folder, and fingered through the papers. I announced, "Corrigan lives at one-forty-five East Thirty-sixth Street. Phelps lives at three-seventeen Central Park West. Kustin lives at nine-sixty-six Park Avenue. Briggs lives at Larchmont. O'Malley lives at two-oh-two East Eighty-eighth."

I put the folder back and locked the cabinet. "Am I going to bed now?"

"No."

"I thought not. What, sit here and wait? Even if they

find a corpse they might not get around to us until morning. It would take a taxi five minutes to go crosstown to Thirty-sixth and Lexington. The fare would be fifty cents including tip. If it's a blank I can walk home. Do I go?"

"Yes."

I went to the hall for my hat and coat, let myself out, and walked a block north. At Tenth Avenue I flagged a passing taxi, got in, and gave the driver the address.

A radio car was double-parked in front of 145 East Thirty-sixth, with no one in it. I entered the building. On the list of names on the wall of the vestibule, Corrigan was at the top, fifth. I went on in. It was an old private dwelling done over into apartments, with a self-service elevator. The elevator was there at that floor. From somewhere below came a faint sound of voices, but there was no one in sight. I opened the elevator door, entered, pushed the 5 button, and was lifted. When it stopped I emerged. There was only one door, at the right of the small hall, and standing at it was a cop.

"Who are you?" he asked, not sociably.

"Archie Goodwin. I work for Nero Wolfe."

"What do you want?"

"I want to go to bed. Before I can do so I have to find out if we got imposed on. We reported this. The guy that lives here, so he said, phoned us and told us to listen, and then a gun went off or a good imitation of one. He didn't hang up but he was gone, and we phoned Homicide. We don't know if the phone call was from here, and I came to see."

"Why Homicide?"

"This might be connected with a case they're on. We have friends there—sometimes friends, sometimes enemies, you know how it is. Is your colleague inside?"

"No. The door's locked. He went down for the superintendent. What did the guy say on the phone?"

"He just said we ought to hear something and told us to listen, and bang. May I put my ear to the door?"

"What for?"

"To listen to the radio."

"Yeah, I've heard of you. Full of gags. Should I laugh?"

"No gags tonight, I'm too sleepy. We heard the radio on the phone, and I thought I'd check. If you don't mind?"

"Don't touch the door or the knob."

"I won't."

He stepped aside, and I got my ear close to the angle of the door and the jamb. Ten seconds was enough. As I listened there was another sound in the hall, the elevator starting down.

I moved away. "Right. Bill Stern. WNBC."

"It was Bill Stern on the phone?"

"No, but it was WNBC. 'The Life of Riley.' Bill Stern goes on at ten-thirty."

"The Yankees look good, don't they?"

I'm a Giant fan, but I wanted to get inside and had to be tactful. So I said, "They sure do. I hope Mantle comes through."

He did too, but he was skeptical. He thought these wonder boys seldom live up to their billing. He thought various other things, and was telling about them when the elevator returned and its door opened, and we had company. One was his colleague and the other was a little runt with very few teeth and a limp, wearing an old overcoat for a dressing gown. The cop, surprised at sight of me, asked his brother, "Who's this, not precinct?"

"No. Nero Wolfe's Archie Goodwin."

"Oh, him. How come?"

"Save it. Hey, get away from that door! Gimme that key!"

The runt surrendered it and backed off. The cop in command inserted the key and turned it, used his handkerchief to turn the knob, which made me suppress a snicker, pushed the door, and entered, with his colleague at his heels. I was right behind. We were in a narrow hall with a door at either end and one in the middle. The one at the right was open, and the cop headed for that and on through. Two steps inside he stopped, so I just made the sill.

It was a fairly big living room, furnished comfortably by a man for a man. That was merely the verdict of one sweeping glance, for any real survey of the furniture, if required, would have to wait. On a table at the far side, between two windows, was the phone, with the receiver off, lying on the floor. Also on the floor, six inches from the receiver, was the head of James A. Corrigan, with the rest of him stretched out toward a window. A third item on the floor, a couple of feet from Corrigan's hip, was a gun—from where I stood I would have said a Marley .32. The lights were on. Also on was a radio at the end of the table, with Bill Stern telling what he thought of the basketball stink. There was a big dark spot, nearly black at that distance, on Corrigan's right temple.

The cop crossed to him and squatted. In ten seconds, which wasn't long enough, he got upright and spoke. "DOA." There seemed to be a little shake in his voice, and he raised it. "We can't use this phone. Go down and call in. Don't break your neck."

The colleague went. The cop kept his voice up. "Can you see him from there, Goodwin? Come closer, but keep your hands off."

I approached. "That's him. The guy that phoned. James A. Corrigan."

"Then you heard him shoot himself."

"I guess I did." I put one hand on my belly and the other on my throat. "I didn't get any sleep last night and I'm feeling sick. I'm going to the bathroom."

"Don't touch anything."

"I won't."

I wouldn't have been able to get away with it if the radio hadn't been going. It was plenty loud enough to cover my toe steps through the outer door, which was standing open, and in the hall to the door to the stairs. Descending the four flights, I listened a moment behind the door to the ground-floor hall, heard nothing, opened it, and passed through. The runt was standing by the elevator door, looking scared. He said nothing, and neither did I, as I crossed to the entrance. Outside I turned right, walked the half short block to Lexington Avenue and stopped a taxi, and in seven minutes was climbing out in front of Wolfe's house.

When I entered the office I had to grin. Wolfe's current book was lying on his desk, and he was fussing with the germination slips. It was comical. He had been reading the book, and, when the sound came of me opening the front door, he had hastily ditched the book and got busy with the germination slips, just to show me how difficult things were for him because I hadn't made the entries from the slips on the permanent record cards. It was so childish I couldn't help grinning.

"May I interrupt?" I asked politely.

He looked up. "Since you're back so soon I assume you found nothing of interest."

"Sometimes you assume wrong. I'm back so soon because a flock of scientists would be coming and I might have been kept all night. I saw Corrigan. Dead. Bullet through his temple."

He let the slips in his hand drop to the desk. "Please report."

I did so, in full, including even the cop's thoughts about the Yankees. Wolfe was scowling some when I started and a lot more by the time I finished. He asked a few questions, sat a while tapping with a forefinger on the arm of his chair, and suddenly blurted at me, "Was the man a nincompoop?"

"Who, the cop?"

"No. Mr. Corrigan."

I lifted my shoulders and dropped them. "In California he wasn't exactly brilliant, but I wouldn't say a nincompoop. Why?"

"It's absurd. Totally. If you had stayed there you might have got something that would give some light."

"If I had stayed there I would have been corralled in

a corner for an hour or so until someone decided to start in on me."

He nodded grudgingly. "I suppose so." He looked up at the clock and put his thumbs at the edge of his desk to shove his chair back. "Confound it. An exasperating piece of nonsense to go to bed on."

"Yeah. Especially knowing that around midnight or later we'll get either a ring or a personal appearance."

But we didn't. I slept like a log for nine hours.

19

SATURDAY morning I never did finish the newspaper accounts of the violent death of James A. Corrigan, the prominent attorney. Phone calls interrupted my breakfast four times. One was from Lon Cohen of the *Gazette*, wanting an interview with Wolfe about the call he had got from Corrigan, and two were from other journalists, wanting the same. I stalled them. The fourth was from Mrs. Abrams. She had read the morning paper and wanted to know if the Mr. Corrigan who had shot himself was the man who had killed her Rachel, though she didn't put it as direct as that. I stalled her too.

My prolonged breakfast was ruining Fritz's schedule, so when the morning mail came I took my second cup of coffee to the office. I flipped through the envelopes, tossed all but one on my desk, glanced at the clock and saw 8:55. Wolfe invariably started for the plant rooms at nine sharp. I went and ran up the flight of stairs to his room and knocked, entered without waiting for an invitation, and announced, "Here it is. The firm's envelope. Postmarked Grand Central Station yesterday, twelve midnight. It's fat."

"Open it." He was standing, dressed, ready to leave.

I did so and removed the contents. "Typewritten, single-spaced, dated yesterday, headed at the top 'To Nero Wolfe.' Nine pages. Unsigned."

"Read it."

"Aloud?"

"No. It's nine o'clock. You can ring me or come up if necessary."

"Nuts. This is just swagger."

"It is not. A schedule broken at will becomes a mere procession of vagaries." He strode from the room.

My eye went to the opening sentence.

I have decided to write this but not sign it. I think I want to write it mainly for its cathartic value, but my motives are confused. The events of the past year have made me unsure about everything. It may be that deep in me much is left of the deep regard for truth and justice that I acquired in my youth, through both religious and secular teaching, and that accounts for my feeling that I must write this. Whatever the motive—

The phone rang downstairs. Wolfe's extension wasn't on, so I had to go down to get it. It was Sergeant Purley Stebbins. Purley would always just as soon talk to me as Wolfe, and maybe rather. He's not dumb by any means, and he has never forgotten the prize boner that Wolfe bluffed him into on the Longren case.

He was brusque but not thorny. He said they wanted to know firsthand about two things, Corrigan's phone call the night before, and my performance in California, especially my contacts with Corrigan. When I told him I would be glad to oblige and come down, he said that wouldn't be necessary because Inspector Cramer wanted to see Wolfe and would drop in at eleven or shortly after. I said that as far as I knew we would let him in, and Purley hung up without saying good-by.

I sat at my desk and read:

Whatever the motive may be, I am going to write it and then decide whether to mail it or destroy it.

Even if I mail it I will not sign it because I do not want to give it legal validity. You will of course show it to the police, but without my signature it will certainly not be released for publication as coming from me. Since the context will clearly identify me by inference, this may seem pointless, but it will serve all desired purposes, whatever my motive may be, without my signature, and those purposes are moral and not legal.

I will try not to dwell at length on my motives. To me they are of more concern than the events themselves, but to you and others it is the events that matter. All you will care about is the factual statement that I wrote the anonymous letter to the court giving information about O'Malley's bribery of a juror, but I want to add that my motive was mixed. I will not deny that moving up to the position of senior partner, with increased power and authority and income, was a factor, but so was my concern for the future of the firm. To have as our senior partner a man who was capable of jury-bribing was not only undesirable but extremely dangerous. You will ask why I didn't merely confront O'Malley with it and demand that he get out. On account of the source and nature of my information, which I won't go into, I did not have conclusive proof, and the relations among the members of the firm would have made the outcome doubtful. Anyway, I did write the informing letter to the court.

Starting a habit, I said to myself, of not signing things. I resumed.

O'Malley was disbarred. That was of course a blow to the firm, but not a fatal one. I became senior partner, and Kustin and Briggs were admitted to membership. As the months passed we recovered lost ground. In the late summer and fall of last year our income was higher than it had ever been, partly on account of Kustin's remarkable performance as a trial lawyer, but I think my leadership was equally responsible. Then, on Monday, December 4, a date I would never forget if I were going to be alive to remember and forget, I returned to the office in the evening to do some work and had occasion to go to Dykes's desk to get a document. It wasn't where I expected to find it and I went through the drawers. In one of them was a brown fiber portfolio and I looked inside. The document wasn't there. It contained a stack of neatly assembled sheets of paper. The top sheet, typed like a title page, said "Put Not Your Trust, A Modern Novel of a Lawyer's Frailty, by Baird Archer." Through curiosity I looked at the next sheet. It began the text, and the first sentence read "It is not true that all lawyers are cutthroats." I read on a little and then sat in Dykes's chair and read more.

It is still almost incredible to me that Dykes could have been such a fool. Through his connection with our office he knew something of the libel law, and yet he wrote that and offered it for publication. Of course it is true that lawyers themselves will do incredible things when their vanity is involved, as O'Malley did when he bribed a juror, and Dykes probably thought that the use of an assumed name would somehow protect him.

The novel was substantially an account of the activities and relationships of our firm. The names were different and most of the scenes and circumstances were invented, but it was unmistakably our firm. It was so badly written that I suppose it would have bored a casual reader, but it did not bore me. It told of O'Malley's bribery of a juror (I use our names instead of those Dykes used) and of my learning of it and sending an anonymous letter to the court, and of O'Malley's disbarment. He had invented an ending. In the novel O'Malley took to drink and died in the alcoholic ward at Bellevue, and I went to see him on his deathbed, and he pointed at me and screamed, "Put not your trust!" In one way the novel was ludicrous. Its ending assumed that O'Malley knew I had informed on him, but there was no adequate explanation of how he had found out.

I took the manuscript home with me. If I had found it by accident and read it, someone else might, and I couldn't risk it. After I got home I realized that I would be unable to sleep, and I went out again and took a taxi to Sullivan Street, where Dykes lived. I got him out of bed and told him I had found the manuscript and read it. In my agitation I did something incredible too. I took it for granted that he knew I had informed on O'Malley and asked how he had found out. I should have assumed that he had invented that.

But it didn't matter. He really had found out. I had not written the informing letter to the court on my typewriter here at my apartment, on which I am writing this. I had taken the precaution of writing it on a machine at the Travelers Club. There wasn't more than one chance in a billion of any risk in that, but that one had been enough. In connection with our defense of O'Malley on the bribery charge, we had photostats of all the exhibits, including the anonymous letter to the court. Dykes had made himself a fairly good expert on documents, and as a matter of routine he inspected the photostat of the anonymous letter. He noticed that the "t" was out of line, crowding the letter to its right, and slanted a little, and he remembered that he had observed the same defect in some other document. And he found it. He found it in a typed memorandum to him which I had typed two months previously on that same machine at the Travelers Club. I had forgotten about it, and even if I had remembered it I would probably have considered the risk negligible. But with that hint to start him, Dykes had compared the photostat with the memorandum under a glass and established that the two had been typed on the same machine. Of course that was not conclusive proof that I had typed and sent the letter to the court, but it convinced Dykes.

It bowled him over that I had found and read the manuscript. He swore that he had had no intention or desire to expose me, and when I insisted that he must have told someone, possibly O'Malley himself, he swore that he hadn't, and I believed him. He had the carbon of the manuscript there in his room. The original had been returned to him by a firm of publishers, Scholl & Hanna, to whom he had submitted it, and he had put it temporarily in his desk at the office, with the intention of putting it in the hands of a literary agent. The longhand manuscript, written by him in longhand, from which the typist had worked, was also there in his room. He turned both the carbon copy and the longhand script over to me, and I took them home when I went and destroyed them. I also destroyed the original of the typed script two days later, after I had reread it.

I felt that I was fairly safe from exposure. I had of
course done nothing actionable, but if it became known
that I had informed on my partner in an anonymous
letter the effect on my career and reputation would have
been disastrous. It was not so much anything O'Malley
himself could or might do as the attitude of others, particularly two of my present partners and certain other
associates. Actually I would have been a ruined man.
But I felt fairly safe. If Dykes was telling the truth, and
I believed he was, all copies of the manuscript had
been destroyed. He gave me the most solemn assurances
that he would never speak of the matter to anyone, but
my chief reliance was in the fact that it was to his own
self-interest to keep silent. His own future depended on
the future welfare of the firm, and if he spoke the firm
would certainly be disrupted.

I saw Dykes several times at his room in the evening,
and on one of those occasions I did a foolish and
thoughtless thing, though at the time it seemed of no
consequence. No, that's wrong—this occasion was not at
his room but at the office after hours. I had taken from
the file the letter of resignation which he had written
months previously, and it was on my desk. I asked him,
for no special reason that I remember, if the title "Put
Not Your Trust" was from Shakespeare, and he said no,
that it was in the 3rd verse of the 146th Psalm, and I
scribbled it in a corner of his letter of resignation, "Ps
146-3."

The phone was ringing, but I finished the paragraph
before I answered it. It was Louis Kustin. He didn't
sound as if his eyes were looking sleepy. He wanted to
speak to Wolfe, and I told him he wouldn't be available
until eleven o'clock.

"I suppose he's available to you?" he asked curtly.

"Sure, I live here."

"My associates and I are conferring, and I am speaking on their behalf as well as my own. I'm at my office.
Tell Wolfe I want to speak to him as soon as possible.
Tell him that the suicide of our senior partner is an
irreparable blow to us, and if it can be established that

Wolfe willfully and maliciously drove him to it he will be held accountable. Tell him that?"

"It'll ruin the day for him."

"I hope to ruin all his days."

The connection went. I wanted to resume my reading but thought I'd better pass it on and buzzed the plant rooms on the house phone. Wolfe answered. I reported the conversation.

"Pfui," he said shortly and hung up. I went back to Corrigan.

I felt that I was fairly safe, though I was not completely easy. Toward the end of December I was shocked into a realization of my true position. Dykes came into my office, during office hours, and asked for a raise in pay of 50 per cent. He said that he had expected to make a considerable sum from the sale of his novel, and now that he had surrendered that source of income he would have to have a substantial raise. I saw at once what I should have seen clearly before, that I would be at his mercy for years if not for life, and that his demands would be limited only by his desires. I was literally in a panic but concealed it successfully. I told him that I had to consider the problem of justifying so large a raise to my associates, and asked him to come to my apartment the following evening, Saturday, December 30, to discuss the matter.

By the time he arrived for the appointment I had decided that I would have to kill him. It proved to be an absurdly easy thing to do, as he did not suspect my intentions and was not on guard. As he sat I went to his rear on some trivial excuse, picked up a heavy paperweight, and hit him on the head. He crumpled without a sound, and I hit him again. During the four hours that I waited for the deserted streets of late night, or early morning, I had to hit him three more times. During those hours I also went for my car and parked it directly in front. When the time came I got him downstairs and into the car without being observed, I drove uptown to an unused East River pier in the Nineties and rolled the body into the water. I must have been less calm and cool than I thought I was, for I thought he was dead. Two

days later, in the newspaper account of the recovery of
the body, I learned that he had died of drowning, so
when I rolled him in he was only stunned.

It was then two in the morning, and I was not through.
I drove downtown to Sullivan Street and let myself into
Dykes's apartment with the key I had taken from his
pocket. With my bare hands an hour there would have
been enough, but with gloves on it took three hours to
make a thorough search. I found only three items, but
they were well worth it. Two of them were receipts
signed by Rachel Abrams for payments for typing made
by Baird Archer, and the third was a letter addressed to
Baird Archer at General Delivery, Clinton Station, on
the letterhead of Scholl & Hanna, signed by Joan Wellman. I said I made a thorough search, but there were
many books on the shelves, and there wasn't time to turn
through every page of them even if I had thought it
necessary. If I had done so I would have found the
sheet of paper on which Dykes made that list of names
with Baird Archer among them, and you would never
have seen it, and I wouldn't be writing you this now.

For a while, a week or so, I had no intention of doing
anything about Joan Wellman or Rachel Abrams, but
then I began to worry. One of them had typed the script
and the other had read it. The trial of O'Malley and the
juror and the disbarment proceedings had of course been
fully reported in the papers, only a year ago. What if one
of those women or both of them had noticed the simi-
larity, or rather the sameness, between the actual happening and Dykes's novel? What if they had mentioned
it or an occasion arose for them to mention it in the
future? They were less dangerous than Dykes, but they
were dangerous, or might be.

That was more and more on my mind, and finally I
did something about it. The last day of January, a Wednesday, I phoned Joan Wellman at her office. I told her
I was Baird Archer, and offered to pay her for advice
about my novel, and made an appointment with her for
the next day but one, Friday, at five-thirty. We met in
the Ruby Room at the Churchill and had drinks and
talked. She was attractive and intelligent, and I was
thinking that it would be impossible to do her any serious
harm, when she asked me point blank about the remark-

able resemblance between the plot of my novel and an occurrence in real life here in New York a year ago. She said she wasn't sure she remembered the name of the disbarred lawyer, she thought it was O'Mara, but probably I remembered it.

I said I didn't. I said I hadn't consciously used any happening in real life when I was plotting the novel, but of course it might have been in my subconscious. She said that as far as she remembered it hadn't come out that O'Mara had been betrayed by one of his partners, and it would be interesting to look into it and see if my subconscious had not only copied what had been published but had also, by insight or intuition, divined what had not been published. That was enough for me, more than enough.

I guided the talk, while we were having dinner, to a point where it was appropriate for me to suggest that we drive to my apartment in the Bronx so I could get the manuscript. She gave me a bad moment when she asked, if I lived in the Bronx, why had I given my address as General Delivery, Clinton Station, but I gave her an answer that satisfied her. She said she would go with me to get the manuscript but let me know that she wouldn't go up to my apartment. I was sorry I had met her in so public a place as the Ruby Room, but neither of us had seen anyone we knew and I resolved to go ahead.

I went alone to get my car and picked her up in front of the Churchill and drove to Washington Heights. There, in a side street, it was as simple as it had been with Dykes. I remarked that the windshield was misted on the inside and reached behind me as if for my handkerchief, got a heavy wrench I had placed there when I went for my car, and hit her with it. She didn't even groan. I tried to prop her up but couldn't, and lifted her over into the back onto the floor. On the way to Van Cortlandt Park I stopped several times to take a look at her. Once she seemed to be stirring, and I had to hit her again.

I drove to a secluded road in the park. There was no one in sight, but it was only ten o'clock and there was a chance that a car might come along at the worst moment, even in February, so I left the park, drove around for two hours, and then returned to the park and the secluded road. The risk was then at a minimum, and anyhow I had to take it. I took her out of the car, put her on the road near the edge, and ran the car over her. Then I drove away fast. When I was miles away I stopped under a light and inspected the car for signs of blood or other evidence, but I had been careful to go slowly when passing over her and I could find nothing.

I put the thing down on my desk, looked at my watch, and saw 9:35. In Peoria, Illinois, it was 8:35, and John R. Wellman, according to the schedule he had given me, would be at his place of business. I reached for the phone and put in a call and soon had him.

"Mr. Wellman? Archie Goodwin. I promised to let you know immediately if anything broke. Corrigan, senior partner in that law firm, was found dead on the floor of his apartment last night with a hole in his head and a gun lying nearby. I would—"

"Did he shoot himself?"

"I don't know. As a purely personal opinion, it looks like it. I would call that a break, but whether good or bad is for Mr. Wolfe to decide, not me. I'm just keeping my promise and telling you. As it stands this minute, that's all I can say. Mr. Wolfe is busy upstairs."

"Thank you, Mr. Goodwin. Thank you very much. I'll go to Chicago and take a plane. I'll call you when I reach New York."

I told him that would be fine, hung up, and returned to my reading.

There was only one other living person who knew the contents of that manuscript, Rachel Abrams, who had typed it. There was only one logical and sensible thing to do.

Until three months ago I had never been conscious of anything in my mind or heart to justify any concept of myself as a potential murderer. I believed that I understood myself at least as well as most people. I was aware that there was an element of casuistry in my self-justification for what I had done to O'Malley, but without that intellectual resource no man could preserve his self-esteem. At any rate, I was an altogether different being from the moment I rolled Dykes's body from the pier into the water. I didn't know it at the time, but I do now. The change was not so much in my conscious mind as in the depths. If the processes of the subconscious can be put into rational terms at all, I think mine were something like this: (a) I have murdered a man in cold blood; (b) I am a decent and humane person, as men go, certainly not vicious or depraved; therefore (c) the conventional attitude toward the act of murder is invalid and immoral.

My inner being could not permit me to feel any moral repulsion at the thought of killing Joan Wellman, certainly not enough to restrain me, for if killing her was morally unacceptable how could I justify the killing of Dykes? By killing Joan Wellman the process was completed. After that, given adequate motive, I could have killed any number of people without any sign of compunction.

So in contemplating the murder of Rachel Abrams my only concerns were whether it was necessary and whether it could be performed without undue risk. I decided it was necessary. As for the risk, I left that to circumstances. With her I could not use the same kind of subterfuge I had used with Joan Wellman, since she had known Dykes as Baird Archer. My plan was so simple that it was really no plan at all. I merely went to her office one rainy afternoon, unannounced. If she had had an associate there with her, or if any one of a dozen other possible obstacles had arisen, I would have gone away and devised a procedure. But she had only one room and was there alone. I told her I wanted a typing job done, approached her to show her what it was, grasped her throat, had her unconscious in half a minute, opened the window, and lifted her and pushed her out. Unfortunately I had no time to search for records; of course I had no time at all. I left, ran down the stairs to the next floor, and took the elevator there, having got off there on my way up. When I left the building her body was on the sidewalk and a crowd was already collecting. Three days later, when my associates and I came to see you, I learned that I had been ahead of your man Goodwin by not more than two minutes. I took that as conclusive evidence that luck was on my side, even though he found entries in her records that connected her with Baird Archer. If he had got to her alive he would have learned the contents of the manuscript.

By that time, the day we called on you, nine days ago, I knew I was in danger but was confident that I could ward it off. You knew of Baird Archer and the manuscript and had connected them with Dykes and therefore with our office, but that was all. Your noticing that scribbled "Ps 146-3" on Dykes's letter of resignation in my handwriting, and correctly interpreting it, increased the danger only slightly if at all, since my plain square hand can be easily imitated by almost anyone and my associates unanimously supported me in convincing the police that you must have made the notation yourself in an effort to trick us.

Wednesday, when the letter from Mrs. Potter arrived, I did not suspect that you had anything to do with it. I thought it was a deadly blow that fate had dealt me at the worst possible moment. It was brought to me, but since it had been addressed not to an individual but to the firm our mail clerk had read it, and therefore I had to show it to my associates. We discussed it and agreed with no dissent that it was essential for us to learn what was in the manuscript, and that one of us must go immediately to California. There was a division of opinion as to who should go, and of course I had to insist that it must be me. Since I was the senior partner my view prevailed and I left by the first available plane.

You know what happened in California. I was in great peril, but I was not desperate until I went to Finch's room in his absence and found Goodwin there. From that moment my position was manifestly hopeless, but I refused to give up. Since, through Goodwin, you had certainly learned the content of the manuscript, my betrayal of O'Malley was sure to be disclosed, but it might yet be possible to avoid a charge of murder. All night, on the plane, with Goodwin seated there only a few feet from me, I considered possible courses and plans.

I had phoned one of my partners from Los Angeles, and they were all at the office when I arrived this morning, going directly from the airport. Their unanimous opinion was that we should call on you and demand to be told the substance of the manuscript. I argued strongly for an alternative course but could not sway them. When we went to your office I was prepared to face the disclosure of my betrayal of O'Malley, supposing that you would tell about the manuscript, but instead of that you dealt me another blow. You told us nothing, saying that you were not quite ready to act and that you still needed a fact or two. For me that could have only one meaning. You did not intend to expose my betrayal of O'Malley until you were fully prepared to use it as evidence on a charge of murder, and you would not have said that to us unless you expected soon to be prepared. I didn't know which fact or two you still needed, but it didn't matter. Obviously you had me or you would soon get me.

My associates wanted a luncheon conference, but I pleaded fatigue from my night on the plane and came here to my apartment. Again my subconscious had taken command, for it came to me in a rush of sudden surprise that I had irrevocably determined to kill myself. I did not dispute the decision. I calmly accepted it. The further decision, whether to leave behind me an account of my disaster and what led to it, has not yet been made. I have spent hours writing this. I shall now read it over and decide. If I send it at all it will go to you, since it is you who have destroyed me. Again here at the end, as at the beginning, what interests me most is my motive. What is it in me that wants to send this to you, or to anyone? But if I start on that I will never end. If I do send it I will not attempt to tell you what to do with it, since in any case you will do as you see fit. That is what I am doing; I am doing as I see fit.

That was all. I jiggled the sheets together, refolded them, slipped them into the envelope, and went and mounted the three flights to the plant rooms. Wolfe, wearing one of his new yellow smocks, was in the potting room inspecting the roots of some Dendrobiums he had knocked out of the pots. I handed him the envelope and told him, "You'll have to read this."

"When I come down."

"Cramer is coming at eleven. If you read it with him

sitting there he'll get impatient. If you talk with him
without reading it I would prefer not to be present."

"What does it say?"

"A full confession. Betrayal of his partner, O'Malley,
three murders—the works."

"Very well. I'll wash my hands."

He went to the sink and turned the faucet on.

20

"THIS," Wolfe told Inspector Cramer, "is correct not only
in substance but also in text."

He held in his hand a typed copy, brought by Cramer,
of what Corrigan had said to us on the phone just before
the bang, as reported by Wolfe to Sergeant Auerbach.

Cramer looked at me. "You were on the line too,
Goodwin? You heard it?"

I nodded, arose, got the paper from Wolfe, read it,
and handed it back. "Right. That's what he said."

"I want a statement to that effect signed by both of
you."

"Certainly," Wolfe acceded.

Cramer was in the red leather chair, leaning back
comfortably, like a man intending to stay a while.
"Also," he said, not belligerently, "I want a statement
from Goodwin giving all details of his trip to California.
But first I would like to hear him tell it."

"No," Wolfe said firmly.

"Why not?"

"On principle. Through habit you put it as a demand,
and it's a bad habit. I don't like it."

"What he did in California led to a violent death in
my jurisdiction."

"Establish that."

"Nuts," Cramer growled. "I ask it as a favor. Not to me, to the People of the State of New York."

"Very well. Having had an authentic discovery of mine, the notation in Corrigan's handwriting on Dykes's letter, denounced by them and you as a trick, I thought it only fair to even up by contriving a trick. I needed—"

"So you still claim that notation was made by Corrigan?"

"No. I never made that claim. I only denied that it was made by Mr. Goodwin or me. I needed to demonstrate that someone in that office was involved in Baird Archer's manuscript and therefore in the murders, and I proceeded to do so. Tell him about it, Archie."

"Yes, sir. Leaving out what?"

"Nothing."

If I had been alone with Cramer and he had told me to leave out nothing I would have had some fun, but under the circumstances I refrained. I gave it to him straight, accurate and complete, from my checking in at the Riviera to my last view of Corrigan's rear at La Guardia Airport as he trotted out to a taxi. When I finished he had a few questions, and I answered them straight too.

He was chewing an unlit cigar. He took it from his mouth and turned to Wolfe. "What it amounts to, you tricked—"

"If you please," Wolfe interposed. "Since you have part you should have all. Yesterday morning, less than three hours after Corrigan's return, they came here—all five of them. They demanded that I tell them what was in the manuscript, and I refused. I would have had to refuse in any case, since I didn't know, but I told them that I wasn't quite ready to act, and I needed one or two more facts. I permitted them to assume that my preparations were all but complete."

Cramer nodded. "You tricked him into killing himself."

"Did I? Did he kill himself?"

"Goddam it, didn't he?"

"I don't know. You have investigated, I haven't. What have you concluded?"

Cramer scratched his ear. "There's nothing against suicide. It was his gun, fired at contact. Smudges on it, no clear prints. His prints on the phone. He had been dead less than an hour when the examiner arrived. No evidence so far of anyone else being there. He had been struck a hard blow on the side of the head but could have got it from the corner of the table when he fell, and probably did. There was—"

Wolfe waved it away. "From you, 'nothing against suicide' is enough. On that sort of thing you are not to be impugned. But it is still open?"

"It's not closed. That's why I'm here. I just said you tricked him into killing himself, and you may or may not hear more about that, but right now I want a lot more than you've given me. If it was suicide, why? Because he thought you knew what was in that damn manuscript? Because he thought you had him? For what? Murder? I want a lot more, a hell of a lot, and I'm here to get it."

Wolfe pursed his lips. "Well." He opened a desk drawer. "This came in my morning mail." He took a fat envelope from the drawer. "See if that answers your questions." He held it out.

Cramer got up to take the envelope and sat down again. He inspected the outside of the envelope before he removed the contents. He unfolded the sheets, read a little, looked at Wolfe, made a growling noise, and read some more. As he finished the first page and transferred it to the back, he inquired, "You say this came this morning?"

"Yes, sir."

He had no more to say or to ask until he got to the end. Wolfe leaned back, shut his eyes, and relaxed. I kept my eyes open. I kept them on Cramer's face, but all I saw was a man so intent and absorbed that he had no expression at all. When he finished he went back to a place on the third or fourth page and read it over. Then he looked at Wolfe, with his lips tightened to a thin line.

"You got this three hours ago," he muttered.

Wolfe opened his eyes. "I beg your pardon?"

"You got this three hours ago. You know how to phone my office. You know how to phone my office. Sergeant Stebbins talked to Goodwin at nine o'clock. Goodwin didn't mention it."

"I hadn't read it yet," I stated. "It had just come."

"You know my number."

"Bosh," Wolfe said testily. "This is ridiculous. Have I concealed it or destroyed it?"

"No, you haven't." Cramer wiggled the sheets. "What evidence is there that Corrigan wrote this?"

"None."

"What evidence is there that you didn't dictate it to Goodwin and he wrote it?"

"None." Wolfe straightened up. "Mr. Cramer. You might as well leave. If you are in a frame of mind to think me capable of so extravagant an imbecility, all communication is blocked." He wiggled a finger. "You have that thing. Take it and go."

Cramer ignored it. "You maintain that Corrigan wrote this."

"I do not. I maintain only that I received it in today's mail, and that I have no knowledge of who wrote it beyond the thing itself. I suppose other evidence is procurable. If there is a typewriter in Corrigan's apartment, and if investigation shows it was written on that machine, that would be pertinent."

"You have no knowledge of it whatever beyond what you've told me?"

"I have not."

"Do you know of any evidence other than this that Corrigan committed the murders?"

"No."

"Or that he betrayed his partner O'Malley?"

"No."

"Do you believe this to be an authentic confession by Corrigan?"

"I'm not prepared to say. I've read it only once, rather

hurriedly. I was going to ask you to let Mr. Goodwin make a copy for me, but I'll get along without it."

"You won't have to. I'll see that you get a copy, with the understanding that there is to be no publication of it without my consent." Cramer folded the sheets and put them in the envelope. "It's covered with your and Goodwin's prints now, and mine. But we'll try it."

"If it's a fake," Wolfe said dryly, "I should think that a man capable of contriving it would know about fingerprints."

"Yeah, everybody knows about fingerprints."

Cramer rubbed his kneecaps with his palms, regarding Wolfe with his head cocked. The chewed cigar, which had previously taken no part in the conversation, slipped from his fingers and fell to the floor, but he made no move to retrieve it.

He spoke. "I admit this is damn neat. It will stand a lot of checking, but I admit it's neat. What are you going to do now, send your client a bill?"

"No."

"Why not?"

"My client, Mr. Wellman, has his share of gumption. Before I bill him both he and I must be satisfied that I have earned my fee." Wolfe's eyes moved. "Archie. Trained as you are, can I rely on you for an accurate copy of that communication from—ostensibly—Mr. Corrigan?"

"It's pretty long," I objected, "and I read it once."

"I said I'll send you a copy," Cramer stated.

"I know you did. I would like to have it as soon as possible. It would be gratifying to have it validated, both by your investigation and my scrutiny, since that would mean that I have exposed a murderer and forced him to a reckoning without a scrap of evidence against him. We still have none, not a title, except that unsigned communication."

"I know we haven't."

"Then by all means check it, every detail, every word. Do you want a comment?"

"Yes."

"A focus of interest is the anonymous letter informing on O'Malley. Suppose it was sent not by Corrigan, but by one of the others. In that case that confession may be factually correct in every important detail but one, the identity of the culprit; and the real culprit, finding me too close for comfort, may have decided to shift the burden onto Corrigan, not concerned that the shift required one more murder. So of first importance is the question, was it Corrigan who betrayed O'Malley? You will of course need the informing letter to the court or a photostat of it, and something authentically typed on the machine at the Travelers Club. You will need to know whether any of the others frequented that club or otherwise had access to that machine. With your authority, that kind of inquiry is vastly easier for you than for me."

Cramer nodded. "What else?"

"At present, nothing."

"What are you going to do?"

"Sit here."

"Some day you'll get chair sores." Cramer got up. He saw the cigar on the floor, stooped to pick it up, crossed to my wastebasket, and dropped it in. His manners were improving. He started for the door, halted, and turned. "Don't forget those statements, what Corrigan said—by the way, what about that? Was it him on the phone or wasn't it?"

"I don't know. As I said, the voice was husky and agitated. It could have been, but if not no great talent for mimicry would have been needed."

"That's a help. Don't forget the statements, what Corrigan or somebody said on the phone, what Goodwin did in California, and now getting this thing in the mail. Today."

Wolfe told him certainly, and he turned and went.

I looked at my watch. I addressed my employer. "Kustin phoned nearly three hours ago, as I reported. He wanted you to phone him quick so he can warn you that they're going to hold you accountable. Shall I get him?"

"No."

"Shall I call Sue or Eleanor or Blanche and make a date for tonight?"

"No."

"Shall I think of things to suggest?"

"No."

"Then it's all over? Then Corrigan wrote that thing and shot himself?"

"No. Confound it. He didn't. Take your notebook. We might as well get those statements done."

21

FORTY-EIGHT hours later, Monday morning at eleven, Inspector Cramer was back again.

At our end much had been accomplished. I had got a haircut and a shampoo. I had spent some pleasant hours with Lily Rowan. I had spent half an hour with Wellman, our client, who had called at the office after taking a plane from Chicago and was staying over to await developments. I had had two good nights' sleep and had taken a walk to the Battery and back, with a stopover at Homicide on Twentieth Street to deliver the statements Cramer had requested. I had made five copies of Corrigan's confession, from the copy Cramer had sent us as agreed. I had answered three phone calls from Saul Panzer, switched him to Wolfe, and got off the line by command. I had answered thirty or forty other phone calls, none of which would interest you. I had done some office chores, and had eaten six meals.

Wolfe had by no means been idle. He had eaten six meals too.

One thing neither of us had done, we had read no newspaper account of Corrigan's unsigned confession.

There hadn't been any, though of course the death of a prominent attorney by a gunshot had been adequately covered, including pointed reference to previous regrettable occurrences connected with his firm. Evidently Cramer was saving the confession for his scrapbook, though it wasn't autographed.

Monday morning he sat in the red leather chair and announced, "The DA's office is ready to call it suicide."

Wolfe, at his desk, was pouring beer. He put the bottle down, waited for the foam to subside to the right level so that the tilt would get him beer and would also moisten his lips with foam, lifted the glass, and drank. He liked to let the foam dry on his lips, but not when there was company, so he used his handkerchief before he spoke.

"And you?"

"I don't see why not." Cramer, having accepted the invitation to help with the beer, which he rarely did, had his glass in his hand. "I could tell you how it stands."

"Please do."

"It's like this. The confession was typed on the machine in his apartment. He's had it there for years. He has always done quite a little typing—kept a supply of the firm's paper and envelopes there. His secretary, Mrs. Adams, admits that there is nothing about the typing or the text to cause a reasonable doubt that he typed it."

"Admits?"

"Yes. She defends him. She won't believe he betrayed O'Malley or committed murder." Cramer emptied his glass and put it down. "I can give you more on the confession, plenty more, but the DA isn't prepared to impeach it, and neither am I. We can't challenge any of its facts. As for the dates of the murders, December thirtieth, February second, and February twenty-sixth, of course Corrigan had already been checked on that along with all the others. The file had him alibied for the twenty-sixth, the afternoon Rachel Abrams was killed, but digging into it we find that it's loose. We'd want to dig more on it if he was alive to take to a jury and we had to face a defense, but he's dead and there'll be no jury. We can't check on December fourth, the day he says he was at his office in the evening and found Dykes's manuscript and read it. There are no other dates to check."

Wolfe grunted. "How are the others on the dates? Did you go over that?"

"Some. They're all about the same as Corrigan; there's nothing too tight to rip open. As I think I told you once, none of them is completely eliminated by an alibi—except O'Malley the day Rachel Abrams was killed. He was in Atlanta, but now that we know what was in the manuscript he's out anyway. All it spilled about him was that he had been disbarred for bribing a juror, and God knows that was no secret. Unless you think the confession lies about the manuscript?"

"No. On that point I credit it unreservedly."

"Then it doesn't matter where O'Malley was." Cramer reached to empty his bottle into his glass and settled back. "Now about the typewriter at the Travelers Club. It's still there, in an alcove off of the writing room, but it was overhauled about two months ago. That doesn't stop us, because in the firm's files we found two items Corrigan had typed on it, memoranda to Mrs. Adams. We got the original of the anonymous letter to the court informing on O'Malley and it was typed on that machine, absolutely no question about it. Corrigan used it occasionally. He ate dinner there two or three times a week and played bridge there Thursday evenings. None of the others is a member. Two of them, Kustin and Briggs, have been brought there once or twice by Corrigan for dinner, but that's all. So it looks—"

"This," Wolfe cut in, "is important. Extremely. How closely was it examined? A dinner guest might conceivably have used a typewriter, especially if he needed one that couldn't be traced to him."

"Yeah, I know. Saturday you called it a focus of interest. I had Stebbins handle it himself, with instructions to

make it good, and he did. Besides, look at it. Say you're
Kustin or Briggs, going there as a guest to eat with
Corrigan. Say you use that typewriter for that particular
purpose. You can't do it, you can't even get in that room,
without either Corrigan or an attendant knowing about
it, probably both of them, and that would be pretty
damn dumb. Wouldn't it?"

"Yes."

"So it looks as if Corrigan did inform on his partner.
That alone makes the confession a lot easier to buy,
signed or unsigned, and the DA's office feels the same
way about it. Isn't that practically what you said Saturday? Is there anything wrong with that argument?"

"No." Wolfe made a noise that could have been a
chuckle. "I will accept an apology."

"The hell you will. For what?"

"You accused me, or Mr. Goodwin, of making that
cryptic notation on Dykes's letter of resignation. Well?"

Cramer picked up his glass and drank, in no hurry. He
set the glass down. "Uh-huh," he conceded. "I still say it
looked like a typical Wolfe stunt, and I'm not apologiz-
ing. That's the one detail in that confession that it's hard
to dope. The confession says he made the notation in
December, so of course it wasn't there when they all saw
the letter last summer, that's all right, but it must have
been there a week ago Saturday when the letter was
sent to you. Yet three of them say it wasn't. Phelps asked
his secretary, a girl named Dondero, to see if it was in
the files, and she dug it out and took it to him. O'Malley
had come to the office that morning, for a conference at
Corrigan's request, and was with Phelps in his room
when the girl brought the letter in, and they both looked
at it. They won't swear the notation wasn't on it, but
they both think they would have noticed it if it had
been, and they didn't notice it. Not only that, the girl
says she would testify under oath that there was no such
notation on the letter. She says she would positively
have noticed it if it had been. Phelps dictated his letter
to you, and she typed it, and Phelps signed it, and she

put it and Dykes's letter of resignation, and the other material written by Dykes, into an envelope addressed to you, and sent for a messenger and took the envelope to the anteroom and left it with the switchboard girl to be given to the messenger when he came. So how do I dope it?"

Wolfe upturned a palm. "Phelps and O'Malley leave it open. The girl is lying."

"What the hell for?"

"Force of habit. The etiquette of the sex."

"Nuts. We couldn't brush it off with a gag if we had to take it to a jury. As it is, I suppose we can let it slide. We have to if we're going to buy the confession."

Wolfe turned his head. "Archie. We gave Mr. Cramer the letter from Dykes bearing the notation?"

"Yes, sir."

"The envelope too? The envelope it came to us in?"

"No, sir."

"We have the envelope?"

"Yes, sir. As you know, we keep everything until a case is closed—except what we hand to the cops."

Wolfe nodded. "It may possibly be needed to save us from a charge of accessories." He returned to Cramer. "What about the District Attorney's office? Are they willing to let it slide?"

"They think it's minor. If the rest of the confession stands up, yes."

"Has the confession been shown to Corrigan's associates?"

"Certainly."

"Do they credit it?"

"Yes and no. It's hard to tell because they're half batty. A year ago their senior partner disbarred, and now their new senior partner confessing to three murders and killing himself—they're in a hell of a fix. Briggs thinks they ought to denounce the confession as a fake and hold you liable, but he's just babbling. He doesn't say you or Goodwin shot Corrigan, but he might as well. Phelps and Kustin say that even if the confession is true it's invalid because it isn't signed, and any publication of it would be libelous. They think we ought to bury it. But they also think we should accept it as true. Why not? Corrigan's dead, and that would make the three murders finished business and they could start gathering up the pieces. Their feeling about you is approximately the same as Briggs', but they're realistic about it. None of them will look O'Malley in the eye, though he gives them plenty of chances to. He sticks it in them and twists it. He sent some flowers to the wife of the juror he bribed, with a letter of apology for thinking she informed on him, and before he sent the letter he read it aloud to them with Lieutenant Rowcliff present and asked their opinion of it."

There was only an inch of beer left in Cramer's glass. He got it and drained it and then settled back, not through yet. He rubbed the side of his nose with a fingertip. "I guess that covers it. It looks like a wrap-up. The DA will be ready to give the press a statement as soon as they decide whether to release the confession. Thank God they decide that and not me. But on the main question, do we cross off the murders or don't we, I'll have to go along and maybe I'm ready to, only there's you to think of. That's why I'm here. Once or twice I have kicked a hat that you had hid a brick in, and I don't want a sore toe. You connected Joan Wellman with Dykes by spotting that name, Baird Archer. You tied in Rachel Abrams by having Goodwin there two minutes late. You pulled the stunt that got Corrigan a bullet in his head. So I repeat a question I asked you day before yesterday: are you ready to send your client a bill?"

"No," Wolfe said flatly.

"I thought not," Cramer growled. "What are you waiting for?"

"I'm through waiting." Wolfe struck the arm of his chair with his palm, a gesture so violent that with him it was the next thing to hysterics. "I have to be. This can't go on forever. I'll have to do it with what I've got or not at all."

"What have you got?"

"Nothing that you haven't. Absolutely nothing. It may not be enough, but I see no chance of getting more. If I—"

The phone rang, and I swiveled and got it. It was Saul Panzer. He wanted Wolfe. Wolfe took it and gave me the sign to get off, and I did so. The part of the conversation that Cramer and I listened to was not exciting. Mostly it was grunts, at intervals. Apparently Saul had plenty to say. At the end Wolfe told him, "Satisfactory. Report here at six o'clock," and hung up.

He turned to Cramer. "I'll have to amend that statement. I now have something that you do not have, but it was easily available to you if you had gone after it. I'm better off than I was, but not much. I never will be, and I'm going to act. You're welcome to participate if you care to."

"In what?"

"A risky but resolute effort to expose a murderer. That's the best I can offer."

"You can offer some information. What did you just get, and who is it?"

Wolfe shook his head. "You would insist on further inquiry and let the moment slip, and further inquiry would be fruitless. He has been too smart for you and almost too smart for me. I'm going to close with him and I may get him. You may participate or not, as you please."

"Participate how?"

"By getting them here, all of them. This evening at nine o'clock. Including the ten women that Mr. Goodwin entertained at dinner two weeks ago. I need them all, or I may. And of course come yourself."

"If I get them here I take a hand."

Wolfe sighed. "Mr. Cramer. Three weeks ago we agreed to cooperate. I have done so faithfully. I have given you everything I got, without reciprocation.

Where do we stand? You, utterly routed, are ready to join with the District Attorney in unconditional surrender. You have been bamboozled. I have not. I know him, his motive, and his strategy. I intend to rush him. You say you should take a hand?"

Cramer was not overwhelmed. "I say if I get them here I am officially responsible and I'm in charge."

"Very well, then you decline. Mr. Goodwin will get them here. If you come you will not get in. I hope to be ready to communicate with you before midnight."

Cramer sat and scowled. His lips tightened. He opened his mouth, said nothing, and pressed his lips tight again. I was pretty well acquainted with him, and I knew by his eyes that he was going to take it. But he couldn't just knuckle under, he had to keep his independence and show his spirit and prove that he was by no means cowed. So he said, "I'll bring Sergeant Stebbins along."

22

WE NEEDED seventeen chairs if they all came, and a phone call from Stebbins around four o'clock informed me that they would. With four from the front room, one from the hall, two from my room, and two from Fritz's room, Fritz and I got them collected and arranged in the office. We had an argument. Fritz insisted there should be a table of liquid refreshments, that Wolfe regarded that as a minimum of hospitality for invited guests, and I fought it. Not so much on account of the basic situation, since more than one murderer had been served a highball or other mixture in that room. The trouble was the females, particularly Helen Troy and Blanche Duke. I did not want the former, at some ticklish spot where everything might hang on a word and a tone, to jump up and call out, "Oyez, oyeth!" And if the latter, whose inhibitions were totally unreliable, got a shaker full of her formula mixed and worked on it, she might do or say anything. So I was firm.

Fritz couldn't appeal to Wolfe because he wasn't accessible. He was there at his desk, but not for us. Five minutes after Cramer left he had leaned back, closed his eyes, and started pushing his lips in and out, which meant he was working, and hard. He kept at it until lunch, took only half of his customary hour for the meal, returned to the office, and started in again. He left for the plant rooms at four o'clock as usual, but when I went up there on an errand he was standing in a corner of the intermediate room frowning at a Cochlioda hybrid that had nothing whatever wrong with it, and he wasn't even aware that I was passing through. A little later he phoned down to tell me to send Saul up to him when he came. So I wasn't present at their conference. Nor did I get any kind of an instruction for the evening. If he was planning a charade, apparently it was going to be a solo.

Wolfe did speak to me once, shortly after lunch; he asked me to bring him the letter from Phelps enclosing the material from Dykes, and the envelope it had come in. I did so, and, after he had inspected them with a magnifying glass, he kept them. And I took one step on my own. Wellman was still in town, and I phoned and invited him to attend because I thought he had certainly paid for a ticket. I didn't phone Mrs. Abrams because I knew she wouldn't care for it no matter what happened.

At dinnertime I took another step. As Wolfe sat behind his desk staring at nothing, pulling at his lip with a thumb and forefinger, I saw that he was in no shape to entertain a guest and went and told Fritz that Saul and I would eat in the kitchen with him. Then I returned to the office and announced it to Wolfe. He put his eyes on me without seeing me, let out a low growl, and muttered, "All right, but it won't help any."

"Can I do anything?" I asked.

"Yes. Shut up."

I had spoken not more than twenty words to him since Cramer had left, seven hours ago.

At ten after nine they had all arrived, but Wolfe was still in the dining room, with the door closed. Leaving the front door and the hall to Saul, I had stayed in the office to supervise the seating. I kept the red leather chair for Cramer and put the lawyers in the front row, including O'Malley. Wellman was off in the corner near the globe. Sergeant Purley Stebbins was against the wall, back of Cramer. For Saul Panzer I had put a chair at the end of my desk. My intention had been to group the ten females at the rear of their employers, and I had so placed the chairs, but they had ideas of their own, at least some of them. For about half a minute I stood talking to Cramer with my back to them, and, when I turned, four of them had moved to the couch. From my chair at my desk I couldn't take in the couch without swiveling or twisting my neck ninety degrees, but I decided to skip it. If Wolfe wanted his audience more compact he could say so.

At twelve after nine I sent Saul to tell Wolfe they were all present, and a moment later Wolfe entered. He went straight to his desk, with no halt for a greeting, not even for Cramer, and sat. The murmurs and mutterings stopped. Wolfe got himself settled, taking his time, moved his head slowly over the arc from left to right, and back again. Then his eyes darted left, and he spoke.

"Do you want to say anything, Mr. Cramer?"

Cramer clear his throat. "No. They understand that there's nothing official about this and I'm here as an observer."

"You told us to come," Louis Kustin said aggressively.

"I invited you. You all know the way out."

"May I make a statement?" O'Malley asked.

"What about?"

"I want to congratulate Mr. Wolfe, and thank him. He has found the answer to a question I've been trying to find for a year and couldn't. We're all in his debt and we ought to say so."

"We are not!" It was Briggs, blinking furiously. "I would like to make a statement! In my opinion, what Wolfe has done is actionable. I say this after full consideration. I came here because I am convinced—"

"Shut up!" Wolfe roared.

They gazed at him, astonished.

He gazed back, moving his head to include the lot. "I do not intend," he said coldly, "to let you degrade this to gibberish. We are concerned with death and a dealer of death. I do this work to earn a living, but I am conscious of its dignities and obligations. I hope and believe that in the next two or three hours, here together, we are going to learn the truth about the deaths of four people, and, in doing so, get a start on preparations for the death of one of you. That's what we're here for. I can't do it alone, but I'll have to guide it."

He closed his eyes, tight, and opened them again. "All of you knew Mr. Corrigan, who died Friday evening. You know of a document, ostensibly written by him, in which he confessed that he had betrayed his former partner and had murdered three people." He opened a drawer and took out papers. "This is a copy of that confession. It was shrewdly conceived and brilliantly executed, but it wasn't good enough for me. It has one fatal defect. The writer couldn't possibly avoid including it, because in that detail the facts were known to others, and the incident was an essential part of the story. When Corrigan—"

"Are you impeaching it?" Kustin demanded. "Are you saying that Corrigan didn't write it?"

"I am."

There were noises, including audible words. Wolfe ignored them, waited, and continued.

"When Corrigan was in California his every move was known and reported, so this confession had to accept that record. But that is the fatal defect. According to this confession, Corrigan knew what was in the manuscript written by Leonard Dykes—he had read it through twice. But in Los Angeles all his efforts were focused on one objective: to get a look at the manuscript. That is emphasized by the fact that he left Mrs. Potter's house, with Finch there, to hurry to Finch's hotel room to search for the manuscript. If he already knew what was in it that was senseless. What good would it do him to find it? If you say that he wanted to destroy it, that too would have been senseless, since Finch had read it. According to this confession, he had already killed two women for the sole reason that they had read the manuscript. If he found and destroyed Finch's copy, Finch would be on guard and after him."

Wolfe shook his head. "No. Corrigan's objective, plainly and unmistakably, was to see the manuscript. He wanted to know what it contained. Mr. Goodwin was there and saw him and heard him. Do you agree, Archie?"

I nodded. "I do."

"Then he had never seen the manuscript, certainly he hadn't read it, and this confession is spurious. There is a corroborative point." Wolfe tapped the paper. "It says here that Dykes told him that all copies of the manuscript had been destroyed, there were no others, and that he believed it. Indeed he must have believed it fully, for otherwise he would hardly have undertaken the murders of the two women; but certainly, when the letter came from Mrs. Potter, saying that a literary agent had a copy of the manuscript, he would have suspected a snare and would have proceeded quite differently."

Wolfe turned a palm up. "Well?"

"I would have understood this this morning," Cramer rasped.

"Are you challenging the whole confession?" Phelps inquired.

"Are you saying," O'Malley demanded, "that Corrigan didn't squeal on me?"

"No. To both of you. But a purported confession shown to be clearly false in so important a detail loses all claim to validity, both as to content and as to authorship. It can be credited only in those parts that are corroborated. For instance, Mr. Cramer has verified it that the anonymous letter to the court was typed on a machine at the Travelers Club, that Corrigan had access to it and used it, and that none of the others did. Therefore I accept that detail as established, and also the account of Corrigan's visit to California, but nothing else, and certainly not the authorship. Of course Corrigan didn't write it."

"Why not?" It came from two of the women in unison. It was the first cheep out of them.

"If he didn't know what was in the manuscript, and he didn't, why did he kill people? There is no discernible reason. If he didn't kill people, why does he confess to it? No, he didn't write this."

"Did he kill himself?" Mrs. Adams blurted. She looked ten years older, and she was already old enough.

"I shouldn't think so. If he did, it was he who got me on the phone to hear the shot and told me he had mailed me a letter, meaning this—"

"What's that?" Cramer demanded. "He said he had mailed you a letter?"

"Yes. I left that out of my report to you because I don't want my mail intercepted. He said that. Mr. Goodwin heard it. Archie?"

"Yes, sir."

"And since he didn't write this thing he would hardly tell me he had mailed it to me. No, madam, he didn't kill himself. We might as well deal with that next—unless someone wants to maintain that Corrigan wrote the confession?"

No one did.

Wolfe took them in. "For this a new character is required, and we'll call him X. This will have to be a hodgepodge party, partly what he must have done and partly what he could have done. Certainly he spent some hours yesterday between noon and ten in the evening at Corrigan's apartment, composing and typing this document. Certainly Corrigan was there too. He had been hit on the head, and was either unconscious from

the blow or had been tied and gagged. I prefer it that
he was conscious, knowing something of X as I do, and
that X, as he typed the confession—which may have
been composed beforehand and merely had to be
copied—read it aloud to Corrigan. He wore gloves, and,
when he was through, he pressed Corrigan's fingertips to
the paper and envelope here and there, certainly on the
postage stamp.

"I don't know whether his schedule was left to exigen-
cy or was designed, but I would guess the latter, for X is
fond of alibis, and we'll probably find that he has one
ready for last evening from nine-thirty to ten-thirty.
Anyway, at ten o'clock he turned on the radio, if he
hadn't already done so, hit Corrigan on the head again,
at the same spot as before, with something heavy and
hard enough to stun but not kill, put him on the floor
near the telephone, and dialed my number. While talking to me, making the voice unrecognizable with
huskiness and agitation, he pressed the muzzle of Corrigan's own revolver against his head and, at the proper
moment, pulled the trigger and dropped the gun and
the phone on the floor. He may also have fallen heavily
to the floor himself; I think he would have. If he did he
didn't stay there long. I said he was wearing gloves. He
made Corrigan's dead hand grip the gun, put the gun on
the floor, and left, perhaps twenty seconds after the shot
had been fired. I haven't even inquired if the door had
to be locked from the outside with a key; if it did, X had
had ample opportunity to procure one. He dropped the
letter to me, this confession, into the nearest mailbox. I
lose him at the mailbox. We'll hear of his next move
when we are confronted with his alibi."

Wolfe's eyes moved. "I invite comment."

Three lawyers spoke at once. Cramer outspoke them.
"How much of it can you prove?"

"Nothing. Not a word."

"Then what does it get us?"

"It clears away the rubbish. The rubbish was the
assumption that Corrigan wrote that confession and

killed himself. I have shown that one is false and the other is not invulnerable. Depriving you of a suicide was simple. Giving you a murder, and a murderer, is harder. May I proceed?"

"If you've got something better than guesses, yes."

"I've got a question," Kustin put in. "Is this a buildup for charging someone in this room with murder?"

"Yes."

"Then I want to speak with you privately."

"The devil you do." Wolfe was indignant. To control his emotions, he closed his eyes and waggled his head. Then he told Kustin dryly, "So you're beginning to see something, now that I've cleared away some of the rubbish? And you'd like to point at it? I'll do the pointing, Mr. Kustin." His eyes moved. "Before I go on to particulars, another comment. At my first reading of this"—he tapped the paper—"I saw the flaw that told me that Corrigan hadn't written it: his performance in Los Angeles made it obvious that he had never read the manuscript. But it could have been written by you, Mr. Kustin, or you, Mr. Phelps, or you, Mr. Briggs. It could have been any one of you, instead of Corrigan, who had done the deeds which this document attributes to Corrigan. That was why it was of first importance to learn if any of you had had access to the typewriter at the Travelers Club. Learning that you hadn't, and therefore had not exposed O'Malley, it was clear that if one of you had committed three murders it must have been for some other motive than concealment of a betrayal of your former partner."

"Get down to it," Cramer growled.

Wolfe ignored him. He looked over the heads of the lawyers and inquired abruptly, "Is one of you ladies named Dondero?"

I twisted my neck. Sue was one of the four on the couch. Startled, she stared at him. "Yes, I am." She was a little flushed and pretty as a picture.

"You are Mr. Phelps's secretary?"

"Yes."

"A week ago Saturday, nine days ago, Mr. Phelps dictated a brief letter to me, to be sent by messenger. There were enclosures for it—items of material written by Leonard Dykes, from the files, including a letter of resignation he wrote last July. Do you remember that incident?"

"Yes. Certainly."

"I understand that you have recently been questioned about it by the police; that you have been shown the Dykes letter and your attention has been called to a certain notation, 'Ps one-forty-six, three,' in a corner of it, in pencil, in a handwriting resembling Corrigan's; and that you state flatly that the notation was not on the letter that Saturday morning when it was sent to me. Is that correct?"

"Yes, it is," Sue said firmly.

"Are you positive the notation was not on the letter at the time you enclosed it in the envelope with the other material?"

"I am."

"You're a positive person, aren't you, Miss Dondero?"

"Well—I know what I saw and what I didn't see."

"Admirable and remarkable." Wolfe was terse but not hostile. "Few of us can say that and support it. How many typewriters did you use that morning?"

"I don't know what you mean. I used one. Mine."

"Mr. Phelps dictated the letter to me, and you typed it on your machine. Is that right?"

"Yes."

"And you addressed an envelope to me on the same machine?"

"Yes."

"How positive are you of that?"

"I'm absolutely positive."

"How much chance is there that for some trivial reason, no matter what, you used a different machine for addressing the envelope?"

"Absolutely none. I was there at my desk, and I did the envelope right after I typed the letter. I always do."

"Then we have a problem." Wolfe opened a drawer of his desk and took out a sheet of paper and an envelope, handling the envelope gingerly, holding it by a corner. "This is the letter and the envelope; Mr. Goodwin will attest that and so will I. The variation is apparent to the naked eye, and I have examined them with a glass. They were not typed on the same machine."

"I don't believe it!" Sue exclaimed.

"Come here and look at them. No, please, only Miss Dondero. The envelope must not be touched."

I made room for her to go by. She went to his desk and leaned over for a close-up. She straightened. "That's a different envelope. I didn't type that. I always put 'By Messenger' in caps and lower case and underline it. That's all in caps and it's not underlined. Where did you get it?"

"If you please, Miss Dondero, take your seat." Wolfe returned the sheet and envelope to the drawer, touching only the tip of the envelope. He waited until Sue was back on the couch and he had her face before he told her, "Thank you for being positive. That's a help. But you're sure you put the letter and enclosures into the envelope you had typed?"

"Yes, I am."

"And sealed it?"

"Yes."

"And left it lying on your desk, perhaps, or in a basket?"

"No, I didn't. It was to go by messenger, and I had sent for one. I went immediately to the anteroom and put it on Blanche's desk and asked her to give it to the messenger when he came."

"Who is Blanche?"

"The receptionist. Miss Duke."

Wolfe's eyes moved. "Which of you is Miss Duke?"

Blanche raised a hand, high. "I am. And I get the idea, I'm quick. You're going to ask me if I put the stuff in another envelope, and I'm going to say I didn't. And I don't know who did. But Mr. O'Malley came and said something about something left out and took the envelope away with him."

"Mr. O'Malley?"

"Yes."

"Did he bring it back?"

"Yes."

"How soon? How long was he gone with it?"

"I don't know, I guess three or four minutes. Anyway he brought it back, and when the messenger came I gave it to him."

"Did you notice whether it was the same envelope?"

"My God, no!"

"This is important, Miss Duke. Will you testify that Mr. O'Malley took the envelope from your desk, left the room with it, and shortly returned with it or with a similar one?"

"What do you mean, will I? I am!"

Wolfe's eyes left her to move right and back again, still above the heads of the lawyers. "We seem to be solving our problem," he remarked. "One more detail would help. Clearly we must assume that Mr. O'Malley addressed another envelope and transferred the material to it. If so, it seems likely that one of you ladies saw him do it, though I don't know how the typewriters are placed in that office. What about it? That Saturday morning, nine days ago, did any of you see Mr. O'Malley address an envelope on a typewriter?"

No reply. He had their eyes all right, but not their tongues.

He nodded understandingly. "It may be, of course, that he used a machine that wasn't under observation. Or he may have been seen by one of the staff who is not present, and that will bear inquiry. But I should make sure that all of you understand the situation. This envelope is vital evidence. If Mr. O'Malley handled it and typed an address on it, it will probably show his prints, for I don't suppose he wore gloves in the office that morning. Not only that, it will be a simple matter to learn which machine it was written on. If it was a

machine that is on the desk of one of you ladies, and
you were there that morning, and Mr. O'Malley denies
that he used it, you may find yourself in an uncomfortable spot. The police may properly ask—"

"It was my machine." It was a sullen mutter, so low
that it barely got through, and it came from the beautiful Eleanor, of all people.

"Ah. May I have your name?"

"Eleanor Gruber." She muttered it.

"You will please tell us about it, Miss Gruber."

"I was at the filing cabinet and he asked if—"

"Mr. O'Malley?"

"Yes. He asked if he could use my machine, and I said
yes. That was all."

"Did he address an envelope on it?"

"I don't know. I was at the cabinet with my back
turned. I said it was my machine, but I should have said
it may have been."

"There was a supply of the firm's envelopes in your
desk?"

"Certainly. In the top drawer."

"How long was he at it?"

"I don't—very briefly."

"Not more than a minute or so?"

"I said very briefly. I didn't time it."

"But long enough to address an envelope?"

"Of course, that only takes seconds."

"Did you see an envelope in his hand?"

"No. I wasn't looking. I was busy."

"Thank you, Miss Gruber. I'm sorry your memory
needed jogging, and I'm glad it's refreshed." Wolfe focused on Conroy O'Malley. "Mr. O'Malley, you ought to
have a word. I won't frame a tedious detailed question,
but merely ask, did you do the things these people say
you did that Saturday morning?"

O'Malley was a different man. The bitter twist to his
mouth was gone, and so was the sag of his cheeks. He
was ten years younger, and his eyes gleamed almost like

eyes in the dark with a light on them. His voice had a sharp edge.

"I'd rather listen to you. Until you're through."

"Very well. I'm not through. Is it plain that I'm accusing you of murder?"

"Yes. Go on."

Purley Stebbins got up, detoured around Cramer and Briggs, got an empty chair, put it just behind O'Malley's right elbow, and sat. O'Malley didn't glance at him. Wolfe was speaking.

"Manifestly, establishing that O'Malley got at that letter in order to make that notation on it in Corrigan's hand before it came to me will not convict him of murder. By then all of you had heard the title of Baird Archer's novel, 'Put Not Your Trust,' and anyone could have known or learned that it came from the third verse of the Hundred and Forty-sixth Psalm. But it shows that he wanted to present me with evidence that someone in your office was connected with the manuscript and therefore with the crimes, and that that someone was Corrigan. I am going—"

"Why Corrigan?" Kustin demanded.

"That's what I'm coming to. I'm going to have to tell you things I can't prove, as I did with X. It is still X, only now I call him O'Malley. An odd thing about this confession is that nearly every detail of it is true and strictly accurate. The man who wrote it did find the manuscript in Dykes's desk and read it; he found that its contents were as described; he went to see Dykes and talked with him as related; he killed Dykes essentially for the reason given, fear of what might result from his knowledge of the contents of the manuscript; he killed Miss Wellman and Miss Abrams for a like reason. But it was O'Malley who wrote the confession. He—"

"You're crazy," Kustin blurted. "The manuscript revealed that Corrigan had informed on O'Malley. Is that right?"

"Yes."

"And O'Malley learned that fact by finding and reading the manuscript?"

"Yes."

"So he killed three people to keep it from being
known that Corrigan had informed on him? For God's
sake!"

"No. He killed three people so he could safely kill a
fourth." Wolfe was on his way now. "When he learned
that it was Corrigan who had ruined his career, destroyed him, he determined to kill Corrigan. But no
matter how cleverly he managed it, Dykes would be an
intolerable menace. Dykes knew that O'Malley knew of
Corrigan's treachery, and if Corrigan met a sudden and
violent death, no matter how, Dykes might speak. So
first Dykes had to go, and he did. Then Joan Wellman—
was she also a menace? O'Malley had to find out, and he
arranged to meet her. He may have thought he intended
her no harm—the confession says so—but when she
spoke of the resemblance of the novel's plot to an event
in real life, and even came close to remembering his
name, that, as the confession says, was more than
enough for him. Five hours later she was dead."

There was a noise from the rear of the room, the
sound of a chair scraping. John R. Wellman was on his
feet and moving. Eyes went to him. Wolfe stopped
speaking, but Wellman came on tiptoe, off to one side,
around the corner and along the wall to the chair which
Purley Stebbins had vacated. It had an unobstructed
view of the lawyers.

"Excuse me," he said, apparently to everyone, and sat.

There were murmurs from the women. Cramer shot a
glance at Wellman, evidently decided that he was not
getting set as a nemesis, and looked at Wolfe.

"There remained," Wolfe resumed, "only one source of
possible danger, Rachel Abrams. O'Malley had probably
been told about her by Dykes, but whether he had or
not, he had found the receipts she had given Baird
Archer when he searched Dykes's apartment. I'll read a

few lines from the confession." He fingered the sheets, found the place, and read:

"My inner being could not permit me to feel any moral repulsion at the thought of killing Joan Wellman, certainly not enough to restrain me, for if killing her was morally unacceptable how could I justify the killing of Dykes? By killing Joan Wellman the process was completed. After that, given adequate motive, I could have killed any number of people without any sign of compunction. So in contemplating the murder of Rachel Abrams my only concerns were whether it was necessary and whether it could be performed without undue risk. I decided it was necessary."

Wolfe looked up. "This is indeed a remarkable document. There we have a man relieving his mind, perhaps even soothing his soul, by coolly expounding the stages of his transformation into a cold-blooded killer, but avoiding the consequent penalty by ascribing the deeds and the onus to another person. It was an adroit and witty stratagem, and it would have triumphed if Mr. Wellman had not engaged my services and remained resolute in spite of repeated checks and disappointments.

"But I'm ahead of myself. This confession is all right as far as it goes, but it leaves gaps. By the day he went for Rachel Abrams, the twenty-sixth of February, two weeks ago today, she was more than a remote threat. He knew—"

"You still mean O'Malley?" Kustin cut in.

"Yes."

"Then you're talking too fast. O'Malley was in Atlanta two weeks ago today."

Wolfe nodded. "I'll get to that. By that day he knew that I was on the case and was concentrating on Baird Archer and the manuscript, and the possibility that I might find Rachel Abrams certainly did not escape him. He had to deal with her first, and he did—a scant two minutes before Mr. Goodwin reached her. And there he

was. The preliminaries were completed. He was ready
for what had always been his real objective: the murder
of Corrigan. To abandon it was unthinkable, but now it
was not so simple. Needing to learn how much I knew,
he phoned Corrigan to suggest that all of you should
come here and invite my questions, and you came. It
may be that my asking to see Dykes's letter of resignation first gave him the idea of putting it all onto Corrigan; that's of no moment; in any case, he contrived to
put that notation in Corrigan's hand on the letter before
it reached me, as the first step."

Wolfe paused to glance at Wellman, but our client
was merely gazing at O'Malley, with no apparent intention of taking part. He went on. "When the police confronted you with the notation, of course O'Malley had to
join you in your claim of ignorance and your charge that
I must have made the notation myself. Then came the
letter from Mrs. Potter, and naturally that suited him
admirably. He knew it was a decoy, either mine or Mr.
Cramer's, for he was confident that all copies of the
manuscript had been destroyed. I have had no report of
your conference that day, but I would give odds that he
maneuvered with all his dexterity to arrange that Corrigan should be the one to go to California. The result
met his highest expectations. On Corrigan's return you
came together to see me again and, as it seemed to
O'Malley, I played directly into his hand by refusing to
say anything except that I was about ready to act. That
made the threat, to whoever was its object, ominous and
imminent; that made it most plausible that Corrigan,
granting he was the object, would prefer self-destruction
and would choose that moment for it; and O'Malley
moved swiftly and ruthlessly. It was only ten hours after
he left here with you that he dialed my number to let
me hear the shot that killed Corrigan."

"You foresaw that?" Kustin demanded.

"Certainly not. At the time you left here I had added
only one presumption to my scanty collection: that Corrigan had never seen the manuscript and didn't know

what was in it. Regarding the rest of you I was still at
sea. I was still merely trying to prod you into movement,
and it can't be denied that I succeeded. Are you ready
to say something, Mr. O'Malley?"

"No. I'm still listening."

"As you please. I'm about through." Wolfe looked at
Kustin. "You said that O'Malley was in Atlanta the day
Rachel Abrams was killed. Can you certify that, or do
you only mean that he was supposed to be?"

"He was there on business for the firm."

"I know. In fact it is not true that my eye on you
gentlemen has been totally impartial until two days ago.
The first time you came here O'Malley managed to get it
on the record with me that he had returned to New York
only that morning after a week in Georgia, and I noted it.
I don't suppose you know Saul Panzer?"

"Saul Panzer? No."

"That is Mr. Panzer, there at the end of Mr. Goodwin's desk. If he ever wants to know anything about
you, tell him; you might as well. Four days ago I asked
him to investigate O'Malley's movements during the
week in question, and he has done so. Saul, tell us about
it."

Saul got his mouth open but no words out, because
Cramer suddenly came to life. He snapped, "Hold it,
Panzer!" To Wolfe: "Is this what you got on the phone
this morning?"

"Yes."

"And you're going to hand it to him like this? Just
dump the bag for him? You are not!"

Wolfe shrugged. "Either I go on or you do. This
morning you said you would take a hand and I said no.
Now you're welcome. Take it if you want it."

"I want it." Cramer was on his feet. "I want that letter
and envelope. I want Panzer. I want statements from
the three women. Mr. O'Malley, you'll go downtown
with Sergeant Stebbins for questioning."

O'Malley was not impressed. "On what charge, Inspector?"

"I said for questioning. If you insist on a charge you'll get one."

"I would want my counsel present."

"You can phone him from the District Attorney's office."

"Luckily I don't have to phone him. He's here." O'Malley turned his head. "Louis?"

Kustin, meeting his former associate's eye, didn't hesitate. "No," he said flatly. "I'm out, Con. I can't do it."

It put O'Malley off balance, but it didn't floor him. He didn't try to press, Kustin's tone having settled it. He turned back to Cramer, but his view was obstructed. John R. Wellman had left his chair and was standing there facing him, and spoke.

"I'm Joan Wellman's father, Mr. O'Malley. I don't know, because it's pretty complicated, but I'd like to see something. I'd like to see if you feel like shaking hands with me." He extended his hand. "There it is. Do you feel like it or don't you?"

Into the heavy silence came a smothered gasp from one of the females. O'Malley nearly made it. He tried. Looking up at Wellman, he started to lift a hand, then his neck muscles gave, his head dropped, and he used both hands to cover his face.

"I guess you don't," Wellman said, and turned and headed for the door.

23

ONE DAY last week I made a station-to-station call to a number in Glendale, California. When I got it I began, "Peggy? This is Archie. Calling from New York."

"Hello, Archie. I was thinking you might call."

I made a face. I had been familiar deliberately, with a

specific purpose, to find a flaw. There was just a chance she might fake indignation, or she might be coy, or she might even pretend not to know who it was. Nothing doing. She was still her—too short, too plump, and too old, but the one and only Mrs. Potter.

"It's all over," I told her. "I knew you'd want to know. The jury was out nine hours, but they finally came through with it, first degree murder. As you know, he was tried for Rachel Abrams, not your brother, but that doesn't make any difference. Convicting him for one was convicting him for all four."

"Yes, of course. I'm glad it's over. Thank you for calling. You sound so close, as if you were right here."

"Yeah, so do you. What's it doing out there, raining?"

"Oh, no, bright sunshine, warm and bright. Why, is it raining in New York?"

"It sure is. I guess I bring it on. Do you remember how I looked that day through the peephole?"

"I certainly do! I'll never forget it!"

"Neither will I. Good-by, Peggy."

"Good-by, Archie."

I hung up and made another face. What the hell, I thought, in another twenty years Bubblehead may be dead, and age and contours won't matter much, and I'll grab her.

ABOUT THE AUTHOR

REX STOUT, the creator of Nero Wolfe, was born in Noblesville, Indiana, in 1886, the sixth of nine children of John and Lucetta Todhunter Stout, both Quakers. Shortly after his birth, the family moved to Wakarusa, Kansas. He was educated in a country school, but, by the age of nine, was recognized throughout the state as a prodigy in arithmetic. Mr. Stout briefly attended the University of Kansas, but left to enlist in the Navy, and spent the next two years as a warrant officer on board President Theodore Roosevelt's yacht. When he left the Navy in 1908, Rex Stout began to write freelance articles, worked as a sightseeing guide and as an itinerant bookkeeper. Later he devised and implemented a school banking system which was installed in four hundred cities and towns throughout the country. In 1927 Mr. Stout retired from the world of finance and, with the proceeds of his banking scheme, left for Paris to write serious fiction. He wrote three novels that received favorable reviews before turning to detective fiction. His first Nero Wolfe novel, *Fer-de-Lance*, appeared in 1934. It was followed by many others, among them, *Too Many Cooks, The Silent Speaker, If Death Ever Slept, The Doorbell Rang* and *Please Pass the Guilt*, which established Nero Wolfe as a leading character on a par with Erle Stanley Gardner's famous protagonist, Perry Mason. During World War II, Rex Stout waged a personal campaign against Nazism as chairman of the War Writers' Board, master of ceremonies of the radio program "Speaking of Liberty" and as a member of several national committees. After the war, he turned his attention to mobilizing public opinion against the wartime use of thermonuclear devices, was an active leader in the Authors' Guild and resumed writing his Nero Wolfe novels. All together, his Nero Wolfe novels have been translated into twenty-two languages and have sold more than forty-five million copies. Rex Stout died in 1975 at the age of eighty-eight. A month before his death, he published his forty-sixth Nero Wolfe novel, *A Family Affair*.

NERO WOLFE

He's not much to look at and he'll never win the hundred yard dash but for sheer genius at unraveling the tangled skeins of crime he has no peer. His outlandish adventures make for some of the best mystery reading in paperback. He's the hero of these superb suspense stories.

BY REX STOUT

☐ 24438	CHAMPAGNE FOR ONE	$2.50
☐ 24375	IN THE BEST OF FAMILIES	$2.50
☐ 24269	PRISONER'S BASE	$2.50
☐ 24191	TRIO FOR BLUNT INSTRUMENTS	$2.50
☐ 24247	TROUBLE IN TRIPLICATE	$2.50
☐ 24032	A RIGHT TO DIE	$2.50
☐ 23803	THREE AT WOLFE'S DOOR	$2.50
☐ 23995	GOLDEN SPIDERS	$2.50
☐ 23721	THE DOOR BELL RANG	$2.50
☐ 23591	TRIPLE JEOPARDY	$2.50
☐ 23513	DEATH OF DOXY	$2.50
☐ 23497	THE SILENT SPEAKER	$2.50
☐ 23446	HOMICIDE TRINITY	$2.95
☐ 24594	THE SECOND CONFESSION	$2.95
☐ 24737	THE MOTHER HUNT	$2.95
☐ 24813	THREE FOR THE CHAIR	$2.95
☐ 24498	CURTAINS FOR THREE	$2.95

Prices and availability subject to change without notice.

Buy them at your local bookstore or use this handy coupon for ordering:

CATHERINE AIRD

For 15 years, Catherine Aird's mysteries have won praises for their brilliant plotting and style. Established alongside other successful English mystery ladies, she continues to thrill old and new mystery fans alike.

☐	24601	PARTING BREATH	$2.75
☐	23677	LAST RESPECTS	$2.50
☐	24600	HENRIETTA WHO	$2.75
☐	24083	A MOST CONTAGIOUS GAME	$2.75
☐	24079	PASSING STRANGE	$2.75
☐	25109	A SLIGHT MOURNING	$2.95
☐	24603	HIS BURIAL TOO	$2.75
☐	24316	A LATE PHOENIX	$2.75
☐	24602	THE RELIGIOUS BODY	$2.75
☐	25110	SOME DIE ELOQUENT	$2.95
☐	24078	STATELY HOME MURDER	$2.75

Prices and availability subject to change without notice.

SPECIAL
MONEY SAVING
OFFER

Now you can have an up-to-date listing of Bantam's hundreds of titles plus take advantage of our unique and exciting bonus book offer. A special offer which gives you the opportunity to purchase a Bantam book for only 50¢. Here's how!

By ordering any five books at the regular price per order, you can also choose any other single book listed (up to a $4.95 value) for just 50¢. Some restrictions do apply, but for further details why not send for Bantam's listing of titles today!

Just send us your name and address plus 50¢ to defray the postage and handling costs.

Masters
of
Mystery

With these new mystery titles, Bantam takes you to the scene of the crime. These masters of mystery follow in the tradition of the Great British and American crime writers. You'll meet all these talented sleuths as they get to the bottom of even the most baffling crimes.